AF541781

TRANSFORMING THE STEEL FRAME

'This is a very important book. The Indian Civil Services used to be one of the best in the world. I support the aspiration of the distinguished editor, Mr Vinod Rai, and the essayists to improve the quality and integrity of the Indian Civil Services. India needs world-class civil services.'

—Tommy Koh

Ambassador-at-Large, Ministry of Foreign Affairs, Singapore

'As the edifice that holds the entire Indian polity together, the Indian Civil Services are huge, complex and ubiquitous. This commendable collection of essays offers insightful and honest analyses of key aspects of the current state and possible future of the civil services, from recruitment to value systems and innovation, among others. This is an impressive volume and I congratulate Vinod Rai and the distinguished contributors for undertaking this important and comprehensive study.'

—Tan Tai Yong

Chairman, Institute of South Asian Studies,
National University of Singapore; and
President, Singapore University of Social Sciences

'Mr Rai, a distinguished civil servant has done a great service by integrating and editing this volume on civil services reforms in India. He has succeeded in bringing together complex issues, comprehensively and analytically, with a sense of history and vision of the future, from national leaders in the public and private sector in India, impacting over one-fifth of the population of the world.'

—Y. Venugopal Reddy

IAS officer (Retd),
Former Governor, Reserve Bank of India

TRANSFORMING THE STEEL FRAME

PROMISE AND PARADOX OF CIVIL SERVICE REFORM

EDITED BY

VINOD RAI

RUPA

First published by
Rupa Publications India Pvt. Ltd 2023
7/16, Ansari Road, Daryaganj
New Delhi 110002

Sales Centres:

Prayagraj Bengaluru Chennai
Hyderabad Jaipur Kathmandu
Kolkata Mumbai

P-ISBN: 978-93-5702-112-8
E-ISBN: 978-93-5702-108-1

First impression 2023

10 9 8 7 6 5 4 3 2 1

Printed in India

CONTENTS

INTRODUCTION

Vinod Rai

The world over, the term 'bureaucracy' evokes more negative than positive sentiments. Bureaucracy is usually seen more as a 'stumbling block' than a progressively inclined, constructive agency engaged in the task of good governance. While people like Cyril Northcote Parkinson have described a bureaucrat as engaged in 'wanting to multiply subordinates, not rivals' and even described how 'officials make work for each other'; Frank Herbert, the author of *Heretics of Dune*, a science-fiction novel, has amplified this idea further and gone on to describe bureaucracy in the following words: 'Bureaucracy destroys initiative. There is little that bureaucrats hate more than innovation, especially innovations that produce better results than the old routines. Improvements always make those at the top of the heap look inept. Who enjoys appearing inept?'

Indian bureaucracy is no exception.

Barack Obama, in his book *A Promised Land*, writes of the country's bureaucracy: 'Despite its genuine economic progress, though, India remained a chaotic and impoverished place: largely divided by religion and caste, captive to the whims of corrupt local officials and power brokers, hamstrung by a parochial bureaucracy that was resistant to change.'[1]

Indian bureaucracy is often referred to as the 'steel frame' for the administration of the country. However, in recent years, it has faced more barbs than accolades for its performance. It is, in fact, pejoratively referred to as 'babudom'[2]. Its performance over the years,

---

[1]Obama, Barack, *A Promised Land*, Penguin Random House LLC, 2020, pp. 337–8.

[2]'Babus' is a colloquial expression referring to clerks in India. So, civil servants being referred to as babus indicate that they have a mindset only of clerks, viz., lacking dynamism, initiative, innovation and capability.

largely because of its rigid attitude and alignment to the party in power, has drawn widespread criticism. How its reputation, from the 'steel frame' days to being seen as 'laidback and laggard' has undergone a change, needs to be introspected. This has to be analysed and remedied as India aspires to be a leading economic power requiring sustainable economic development. Such consistent economic development can only be premised on the edifice of a transparent, accountable and ethical governance structure. This is the role that the civil service is meant to play.

The Need for Urgent Reform

With the passage of time, cracks have been observed in the quality of the service. Critics feel it has become insensitive and unresponsive to the needs of citizens, for whose welfare the administration functions. The officers are also seen to be functioning from their 'ivory towers' without really appreciating grassroots issues. In fact, some even feel that the bureaucracy has become the single dominating entity resisting change to bring about a flexible and people-oriented administration.

Sustainable economic development requires good governance. The quality of administration ensures fulfilment of the stated objectives of any elected government in terms of inclusive development and targeted delivery of specialized schemes, such as guaranteed rural employment, assured primary education programmes and rural health missions. It is recognized that the civilian administration has become far more complex now than in the last century. Considering the fact that bureaucrats do not function in a vacuum and are subject to political interference and regional pressures, their objectivity in functioning has come up for adverse scrutiny at times. This factor, coupled with the deep-seated suspicion that career advancement does not take place only on merit, has created serious motivational issues. The service is often perceived as lacking in competence and professionalism, harbouring political biases and suffering declining independence and, of course, concerns around malfeasance.

We have had Administrative Reforms Commissions provide detailed recommendations to bring in reforms. However, successive governments have either been non-serious about accepting these recommendations or have just not been concerned about them. There have been another set of recommendations which have been advocated by the highest court of the land. These have also been disregarded. Recommendations such as fixed tenure for key posts like the cabinet secretary and the home secretary and a civil services board for postings, stand ignored.

The bureaucracy is the continuous element in administrations. Since governments may change, the framers of the Constitution provided for an impartial and permanent bureaucracy. An impartial, dynamic and accountable civil service can ensure that objectives of rapid and inclusive growth and welfare are actually achieved. The stakes in having such a service are very high—the government and the political executive must work towards ensuring a spirited and impartial civil service structure designed to cater to the needs of the nation.

So, is there a felt need for reform in the civil service? If so, we propose to deliberate on a road map for any seriousness that the government may show to address the situation.

Time to Change Gears

The issues that afflict the civil services indicate that piecemeal and peripheral attempts at tinkering will not bring about any perceptible reform in officers' capability to deliver objectively. Irrespective of the form of government, viz., a monarchy, theocracy, communist regime, dictatorship or parliamentary democracy, there is a permanent bureaucracy which functions below the dominant regime for implementation of government policies. Civilian administration has had to keep pace with the altered models of governance across all geographies and regimes in the world today.

It is well recognized that for economic development to be sustained over the long term, it has to be premised on an edifice of a good governance system. There is thus a need to make the bureaucracy much more effective, independent and efficient. A thorough overhaul of the recruitment norms, training and reskilling, and indemnification from political interference to ensure objectivity, will have to be contemplated urgently for administration to encourage and support rapid economic growth. The government is also seized of the need to reskill and reorient government official's professional skills and have thus launched Mission Karmayogi[3], in which civil servants will be trained to be more creative, constructive, imaginative, innovative, proactive, professional, progressive, energetic, enabling, transparent and technology-enabled.

While widespread consultations have been done by the government for formulating the mission, it was felt that we need to obtain the views of distinguished personalities from the service and others who have either collaborated with the government or watched the functioning of the service from a distance. So, in this volume, we have brought together essays of a galaxy of eminent former civil servants who have connected at different stages of their career as a civil servant, such as recruitment, training and personnel management. Some of these former civil servants have also held constitutional appointments. The attempt is to ascertain their views on the reforms required in the services to ensure a more effective, capable, independent, professional and upright service. We also sought the views of reputable personalities from the corporate sector who have closely functioned with the government to ascertain their impressions of the strengths and weaknesses of officials and how to bring about improvement. We have also received the views of some very illustrious international civil servants who have the distinction of serving in multinational institutions such as the United Nations (UN) or Commonwealth Secretariat.

---

[3]'Karmayoga' is a term described in the holy book, Bhagavad Gita. A karma yogi is a person with the mental discipline to perform the acts that are ordained for him, irrespective of his state or status. He should do it purely with the firm faith that it is required of him to perform that role or act.

A Comprehensive Approach to Reform

The making of a civil servant begins from the recruitment process, which is undertaken by the Union Public Service Commission (UPSC). Deepak Gupta, who was the chairman of the UPSC, in his essay on developing excellence in the civil services, draws attention to the recommendation made by every administrative commission to lower the age of recruitment, as entrants to the service at an advanced age lack the qualities to be aspirational and come with the 'baggage of entrenched mindsets'. Such entrants can hardly be moulded and run the risk of not being able to rise up to the top. The adverse consequences for reserved candidates, who have yet higher age limits for taking the examination, is far more, since they will see their colleagues continue longer in the service and thereby achieve higher positions, while their career span will be much shorter. He has also expressed his views on the 'generalist versus the specialist'. He maintains service officers have a long-term stake in the system as against lateral entrants, who may have limited appreciation of ground realities or implementation challenges. Indian Administrative Service (IAS) officers do attain a certain degree of domain expertise and are appointed to sectors which are in their area of specialization. Gupta strongly advocates a 'cleansing process', wherein incapable and corrupt officers get weeded out. He believes such a process will be objective only when the appraisal system is made more transparent and entrusted to the UPSC.

The three All-India Services—IAS, Indian Police Service (IPS) and Indian Forest Service (IFS)—are required to function at the state and federal level. The unique requirement from an IAS officer is that he is called upon to function at the district, state and union government, where the job requirements at each level are very distinct. There is also substantial variation between regions. The skill sets and sensitivities required in the northeastern states are very different from the southern states or Jammu and Kashmir. The initial training of such officers has to be designed to prepare them for functioning in all diverse situations. Sanjeev Chopra, a former director of the

Lal Bahadur Shastri National Academy of Administration, which trains new entrants to the civil services, refers to the changing profile of an IAS officer. The two-year training of civil service entrants is divided into the foundation course and the professional course. The course design for the former is common across services, whereas the latter prepares each service officer for the unique requirements of their service. In 2019, the foundation course was reoriented to dismantle the artificial barrier between technology, human resource and environment. It was designed so as to embed technology as a driving force in major sectors such as health, agriculture, education and urban mobility. The academic component of professional training has been undergoing change with the training pedagogy involving a greater emphasis on syndicate work and practical training. In the first decade of their service, officers are trained to manage administration at the district level. After that stint, the mid-career training programmes take over, which have been designed along the recommendations of the Second Administrative Reforms Commission. Officers are expected to choose any one of the specializations in the fields such as economic management, industrial development, agricultural and rural development, health, education, social sector, personnel management and financial security.

One of the problems plaguing the services is the issue of integrity. The malaise seems to be spreading and instances of misdemeanour appear to be raising fewer eyebrows now. Has our appetite to condone malfeasance become so large? Dealing with the subject of combating corruption in the civil services, Pradeep Kumar emphasizes the distinction between preventive and punitive vigilance and feels that while preventive vigilance is an ongoing process and is necessary to reduce the scope and opportunities of corruption, it is not sufficient by itself to curb corruption. It is essential that the delinquent and corrupt are punished strictly and swiftly. Punitive vigilance is vital for fighting corruption and should go hand in hand with preventive vigilance. He emphasizes the need to create an environment that provides for 'honest mistakes'. This will ensure that the well-meaning and competent officers can work without fear and the corrupt are punished speedily. He advocates that to encourage ethical behaviour, an appropriate mix of incentives to reward good behaviour and disincentives to punish bad behaviour should be put in place. He emphasizes that from the societal perspective, family, community leaders and the education system play an important part in moulding human behaviour towards inculcating the qualities of probity, ethical values and ethical conduct. The role of the political leadership in this struggle is highlighted by him to implement large-scale reforms towards a clean and objective system.

The Supreme Court created a sensation when it termed the Indian premier crime investigation body, the Central Bureau of Investigation, to be a 'caged parrot'.[4] This observation was made to project the helplessness of the agency at the hands of its political masters. This indeed is a rising tendency since the public services are very susceptible and vulnerable to political influence. Manish Sabharwal makes the case that the Indian steel frame has also become a steel cage and to transform it to make it an edifice on which India's economic development can be premised requires a major reboot of the human capital regime faced by our burgeoning civil services. He proposes a radical revisit of the present human capital regime through reorientation in seven areas of: structure, staffing, training, performance management, compensation, culture and human resources. He is very critical of the current performance management system, which does not differentiate between a 'performer' and an incompetent dead wood.

He is also opposed to the huge bureaucratic set-up and feels that there needs to be a rightsizing of ministries and departments by halving each. His hypothesis advocates only 25 secretary-level officials in the central government and not more than two directors general of police in each state. Sabharwal distinguishes between 'promotable' and 'postable' officers, with the latter comprising a category with less productive officials who are not wanted by any department. He is also a strong proponent of lateral entry of professionals to

[4]Colvin, Ross, and Satarupa Bhattacharjya, 'A "Caged Parrot"—Supreme Court Describes CBI', Reuters, 10 May 2013, https://reut.rs/3G9hiWE. Accessed on 21 December 2022.

renew imagination, skills and energy. A new theme introduced by Sabharwal is to devise a compensation framework based on a 'cost-to-government' structure, which monetizes benefits. He is of the view that a culture of probity, which penalizes corrupt behaviour, operates less on a hierarchical culture and measures outcomes. The human resource management system in government, he maintains, needs to be no longer based on personnel and training processes and should be revolutionized with greater resources and focus.

For all the blame that Indian bureaucracy faces, it is undeniable that if permitted independence from the political executive, it displays professional excellence. A case in point is the central Election Commission of India, which has the remarkable record of delivering 17 general elections, the last of which was in 2019. In this election, 67.11 per cent of the population, viz., 88 million people, cast their votes. Highlighting this role of the bureaucracy in ensuring free and fair elections in the country, N. Gopalaswami, a former chief election commissioner, credits T.N. Seshan, India's tenth election commissioner, for having played a stellar role in making the electoral photo identity card compulsory, though all political parties opposed it. The Supreme Court had to step in and validate the decision of the election commissioner. The introduction of the electronic voting machine constituted a historic step. Challenged multiple times and in multiple courts, the voting machine has established its credibility and added to the efficiency of the election process. Gopalaswami refers to the challenges faced by election commissioners when their independent and objective actions become unpalatable to the ruling dispensation. Appointment of multiple election commissioners by the government was an attempt to blunt the constitutional body and try to ensure its acquiescence. However, the commission has remained steadfast in maintaining its independence and even ensuring the commitment of political parties to the model code of conduct, which is a unique feature of Indian elections. He bemoans the palpable erosion of values in the election arena as winning becomes the sole objective. Drawing attention to the high proportion of Members of Parliament with serious criminal cases against them, he considers political party funding a grey area with no transparency in the source of funds. He concludes by seeking a persistent citizen campaign to induce political parties to undertake reforms.

One of the landmark initiatives taken by the Indian parliament to introduce transparency in actions of the government was the introduction of the Right to Information (RTI) Act in 2005. This act gives Indian citizens the right to access information from any public authority or institution. Satyananda Mishra, a former chief information commissioner, feels that RTI was the first serious attempt by the government to permit some transparency in the decision-making process. He feels that the advent of measures such as direct benefit transfer, Aadhaar and cheap access to mobile telephony has eliminated unwanted middlemen and leakage in the delivery of services by the government. He is of the view that with the advent of measures such as Mission Karmayogi, the government must ensure an interference-free working environment in which objective, impartial and balanced decision-making is feasible. Posting civil servants on the assurance of their loyalty may reap dividends in the short run but will adversely impact the efficiency of decision-making. So, the need of the day is selection of officers for designated jobs on their aptitude and proven track record. Mishra feels that for accountability to be made more effective, the information barrier between any government and its citizens must become sufficiently transparent if it cannot be done away with. The intent of the law on RTI was strengthening democracy by enhancing transparency in the functioning of the government and to contain corruption. He feels that the appointment of information commissioners at the state and central levels is being done increasingly as an act of patronage rather than the competence and impartiality of the person concerned. Mishra perceives a widespread feeling that the RTI is losing steam as a tool of citizen empowerment. It is thus incumbent on the state to carry forward the spirit of the reform process that was initiated by Parliament in 2005.

It is widely believed that Indian bureaucracy suffers from an overload of seniority and number of years in the service, for upward movement, rather than professionalism and merit. S. Ramadorai, with his vast corporate experience, has expressed the opinion that a new-age civil service should be identified by meritocracy and values, such that the country's most talented contribute to nation-building while maintaining the highest standards of integrity, objectivity and impartiality. He argues for a policy framework to mainstream lateral entry of experts from the private sector into the bureaucracy. In the recruitment procedure, he proposes a metrics-driven approach with inclusion of psychometric tests to get an insight into the candidate's attitude and aptitude. Quite in sync with the Administrative Reforms Commissions which have advocated a reduction in the age of recruitment, Ramadorai is a proponent of making the civil service a career option at the 10+2 level itself. He lays stress on reskilling officers at regular intervals since knowledge redundancy is fairly rapid. He suggests that the government create a single platform to automate every touchpoint between government, citizens and businesses. Ramadorai feels that the permanent service must focus on the attainment of sustainable development goals, in the process maintaining the centricity of the man on the road. Emphasizing the fact that the process of reforms is a journey and a not a one-time effort, he stresses the need for strengthening the civil service officers on aspects such as emotional intelligence, ethical values, empathy, learnability and the ability to work in a collaborative environment. While stressing on these factors, he also feels that any reform process must address issues connected with frequent transfers, tenure, political influence and systematic performance evaluation.

Dr Prajapati Trivedi, a professor at Harvard Kennedy School, was tasked with implementing a performance management system for government departments. He prepared a 'Results Framework' document to calculate a composite score for each department at the end of the year. A score of 100 per cent implied that all commitments were met. This enabled a performance-related incentive scheme, which could have been an excellent motivator for officials. However, the scheme, though approved in principle, could not be ordered for implementation, as the government underwent a change, and thus remained incomplete in application. Dr Trivedi has come to the conclusion, after observing the functioning of officials in the government, that while political will matters, bureaucratic skill is equally essential. If the government wishes to implement something that is outside the experience and competence of the regular civil servants, leaders must have the confidence, courage and determination to supplement bureaucratic skill with appropriate technocratic skill. He feels that civil service officers must gain some domain knowledge when they attain senior levels.

The 73rd and 74th amendments sought democratic decentralization of power and resources among the central government and local bodies such as Panchayati Raj Institutions to create more engagement of the public in governance. Subhomoy Bhattacharjee, a journalist with loads of experience in dealing with the government administration and civil servants, draws attention to some egregious examples of bureaucratic overreach in the third tier of government. Officials expand their remit at the expense of the political executive, taking advantage of the dis-balanced power structure written in the laws. The trend, he believes, has grown so pervasive that it has become the signature in any state administration, irrespective of whether the political formation running the state is a coalition or a single party. Effectively, the civil services hold the key to most economic activities. This is not just a game of one-upmanship but has far-reaching consequences, as India urbanizes massively through this decade, leading to demands for more involved policymaking. In effect, the non-elected executive is freed of any popular oversight, which the political executive is supposed to bring in. The only role left for the political groups, in or out of power, is to seek to be co-opted in the delivery mechanism to secure a larger share for the interest groups they represent.

One of the most severe criticisms about the civil service officers is that they are inaccessible in their ivory towers and are impervious to public opinion and sensitivities. Modern-day administration has become complex and merits wide consultation among citizen's groups when dealing with issues concerning infrastructure development in urban areas. Urban self-governing bodies were empowered by the constitutional amendments to practise participative governance so as to effectively address societal concerns. Kiran Mazumdar-Shaw, a very successful entrepreneur and one of India's pioneers and best-known biotechnology professionals, has been at the forefront of citizen's organization for improving governance for the welfare of the common man. Leading the Bangalore Political Action Committee, she shares her experiences on how collaborative and accessible officials have been successful in associating with citizen's groups to upgrade governance to the advantage of citizens. She maintains that non-participative and the not-too-constructive mindset of officials needs to undergo a change. Officials must function hand in hand with citizen's groups to bring about any upgradation in the life of citizens. Such an approach can help enlist the support of experts in different fields of urban management.

Arguing for civil servants to be mindful of technological developments to spur innovation, Dr Pushpendra Rai, a former deputy director general of World Intellectual Property Organization, maintains that technology and innovation promotion are the main drivers of development models today and so it is imperative for civil servants to focus on integrating these elements in all government policies and programmes. They need to institute systems under which officers strenuously work towards creating institutional links between research and industry to tap the innovative potential of all sectors. Innovation is not merely the physical part of such programmes but also its associated practices, ensuring that service delivery conforms to the highest standards, and the customer is the nucleus of the entire paradigm. He draws attention to recent civil service reform measures which have laid stress on these aspects, therefore making it incumbent on civil servants to moderate their approach towards the implementation of development programmes and adjust behavioural patterns accordingly.

Another advocate for civil servants to adopt a participative approach, Naina Lal Kidwai, after a successful banking career, has been championing the cause of collaborative governance by better accessibility and cooperation between citizen's groups and the administration. She has been an apostle for skilling women into hitherto unexplored professions for females, such as masonry and *jal sahiyas* (a cadre of drinking water service delivery at the grassroots). She advocates a partnership of trust and collaboration as the cornerstone for effective delivery of government schemes in far-flung areas, and this requires a genre of civil servants who are trained to be collaborative and accessible in their approach.

The Comptroller and Auditor General of India (CAG) reports are not the most welcome of documents to any administration. They are perceived to be 'fault-finding' documents which serve as 'stumbling blocks' for smooth administration. I have argued in my essay that the CAG should serve to be the 'change agent' by identifying itself with the executive and by collaborating to upgrade governance. Positive reporting and wide dissemination of audit reports to create a more aware citizenry is the order of the day. Digital auditing and sustainability reporting also need to be resorted to. It is also essential that the public accounts committee of Parliament has more structured and fixed schedule of meetings. This will help create greater accountability, thereby enhancing the trust between the government and its citizens.

All the contributors to the volume have had extensive experience with the civil service. Some have been 'insiders' in having been a member of the service themselves. Others have worked in close collaboration with the administration and drawing from their own multifaceted experiences, have expressed candid and practical opinions on the road forward for the service to upgrade governance and ensure inclusive and sustainable economic growth. The civil service has a very significant role to play for the fruits of development to flow down to the poor and deprived. Market forces or the champions of laissez-faire will not be able to ensure the delivery of welfare measures undertaken by the government. The civil service is the only vehicle which provides the connect between policy initiatives of the government and that strata of society who are meant to be beneficiaries of these welfare measures. Its role is critical. Those seeking to enrol in the administration need to have a mindset of 'service' more than seeking an 'employment'. They have to be non-partisan in their approach, be sentinels of unimpeachable integrity and work amid the citizen rather than from a pedestal of an overlord. Even as India surges to become one of the largest economies in the world, the well-being of the lowest common denominator at the bottom of the income pyramid can be uplifted only by a dedicated, conscientious and even-handed civil service.

1
IN SEARCH OF EXCELLENCE
Selection, Promotion and Retention

Deepak Gupta

When the country got Independence, the question of the nature and structure of the civil services led to an intense discussion, especially since the extant Indian Civil Services (ICS) was seen as an instrument of the imperial power. The provinces wanted their own services, as opposed to a central one, so that they could control them. Seeing the chaos of that time, the need to unite India and wary of the dangers of politicization, Sardar Vallabhbhai Patel led the successful battle to design the Indian Administrative Service (IAS), modelled on the ICS.

The gap over time, between the expectations of service delivery from the IAS and the debatable but nevertheless widespread perception of its progressive failure to meet them, raises fundamental questions of what has gone wrong and why and how to improve its institutional functionality and make it more internally competent. There can be no doubt that it has to be at the 'top of the ladder', in a manner of speaking, becoming a 'meritocracy'; i.e. having superior abilities, qualities and values than others. The debate must be about what kind of civil servant or service, the nation should have.

To a great extent, all this is dependent on 'systemic' aspects such as, the conditions of service and processes through which officers enter the service, how the subsequent career progression is governed and navigated and even the manner of exit. While some of these processes had inbuilt problems which have become evident or deepened over time, there have been conscious changes made and practices adopted by politicians that have impacted adversely both the ability of the service and the individual officer to play the expected role. In this essay, I discuss some of the important possible procedural changes related to these aspects.[1] All things remaining the same, these will positively impact the attitude, morale, performance and effectiveness of individual IAS officers, while strengthening the defining characteristics and professionalism of this premier civil service of India.

Excellence and Democratization

The manner of selection into the IAS is the first issue that needs to be addressed. The liberal response against patronage in early nineteenth-century Britain led to the demand for a new type of civil service, selected for competence, not connection; and promoted for ability, not seniority, promising a revolution in the quality of government. *The Northcote-Trevelyan Committee Report* (1854) recommended that superior posts in the East India Company be filled by the 'most promising young men of the day' through a merit-based competitive examination on a level with the 'highest description of education' in the country.[2] This was a development of fundamental importance. Fortunately, this principle in India was retained post 1947.

Over a period of time, the objective has increasingly been to democratize the process and make it less 'elitist' by having lower standards and to make the selection more representative through quotas. Both these were perhaps necessary and desirable. However, this has led successive governments to make many changes through ad hoc decisions related to maximum age, chances for sitting, structure of papers, etc. emanating from a continuous demand for more and more concessions couched in the language of 'sociopolitical compulsions'. Political populism, or the so-called political imperative, has had an

[1]These issues are discussed in detail in my book, *The Steel Frame: A History of the IAS*, Roli Books, Delhi, 2019.

[2]*The Northcote-Trevelyan Report*, March 1954, Wiley Online Library, https://bit.ly/3tXBgwF. Accessed on 24 November 2022.

adverse impact on the structure and quality of India's premier services, diluting its standards and even questioning the fundamental principle of merit per se.

This approach has affected the content and design of the national examination for entry into the premier civil services of the country, which must not be trivialized by a common denominator approach. Its prestige, rigour and exacting nature must be protected. There is a rare unanimity of opinion against the present system among experts, various stakeholders and civil servants, as reflected in the many reports of committees set up to review the scheme of examination from time to time and large number of articles. But there is a complete divergence of views within a wide spectrum of the political class. Even though the examination remains highly competitive and continues to give confidence that the all-India and central civil services have merit and are selected on that basis; there is a need for improvement in this process and even to roll back some of the changes made, howsoever difficult it might be politically. It is too important to be ignored. Some of the issues and suggested changes are discussed below.

The maximum age limit and number of attempts

During the nineteenth century, for good reason, there was a strong belief that only youngsters should be selected for the service. That is why the maximum age limit was always kept low and never more than 23, going as low as 19. In independent India, however, it has been increasing gradually from 24 in 1951, mostly in an ad hoc manner. The current age limit for general candidates is a very high 32. For the Other Backward Classes (OBCs) and Schedule Castes (SCs)/Schedule Tribes (STs) it is 35 and 37, respectively. The number of attempts have also correspondingly increased from two (1951) to three (1973), four (1990) and six (2014). For OBC, the number of attempts is nine, while there are no limits for SC/ST up to their age limit.

Every committee set up over the years to review the scheme of examination, including the Baswan Committee, which was the latest in 2016, has consistently recommended lower limits for both maximum age and the number of attempts. The reasons given in these reports and commented on in many articles can be summarized thus. First, younger officers would be more energetic, aspirational, enthusiastic, achievement-oriented and ready to take up challenges. Second, the Second Administrative Reforms Commission had stated that a civil servant entering at a later stage finds it difficult to adapt to and internalize, the core and intrinsic values demanded of a civil service.[3] People at the so-called ripe age have seen a bit of life, lack the moral or ideological commitment of a fresher from a university and come with a '"baggage" of entrenched mindsets'[4]. Finally, a higher age at entry makes reaching the top impossible. Thus, a driving force for good performance goes away, while simultaneously creating perverse incentives as a consequence. The problem is the same for the reserved categories.

These arguments are so persuasive that it is surprising that no heed is given to them. Therefore, we must restrict the maximum age to 26 for all categories, starting first by lowering the age to 28. It follows that no more than three attempts should also be permitted for them. The service does not need plodders who may succeed only because of taking the exam repeatedly.

Common examination and optional papers

Recruitments to the ICS and Indian Police (IP) used to be done separately. However, examinations in independent India were made common for the All-India and Central Services. The IAS, however, is clearly the first choice. Those officers who join other services continue taking exams for the IAS, sometimes through repeated attempts. This justifies making the examination separate and tougher for IAS aspirants, as it used to be. Moreover, different services have their own requirements. A possible alternative could be to have common preliminary and mains examinations with additional selected paper(s) for different services.

---

[3]*Refurbishing of Personnel Administration—Scaling New Heights*, Second Administrative Reforms Commission, Tenth Report, 2008, p. 96, https://bit.ly/3BWl4jE. Accessed on 22 December 2022.

[4]Ibid. 81.

Ever since the examinations started in England, it was felt that an excellent general education would be both desirable and sufficient for the examinations. It was also emphasized that only the general intellectual resources should be tested. Other requirements could be acquired later. This was the trend in the early decades in independent India too, when the humanities dominated the numbers who sat for as well as qualified for the examination. The trend now shows a huge preponderance of engineering and medical graduates qualifying.[5] They have been opting for primarily four humanities subjects—geography, history, sociology and public administration—making a cross-domain shift to humanities. Committees have noted that 'scorability' becomes the chief criterion while choosing optional subjects. Moreover, the threshold of difficulty is not the same, besides the complexity of preparing question papers of a uniformly high standard across a wide range of subjects. Therefore, the time has come to simply do away with all subject-optional papers and have only compulsory papers which cover all knowledge issues expected of candidates aiming to join the higher civil services.

Many State Public Service Commissions have already replaced optional papers with compulsory ones. The feedback suggests that this has been welcomed, because it has provided a level playing field at a stroke.

The IAS and the Federal Structure

At the time of Independence, most provincial leaders strongly opposed formation of All-India Services as provincial services permitted them to exercise greater control over the administration. Sardar Patel had recognized these services as a unifying factor. In the debate in the Constituent Assembly on 10 October 1949, he said:

> [There is] .... no alternative to this (All-India Service) administrative system...The Union will go – you will not have a

[5]The year-wise figures are available in the Annual Reports of the UPSC, https://bit.ly/3YF0CO1. Accessed on 22 December 2022.

> united India, if you do not have a good All-India Service, which has the independence to speak its mind, ... This Constitution is meant to be worked by a ring of Service, which will keep the country intact .... These people [All India Service officers] are the instruments. Remove them and I see nothing but a picture of chaos all over the country.[6]

The further rationale for the All-India Services, which Sardar Patel emphasized, was to have local administrators with a national perspective and top policymakers in the Centre to have grassroots knowledge. The practice, however, has been contrary to this principle.

As much as 33 per cent officers of the IAS cadre get promoted from the state services. They rarely go on central deputation and do not go to other state cadres. They are selected on the basis of seniority with the age being up to 56 years. Since Annual Confidential Reports (ACRs) are generally graded 'good/very good', the standards for which are minimalistic, the elevation is almost certain but for exceptional cases where officers are declared unfit. The seniority principle implies officers get promoted towards the end of their careers. It is a moot point as to what contributions can be expected from them at that stage, especially with no prospects of going higher.

There is a system of empanelment of direct recruits to the IAS to select those who can go for deputation to the Centre. Those who do not get empanelled stay in the states. Moreover, they continue to get their promotion in a routine manner and rise to the highest positions in the state. Many officers, empanelled or not, don't go to the Centre by choice. Many from both these categories of officers also belong to the respective state. One could argue, therefore, that state administration then largely remains in the hands of those who either do not want to go out of the state; those who have not been considered good enough to be empanelled; or, generally, those who belong to the state. The political-cum-civil servant nexus thus only gets stronger. This is also one reason why empanelled additional

[6]'Constituent Assembly Of India Debates (Proceedings)—Volume X', Constitution of India, 10 October 1949, https://bit.ly/2K4z8vU. Accessed on 18 January 2023.

secretaries should be sent back to the states.

The above processes have had very adverse consequences. First, they have considerably weakened the federal character of the service. Second, the competency of state administrations has diminished. Third, it has led to a huge shortage of officers on deputation to the Centre, which itself has become a controversial issue. It has also affected the to-and-fro movement between the Centre and states. Therefore, changes are required, urgently.

If the existing system of promotion has to continue, then at the very least, there should be an examination that allows younger officers to compete. When promoted, officers must go out of the state at least for one term and some, to other cadres. I suspect many officers would then not seek promotion, preferring to stay in the comfort of their states.

Serious shortages have developed in the IAS cadre, currently about 20 per cent.[7] A parliamentary committee has recently recommended that the annual intake of direct recruits should increase from 180.[8] Perhaps it would be appropriate to raise this number to 300, considering that some will be pensioned off during their careers. However, this must not lead to more promotions from state services.

This shortage of officers going to the Centre has led to two developments. The first has led to a controversial amendment in deputation rules proposed in January 2022 to ensure that states nominate a proportional number of IAS officers for deputation as per cadre strength. The amendment gives the central government powers to enforce compulsory deputation of officers, officers by name, even if they have not expressed their willingness for central deputation. This has already become another divisive issue in Centre–state relations, which does not bode well for either the service or individual officers. The second is the demand for lateral entry at the Centre, ostensibly

[7]Mishra, Abhinandan, '20% of Total IAS, IPS Posts Vacant in the Country', *The Sunday Guardian,* 3 April 2021, https://bit.ly/3AKFvPY. Accessed on 25 November 2022.

[8]*One Hundred Twelfth Report on Demands for Grants (2022–23) of the Department of Personnel and Training,* Rajya Sabha Secretariat, Parliament of India, March 2022, https://bit.ly/3VHAznl. Accessed on 25 November 2022.

on grounds of a lack of professionalism among the IAS officers, but more triggered by shortage. Since the latter issue has gained salience and many proponents, it is necessary to consider it in more detail.

Lateral Entry and Specialization

The generic issue of generalist versus specialist has drawn the attention of many management experts and thinkers. Some important observations below provide a context before we consider the Indian situation.

Many management experts like Peter Drucker have felt that specialists tend to have a telescopic view, when the need is to see the holistic picture towards 'broader policy premises', which the generalist does by seeing the total picture in perspective.[9] Prakash Tandon, who was one of India's most eminent managers in the private sector, has said that those who go to the top are gently 'despecialized' and 'generalized' so that they develop the capacity to take a broader executive view. They also stated that there was no reason to believe that private-sector managers would necessarily perform better because they would 'immediately become "bureaucrats" themselves'.[10]

It is well recognized that the process of policymaking has become very complex today. A multi-sectoral approach to framing of policy has become necessary. Instead of having a specialist in place, there should be a pool of specialists available having special expertise in an area or areas to assist in the formulation of policy. The coordinating and processing role that the generalist plays has become even more important. They may not be a technical expert but are a 'synthesizer' and 'coordinator' among different views or sub-systems a 'mediator' among contending interests and an 'arbiter' in conflict situations.

More than any other service, the work of an IAS officer brings them into contact with the common people, providing both grassroots experience and a learning to be down to earth. Moreover,

---

[9]Gupta, Deepak, *The Steel Frame: A History of the IAS*, Roli Books, 2019, p. 175.
[10]Ibid.

the interchange between the Centre and states gives a unique perspective and an overall view. Movement to different departments gives a cross-sectoral and holistic picture which goes beyond departmentalism, while serving at different levels provides insights into both policymaking and implementation. It may, therefore, be argued that the IAS officer has actually become a specialist domain expert in the most difficult and complex of domains—public administration.

There are some other valid concerns. First, given the erosion of state capability and institutional credibility at all levels, it runs the risk of degenerating into an uncontrollable 'spoils' system. This has happened in other countries. Pakistan is a good example. Service officers have a long-term stake in the system. Lateral entrants, as 'birds of passage', will necessarily have a short-term agenda, possibly within the time frame of a particular government. There could also be serious concerns about accountability and conflict of interest. In the complete absence of field or grassroots experience, policymaking by lateral entrants will have limited appreciation of ground realities or implementation challenges. Large-scale induction would work against coordination between the Centre and states as well as the modicum of uniformity in administration that the country now has, which will lead to a splintered administration. There are fears that if such a course is pursued seriously, in one generation, there won't be any permanent civil service left, removing a fundamental constitutional construct that safeguards both the country and its democracy, especially so designed by the makers of our Constitution.

This debate, however, underscores the need for officers to develop domain expertise and for structural and systemic reforms to enable and incentivize that. Domain competency comes from good subject-matter knowledge, work experience in that area and academic study or research and training. The design of an officer's career graph and their further appointments in the administration, subsequent to the district tenure, must enable this development. This includes training provisions and opportunities provided to pursue higher studies.

Professionalism can also be an effective moderator of, and even a strong curb on personal feelings and predilections. The intellectual integrity and professionalism of an officer should be greatly valued and positively encouraged; in fact, this is what is often referred to in a positive manner when an officer, in assessment reports, is commended as 'a thinking officer'. It would greatly harm the country if restraints are put on the intellectual capacity or conscience of civil servants, which converts them into mindless automatons.

Lateral entry should therefore not be considered as a general panacea to overcome system faults. Systemic faults need to be treated separately to remedy the fault lines that have crept in. Lateral entry of professionals is a simplistic solution seeking to remedy a very complex problem. Used selectively, it could benefit in limited areas. Used liberally, it could completely destroy the system.

Process Changes

Selection of top personnel

The higher echelons of the bureaucracy have a vital role to perform in policy formulation and implementation. It is thus necessary to ensure that the choice of officers to fill these positions is done with extreme care.

It would be stating the obvious that leadership positions in the administration must be filled by officers of impeccable integrity and proven merit and done in a transparent manner. Otherwise, the administration below will not only be demoralized but tend not to respect hierarchies and values, which will have its own adverse consequences. The message in such cases is that merit is not going to be rewarded.

Central government

Fortunately, the principle of seniority has been generally followed in the appointment of the cabinet secretary at the Centre. It may not get the best man, but ignoring seniority may lead to discretionary appointments often leading to demoralizing the service. The repeated extension in service—for two years and then one year at a time after the extended tenure of two years—which seems to have become the norm in the last decade, is not at all desirable. Nobody is indispensable. Fixed tenures should be respected.

In the previous United Progressive Alliance coalition government at the Centre, a substantive change occurred in the posting of secretaries to the central government. They were chosen only after they had met the minister concerned—for what reason? The messaging was incorrect. Departing from this disreputable practice, the present government has gone to the other extreme of postings, largely determined by the Prime Minister's Office. This role should be primarily performed by the cabinet secretary himself, as it used to be. Specialization and the career graph of the officer should automatically be able to suggest certain desirable options. If a fundamental criticism is against the 'generalist', then it would be highly inappropriate if an officer with specialization is not posted as head of the concerned department simply because they are not wanted and for no good reason. What can be worse than that?

These basic principles must be upheld and become the rule.

State governments

Appointment of chief secretaries in states has increasingly become very controversial. Often, it is no longer by seniority and there are many glaring examples of nepotism. Many go on to become advisors in the office of the chief minister. The identification with the government in power thus becomes complete.

Actually, the parameters within which such selections are made should be defined to ensure that it is not seen as a reward for 'services rendered' in the past. Such latitude has often been misused. The problem is that governments have increasingly tended to look at certain officers as 'personal' favourites who could be expected to do their bidding. If there was no labelling, no undue favours asked and only capable officers were promoted, the 'neutral' and 'committed' bureaucrat would faithfully implement programmes of the government of the day or the incoming government, irrespective of its political colour or their own beliefs.

I must go back to Sardar Patel to refer to the basic spirit behind the Constitution embedded in this concept of a neutral bureaucracy. In April 1948, he wrote to Nehru:

> [A]n efficient, disciplined, and contented service, assured of its prospects as a result of diligent and honest work, is a *sine qua non* of sound administration under a democratic regime even more than under an authoritarian rule. The civil servant must be above party and we should ensure that political considerations [...] are reduced to the minimum, if not eliminated altogether.[11]

During the debate in the Constituent Assembly, he made a pointed reference to the relationship between the 'minister' and the 'secretary' thus said: 'I have told them, "If you do not give your honest opinion for the fear that it will displease your Minister, please then you had better go. I will bring another Secretary," [...] [A]s a man of experience, I tell you, do not quarrel with the instruments with which you want to work.'[12]

Some way has to be found to carefully select the chief secretary and the director general of police (DGP) in states. The Supreme Court has laid down the procedure for the selection of DGPs in states, though the states are trying very hard to veer round it continuously. However, a 2017 Supreme Court judgment also noted that an incoming government could not change the DGP though it, perhaps mistakenly, stated that it could have a different chief secretary—the level at which policymaking is a major function—of its choice. Looking at developments in various states, perhaps some guidelines for appointing chief secretaries are urgently needed, as also about their post-retirement postings.

Empanelment and appraisal

In the IAS, there are separate routes for promotion in service and for empanelment for higher-level appointments in the Government

[11]Noorani, A.G., 'Bureaucracy's Place', Dawn, 20 August 2022, https://bit.ly/3jQ5lMO. Accessed on 4 January 2023.

[12]Constituent Assembly Debates on 10 October, 1949 Part I, https://bit.ly/3V7kh71. Accessed on 25 November 2022.

of India. Almost everyone gets promoted to the higher grades in the states by mere effluxion of time. It is well known that any organization which does not punish its poor performers, and worse, protects and promotes them, punishes its high performers. And a service cannot continue to be called premier if it cannot find a way to get rid of those who do not measure up and where even 'deadwood' can wait, often successfully, like 'hawks for a plum posting'. The artificial distinction between promotion and empanelment must be removed. Those not promoted at each stage should be weeded out with suitable pensions.

The cleansing process must start early because the rot also sets in early. Officers coming out of the district must be clean. Around 10–15 per cent of officers who do not meet minimum standards, or have corruption cases against them, should be weeded out at each of these two stages. This will ensure promotion getting firmly linked to performance and competence, spurring development of professionalism within the service and immeasurably improving the ethical conduct of the officers.

The appraisal system must also change. The criteria-based system for performance appraisal must be made assessment-subjective. Some officers undeservedly got 'outstanding', while others were rated 'good' or 'very good'. The latter would lead to the denial of promotion. The system changed, where certain attributes were given numerical ratings. More importantly, the assessments were to be shown to the subordinate officers who had a right to represent against the grading given. The result has been that high numerical ratings are now given routinely. Since 'outstanding' requires only 8/10, it is safe to give 8.1 if the officer is not so good. While empanelment may not happen, promotion is almost guaranteed.

The present government has introduced a 360-degree system of assessment. Some senior retired officer talks to seniors, juniors, peers, etc. of the concerned officer. Questions are asked related to the officer's integrity, accessibility, decision-making and functional skills, ability to withstand illegitimate pressures, pro-poor orientation, etc. This has, however, so far led to mixed results. While many have welcomed this in principle presuming it has put a premium both on competency and integrity as also positive behavioural traits, others say that it has also introduced a degree of ad hocism and disguised discretion. There is need for further reform and streamlining.

The time has come for this appraisal to be done through the Union Public Service Commission (UPSC). Committees have repeatedly recognized that only those who can demonstrate a credible record of actual performance and possess knowledge and skills required for higher responsibilities should be promoted. The UPSC panel can make this assessment by going into details of their work, various attributes, professionalism, the degree of specialization, etc. Ideally, all the officers should be called for a long interview with a panel of eminent persons headed by the UPSC chairman. They could be asked to send an essay on some subject and also explain in writing, the important work that they have done at different positions. The panel would also have his ACRs as well as the result of the 360-degree exercise. When the UPSC does this review, it should also consider the domain competency the officer has acquired. This change is necessary and urgent.

Regulation of tenures

This is a complex problem. The Second Administrative Reforms Commission had recommended that transfers must be regulated by a national civil services authority, like in Japan. This has been repeatedly endorsed by experts. The Supreme Court has directed that a civil service board should be set up for transfers. This order has simply not been implemented or is circumvented. In essence and in spirit, the board has also not functioned at the Centre. Chief secretaries in states and even the cabinet secretary at the Centre, no longer have the authority they once had in transfers.

Fixed tenure should be legalized into a regulation, but with exceptions, so that the solution also does not become a problem. Transfers may be necessary, and in some individual cases, desirable also, but the board must be involved. One also has to be practical to understand that the ruling dispensation, both at times of change and otherwise, must have some discretion. But this should not become licence and a tool to punish. In the Indian situation, such a crucial reform is a big ask. Politicians are not going to easily let this power of (arbitrary) transfer go.

Post-retirement positions

One of the most pernicious developments has been the conferment of special reward beyond normal conditions of service, largely at the central level but also in states, by sending retiring bureaucrats immediately to post-retirement posts. These have proliferated in recent years by the constitution of regulatory bodies, tribunals, commissions, committees, etc. This trend has led some scholars to voice concerns about a 'sinecure state' in which senior IAS officers and increasingly those of other services, modulate their performance in their final years of service at the expense of 'neutrality' and 'objectivity' to hop onto the 'gravy train' by landing plum post-retirement assignments. Of late, politics seems to be becoming a preferred option, which is even more dangerous. Senior officers resign or take premature retirement and join political parties the next day and even stand for elections immediately. In the *Civil Services Survey: A Report, 2010*, junior officers have commented on this being an important reason for the 'spinelessness of senior civil servants'.[13]

One alternative is that all secretaries, not just a privileged few, must get a minimum of two years' tenure and possibly, even three. All departments are important and so is the principle of minimum tenure. In fact, there is a strong argument in favour of such selected officers retiring only at the age of 62. The experience of capable officers is very valuable. In no case, however, should any extension to any officer be given. This may also help in sorting out the issue of appointments to autonomous bodies. This could be done at the age of 60, and only for three years, so that officers can choose to

[13]*Civil Services Survey: A Report*, Ministry of Personnel, Public Grievances and Pensions, Department of Administrative Reforms & Public Grievances, Government of India, 2010, p. 112, https://bit.ly/3V44KVR. Accessed on 25 November 2022.

go there or be (or remain) secretary to the Government of India till 62. If retirement stays at 60, all such appointments (including joining a political party) should have a cooling-off period of two years post-retirement, or resignation after reaching additional secretary scale.

Developments over time and particularly in the last two years, have brought multiple and multidimensional challenges to the fore—the continuing impact of the pandemic; the almost existential threat of climate change requiring enormous changes in our way of life and transformational change in economic systems; the emerging geopolitical and economic crisis caused by international events; the new-found Chinese aggressiveness, the rising worldwide tide of authoritarianism; extreme politicization; and sadly, the increasing domestic political and social divide. These emphasize, as never before, that good governance has become a country's most important resource. This includes both sound and enlightened political leadership and a competent bureaucratic administration. It is in this larger context that we should see the role of all the services.

The reforms suggested above would lead to younger officers entering the service better attuned to its needs. The system would encourage professionalism and reward merit and competence while the inefficient would be weeded out, ensuring only the really capable reach the top. Political neutrality would lead to better designing of policies and more effective implementation. To my mind, implementation of the reforms mentioned will lead to a sea change in the performance and effectiveness of the IAS and of other services, which the country badly needs. They need to be addressed with the utmost urgency.

2

ENSURING INTEGRITY

Fighting Corruption Within the Civil Services

Pradeep Kumar

> *In looking for people to hire, you look for three qualities—integrity, intelligence and energy. And if they don't have the first, the other two will kill you.*
>
> —Warren Buffett

Righteousness is the foundation of good governance. Having an honest, fair, impartial and accountable civil service is a necessary attribute of a nation, as the service is accountable for key responsibilities. Civil servants help formulate policies that affect the lives of people. They set the rules of the game for conducting business and commerce. They negotiate with private parties, allocate national resources, get projects implemented and facilitate the delivery of services to citizens and are privy to sensitive information. Integrity in their day-to-day functioning is paramount.

As the founding fathers of the Republic of India sought to create a neutral and professionally competent civil service capable of advising the political executive, they made recruitments to all higher ranks of the bureaucracy through the Union Public Service Commission (UPSC), an independent constitutional body. They further provided security of service to the members of civil service by ensuring that they cannot be dismissed, removed or reduced in rank except after concluding a fair enquiry in accordance with the provisions of Article 311 of the Constitution. This independent service, however, is not without its problems, one of the major ones being—corruption.

Corruption is widely prevalent in India. In most national surveys, corruption has invariably been ranked as one of the three most important problems facing the country. According to Transparency International's Corruption Perceptions Index for 2021, which ranks countries by their perceived levels of corruption, India is ranked 85th out of 180 countries, meaning 84 countries are perceived to be less corrupt than India. We ranked lower than China and many African countries, but higher than Pakistan, Bangladesh and Sri Lanka.[1]

Our statutes do not provide any definition of corruption. The meaning of corruption in India consequently has to be appreciated as the common man perceives it and as the law perceives it. Corruption within civil services entails misallocation of resources and distorted investment priorities. Public interest is neglected and the selection of projects and spending of funds is made based on considerations of 'what is in it for me?' There is cost and time overrun in implementing projects and the quality is compromised. There is leakage of funds. The benefits of the government policies and programmes do not reach the intended beneficiaries and the poor suffer the most. The businessmen also suffer because corruption distorts the operation of free markets. Corruption has the effect of weakening our institutions. Every time a person visits a police station or a government office and pays a bribe, their confidence in the rule of law gets undermined. Corruption by civil servants has a devastating impact on the country's developmental efforts and economic growth.

Corruption by civil servants can broadly be classified into two categories: petty corruption and grand corruption.

Petty corruption or retail corruption is coercive in nature and primarily involves the lower ranks of the bureaucracy. It mainly occurs when citizens have to pay bribes to obtain public services, such as a ration card, driving licence or an electricity or water connection. Failure to pay such bribes results in delayed services, unnecessary harassment, raising of needless objections and wastage of time. Poor

---

[1]'Corruption Perceptions Index: 2021', Transparency International, https://bit.ly/3AGiDBq. Accessed on 25 November 2022.

and weaker sections are the worst-affected, as they neither have the influence nor the means to pay. In India, 51 per cent of the bribes are paid for timely delivery of services to which citizens are already entitled.[2] Most of the mature democracies in the developed world have managed to free themselves of this type of corruption and a citizen is not harassed in his day-to-day conduct of business.

Grand corruption involves the grant of undue favours to private parties by higher levels of the government. It involves collusion among politicians, bureaucrats and businessmen in the award of public work contracts; in the procurement of goods and services; grant of permits and licences; other regulatory clearances; food and drugs adulteration; real estate transactions; recruitment, transfer and posting of officials; tax evasion; and allocation of natural resources. An extreme form of grand corruption is called 'state capture', where private interests dictate government policies.

Regulations and Frameworks to Combat Corruption

When India attained Independence, the lofty ideal of building a 'new India' and the fact that the new leadership of the country had been groomed under the moral leadership of Mahatma Gandhi was expected to keep the leadership free from the corrupting influence of power. Post Independence, several political leaders and civil servants, inspired by the ideals of the freedom movement, worked with great dedication, commitment and honesty to hold the country together in the aftermath of Partition. However, sadly, many in the civil services could not resist the temptations of office and the tremendous opportunities of corruption that were created as a result of the socialist policies of the government, the Licence or Permit Raj and the massive expenditures on building infrastructure and other government programmes. As early as 1948, Parliament and the

---

[2]*Global Corruption Report 2009: Corruption and the Private Sector*, Transparency International Report, 14 September 2009, https://bit.ly/3WD3UQ3. Accessed on 23 December 2022.

country were rocked by the Jeep scandal relating to the procurement of jeeps involving high public officials. By the early 1960s, corruption in government had become a matter of grave concern. Lal Bahadur Shastri, the then home minister, said in Parliament, 'Stamping out corruption is a very tough job, but I say so in all seriousness that we would be failing in our duty if we do not tackle the problem seriously and with determination.'[3] A high-level administrative committee under the chairmanship of K. Santhanam was set up to address the issue and submitted its report in 1964.

In pursuance of the recommendations of the Santhanam Committee, the Central Vigilance Commission (CVC) was constituted as a premier integrity institution in 1964, enjoying the same measure of independence as the UPSC. It was established with oversight over all central ministries, public-sector undertakings and other government organizations. The Central Bureau of Investigation (CBI) was established in 1963 as a premier federal agency to investigate cases of corruption against public servants, now under the Prevention of Corruption (PC) Act, 1988. The CBI's power to investigate cases is derived from the Delhi Special Police Establishment Act, 1946. Further, a vigilance set-up was established by the then Department of Personnel and Administrative Reforms in the ministries, public-sector undertakings and other central government organizations.

In 2003, on the basis of the Supreme Court's directive in the Vineet Narain case, the CVC was made a statutory body, independent of government. The Court also issued a number of directions to insulate the functioning of the CBI from government interference. The CVC was entrusted with the mandate of superintendence over the anti-corruption wing of the CBI. It oversees more than 6.5 million central government employees, has superintendence over the vigilance administration and tenders advice in respect of disciplinary and vigilance matters to the central government and its organizations. In

---

[3]Quoted in 'Speech of the President at the Inauguration of Seminar Being Organized on the Occasion of Golden Jubilee Celebrations of Central Vigilance Commission', Press Information Bureau, Government of India President's Secretariat, 11 February 2014, https://bit.ly/3V7Wbcm. Accessed on 25 November 2022.

2004, it was made the designated authority to receive whistle-blower complaints and protect the whistle-blower.

Over the years, successive governments have progressively strengthened the institutional framework for addressing corruption. The PC Act, 1946, was replaced with the PC Act, 1988 to give more teeth to the Act and to extend the definition of criminal misconduct. The Act has been further amended in 2018 to make active bribery an offence and has put bribe givers and bribe takers on equal footing.

The Right to Information Act was passed in 2005. It was a landmark legislation that gave power to citizens to seek information from the government and remove opaqueness from its functioning. Another important development has been the enactment of the Lokpal and Lokayukta Act in 2013 and its coming into force. Parliament enacted the Lokpal Act in response to the people's movement against corruption, led by the social activist, Anna Hazare. The Act has a wide-ranging mandate and was expected to check corruption by senior political leaders. However, the effectiveness and impact of this Act is yet to be assessed. The public interest litigation in the high courts and Supreme Court has become another powerful tool in the hands of citizens to hold the government accountable and keep a check on the exercise of arbitrary power.

India is a signatory to the United Nations Convention Against Corruption and remains actively engaged with other anti-corruption agencies. In a globalized world, we cannot remain isolated from developments in other parts of the world and must remain in step with the best global practices.

Approaches to Fighting Corruption: Preventive and Punitive

Preventive vigilance and punitive vigilance are the two ways by which governments and anti-corruption agencies keep a check on corruption by civil servants. While the former seeks to reduce the scope and opportunities of corruption in an organization, the latter focusses on punishing government servants for errant behaviour under department rules or regulations; and for frauds, malfeasance and other forms of criminal misconduct under the PC Act, 1988.

Corruption in government and its organizations is mainly due to administrative delays, cumbersome and ambiguous rules, discretionary decision-making and excessive state regulations and controls. The CVC has consistently worked with the government and its organizations for making systemic improvements; rationalization and simplification of rules and procedures; reducing human interface; and discretion in decision-making. It has advocated the use of information and communication technology wherever possible.

The Government of India, in a major initiative, has repealed more than a thousand obsolete laws, rules and regulations from its statute books. It has taken major steps to simplify the tax administration by computerizing the filing of income tax returns and their assessment. This has removed a considerable source of harassment and corruption. Similarly, the scheme for the financial inclusion of the poor, the Pradhan Mantri Jan-Dhan Yojana and various direct benefit schemes of the government, which enable the direct transfer of funds to their bank accounts, have transformed the delivery mechanism of government benefits. They have significantly reduced the leakage of funds too.

The explosion of mobile telephony and the spread of internet facilities have made it possible for people to directly access many of the services online, such as obtaining ration cards, birth and death certificates, renewal of driving licence and payment of house taxes, among others. The interface with the intermediary has been eliminated.

This development has helped address petty corruption as well, as it is best addressed by making systemic improvements and deploying technology.

One path-breaking initiative by the government was the dismantling of Licence Raj and unshackling of the Indian economy. The economic reforms initiated in the 1990s significantly reduced many of the old forms of corruption, resulting in faster economic growth and introduction of new areas of economic activity.

On the flip side, it also opened opportunities for corruption. As many private players, both domestic and foreign, entered into sectors that were earlier restricted, they sought to win government contracts along with a larger share of the market in the fast-growing economy, sometimes using dishonest means. In a globalized economy, round tripping and parking of ill-gotten wealth in tax havens abroad became easier. The challenge before anti-corruption authorities is to continuously remain in step with the changes, upgrade their skills and better equip themselves.

It is vital from the perspective of preventive vigilance to identify the areas in an organization that are prone to corruption. Officials with a good track record must be posted to these sensitive areas. They must be rotated periodically so that they do not develop vested interests. Vetting the integrity of public servants at the time of their promotion or appointment to an important public office is a crucial means to ensure that only people with proven integrity and clean records occupy high posts. As a part of the vigilance function, the CVC regularly vets more than 2,300 officers every year (2,371 in 2020). An important step relating to this is the requirement for civil servants to annually declare their immovable assets, which can then be regularly checked to detect if the declared assets are disproportionate to known sources of income.

A critical area prone to corruption is the procurement of goods and services and the award of public contracts. As much as 20 per cent to 22 per cent of India's GDP is spent on public procurement. The CVC and the finance ministry have issued detailed guidelines to ensure adequate competition, fairness and transparency in the procurement process. Recent initiatives such as e-procurement, integrity pact and the establishment of a government e-marketplace (GeM) have helped reduce corruption. Most of the posts held by civil servants also involve public procurement related decision-making. Yet, there is no formal training for officers on procurement or project management. They learn through experience on the job. It is necessary to build the capability of handling complex procurement cases within the civil services.

Preventive vigilance is an ongoing process and is necessary to reduce the scope and opportunities of corruption. But it is not sufficient by itself to curb corruption. The delinquent and corrupt must be punished strictly and swiftly. Punitive vigilance is vital for fighting corruption and should go hand in hand with preventive vigilance.

Punitive action can be either departmental or criminal. The former is taken when there is a preponderance of the probability of wrongdoing by a government official, while the latter is taken where corruption is proved beyond a reasonable doubt.

Credible anti-corruption efforts require that action is taken against big fish. It is not enough to punish the junior staff. The senior ranks of civil services must be held accountable to higher standards of conduct and should be given exemplary punishment. However, the task of acting against the powerful and corrupt is never easy. There is often a nexus between corrupt bureaucrats, politicians and businessmen. The bureaucrat is not above using his proximity to influential politicians and businessmen to derail the action against him. The politicians and businessmen also do not hesitate in enlisting the support of willing bureaucrats in pursuit of their political and business interests. Effective action against corrupt civil servants requires a credible, professionally competent, impartial investigation agency, independent prosecutors and a fair trial.

The challenge before governments is to create an environment in which the honest can work without fear, the corrupt are punished ruthlessly and there are no delays in exonerating the innocent and punishing the guilty. For too long, the rich, powerful and well-connected have thought that the laws of the land do not apply equally to them. There is one set of laws for them and another for the ordinary people. Fortunately, times are changing and as a result of the deepening of democracy, the spread of education, sustained efforts of the civil society, media (print, electronic and social); and accountability institutions like the Supreme Court, high courts, Comptroller and Auditor General of India and the CVC; the people at the grassroots are demanding a corruption-free government. For the first time, government and army officials, industrialists, and politicians are facing criminal action and jail. There is palpable fear among the corrupt. It would be wrong to say that VIP culture has disappeared, but the needle has moved.

The Crucial Role of Leadership

There can be no effective fight against corruption without proper leadership. There is enough evidence to show that organizations whose leadership is personally honest and committed to ethical and moral values fosters an environment supportive of ethical conduct.

The UPSC selects the members of the higher civil services through a rigorous process. They are bright men and women, well-qualified and knowledgeable. However, it is increasingly realized that mere high IQ or EQ is not enough for effective leadership. A leader must have a moral dimension, a moral compass to guide him as he navigates myriad challenges in his journey and is called upon to make difficult choices. His inner resources and character alone will help him to decide what is right and what is wrong. Rabindranath Tagore, on leadership, has been, as usual, practical and forthright in his views: 'Character, not brain, will count at the crucial moment.'

All-India Services and Central Services members are in a leadership role from the day they join the service. Their influence on the functioning of government is way beyond what their limited numbers would suggest. Their conduct sets the tone for other employees. Their ethical and moral moorings are therefore key to good governance. Integrity in their case does not mean mere financial probity but includes moral and intellectual honesty—the courage to speak the truth to those in power.

I fondly recall my days as a probationer in the IAS in LBS National Academy of Administration in the early 1970s. At that time, a term commonly used in the academy was OLQ, meaning 'officer like qualities'. It had no precise definition, but everybody understood what it meant. It implied that officers of the service would act with dignity and honour at all times. It was expected of them to have a sense of 'what is right and what is wrong', 'what is done and what is not'. The officers not adhering to OLQ met with stern disapproval from their peers. There was an unsaid belief in Plato's dictum, 'Good people do not need laws to tell them to act responsibly, while bad people find a way around the laws.'

The informal value system of the service served a useful purpose but was not adequate to ensure ethical behaviour. A more formal compliance to All India Services (Conduct) Rules, 1968 was considered necessary and insisted upon. It incorporated many, if not all, of the dos and don'ts of the OLQ. It is time to consider implementing the recommendation made by the Second Administrative Reforms Commission, 2007, to define the 'public service values' towards which all public servants should aspire and which should be made applicable to all tiers of government. Transgression of these values should be treated as misconduct inviting punishment.

The political and administrative environment in which the All-India Services functions has undergone a sea change since the time I was a probationer at the academy. The polity has moved from a single-party dominance to a highly contested multiparty system, wherein many states are ruled by parties different from the party in power at the Centre. Coalition governments are also not an uncommon feature both at the Centre and state level. All-India Services, which are jointly shared between the Centre and states, have to reckon with this reality. The officers get caught in the crossfire of various political parties with different agendas, many a time, for no fault of theirs.

The political executive, both at the Centre and the states, has made a consistent effort to curtail the power of the civil services to take decisions in administrative matters which are rightly within their domain. Since they could not easily remove the officers, in view of the protection provided to them under Article 311 of the Constitution, they thought of other ways to tame the bureaucracy—frequent transfers, punishment postings, lack of stability in tenure and humiliating officers in public. Unceased political meddling and interference in the working of the administrative apparatus has led to indiscipline, inefficiency, corruption and unaccountability among the employees. It is no wonder that many now say that the 'steel frame' of Indian bureaucracy has corroded.

This has also given rise to a class of unprincipled officers who have no qualms in shedding their political neutrality and objectivity and aligning themselves with the party in power. The politicians reward them with choice postings, smoother career progression and shut their eyes to their many transgressions made in pursuit of their personal gains. They are accountable to nobody except their political masters. The silver lining is that this unholy arrangement does not last forever. Once the political party loses power, their glory ends. Many of them are hounded and face inquiries. This is, however, a small consolation because the damage that they do to the system is enormous and long term.

At the other end of the spectrum, despite a challenging work environment, are a class of All-India Services officers who are honest, dedicated, fair and objective and who adhere to the highest standards of integrity. Sometimes, they may have to pay a price for their convictions, but they remain undeterred. It would be a mistake to conclude that they are not valued. They enjoy credibility and respect among their peers. They even come to earn the grudging respect and appreciation of politicians. Eventually most of them, if not all, get fair, just dues and recognition.

The bulk of officers are in between. If good behaviour is consistently rewarded and bad behaviour consistently punished, the bulk of officers follow the narrow and straight path. On the other hand, if good behaviour is not only not rewarded but is actually fraught with difficulties and bad behaviour is extravagantly rewarded, a bulk of them tend to stray from the honest path.

The path that members of the All-India Services choose to follow in the service is ultimately for them to decide. They will have to deal with the consequences of their choice. But we can make the decision easier for them by reversing the perverse system of incentives that makes corruption a 'high-return, low-risk' activity and institutionalizing an appropriate mix of incentives for the honest and disincentives for the corrupt.

Candidates of character with a strong commitment to public service must be selected at the recruitment stage. During training and in-service programmes, the importance of adhering to ethical conduct needs to be constantly reinforced. There should be no latitude given to those who fail to comply with the ethical norms expected of the members of the higher civil services. As John Adams, one of the founding fathers of USA, said, 'Because power corrupts, society's demands for moral authority and character increase as the importance of the position increases.'

The Need for Reforms

It is generally acknowledged that the criminal justice system of India needs serious reform. The CBI, the premier federal agency to investigate offences of corruption, had acquired an enviable reputation of professional competence after its formation. However, in recent years, its reputation has taken a dent. There have been controversies surrounding its handling of some prominent cases and on the quality of its investigation. With different political parties in power at the Centre and in states, differences have emerged on the CBI's power and jurisdiction to investigate cases with respect to certain states. The Supreme Court has tried to insulate the investigations by CBI from any outside interference by providing a fixed tenure to the director of CBI, whose selection is done by a high-level panel comprising the Chief Justice of India or his representative, the Leader of the Opposition and chaired by the Prime Minister of India. Further, the Supreme Court has mandated superintendence over the CBI's functioning by the CVC. However, the public perception about the CBI continues to be that it is misused by every government and is a handmaiden of the government of the day. The pace of investigation in many important cases involving the high and mighty is often based on political calculations.

The CBI needs to have checks and balances to ensure the integrity of its investigation. It is essential that it develops robust internal systems to monitor corruption within its ranks and eliminates it with an iron hand. It should create a work environment in which the officers and ranks of the CBI are able to take pride in their own professional competence and the work they do; and needs to upgrade its in-house training for officers. In a globalized world, investigating transnational flows and recovering the assets of the proceeds from crime of the corrupt becomes a priority. The CBI needs to focus on building its capability as investigations become more scientific and new techniques of collecting and evaluating evidence are developed.

The CBI functions under the Delhi Special Police Establishment Act, 1946. There is also a felt need of an external oversight mechanism to assess the quality of investigations carried out by the CBI and enhance its accountability. The oversight, of course, has to be carried out in a manner that does not, in any way, compromise the independence of the investigating officer in conducting the investigation. It must be post-facto; of investigations which have already been completed with a view to assess the quality of investigation carried out and the scope for improvement. The oversight could be done either by a parliamentary committee or by a group of retired Supreme Court judges, the CVC and other eminent persons. To address many of these and other issues, there is a strong case for Parliament to replace the existing Special Police Establishment Act and legislate a new Act in tune with the needs of the present times and requirements of a modern federal investigative agency.

If improving the functioning of the CBI is a challenge, equally (if not more) daunting is the challenge posed by the endless judicial delays. On an average, it takes 12 to 18 months to complete the investigation, seven to eight years for the trial court to reach a decision and thereafter, there is appeal and revision to higher courts. The failure of our judicial system to decide cases within a reasonable time frame is a major lacuna.

Table 1
PC Act Cases Pending Trial

Length of Pendency	As on 31 December 2020
Less than three years	1,304
More than three years and up to five years	1,031
More than five years and up to 10 years	2,168
More than 10 years and up to 20 years	1,782
More than 20 years	212
Total	**6,497**

Source: Central Vigilance Commission Annual Report, 2020, https://bit.ly/3VoGZY3, p. 96.

Table 2
Age-Wise Analysis of Pending Appeals and Revisions

Age	Appeals	Revisions	Total
Less than two years	1,810*	443	**2,260**
More than two but less than five years	2,510	315	**2,825**
More than five but less than 10 years	3,420	209	**3,629**
More than 10 but less than 15 years	1,745	79	**1,824**
More than 15 years but less than 20 years	626	17	**643**
20 years	394	3	**397**
Total	**10,512**	**1,066**	**11,578**

Source: Central Vigilance Commission Annual Report, 2020, https://bit.ly/3VoGZY3, p. 97.

*This figure is incorrect in the original

Nearly 1,800 cases are pending in trial courts for more than 10 years and more than 200 cases for more than 20 years. The situation is equally bad if not worse at the appeal stage in the high courts, with more than 2,700 cases in appeal for more than 10 years. If a decade is taken to convict or acquit an accused, it is neither fair to the accused official nor to the government. The corrupt use the loopholes in the system to delay their conviction, whereas the innocent are unnecessarily harassed with their reputation in tatters and career in ruins. The whole system of rewards and punishments gets upended. The government has tried to reduce the heavy pendency of cases by establishing 91 special courts to deal with offences under the PC Act. But as the CVC Annual Report 2020 shows, the pendency continues to remain heavy. The problem of judicial delays is deep-rooted and mere tinkering will not help. Our judicial system needs wide-ranging reforms. 'Justice delayed is justice denied,' is an old maxim.

The role of political leadership is crucial in driving reforms. Without their strong commitment and support, the efforts of the civil services to reform the system can only have limited impact.

The Way Ahead

A challenge as complex as eradicating corruption has no simple or single solution. Preventive and punitive vigilance are effective and practical ways to curb it and support each other's effort, but they have failed to eliminate corruption. Their efforts have not succeeded, mainly because corruption is rooted in human greed, self-interest and the desire to secure an unfair advantage.

In the near and medium term, the only practical way to check corruption is to persevere and make preventive and punitive vigilance more effective. Moreover, to encourage ethical behaviour, an appropriate mix of incentives to reward good behaviour and disincentives to punish bad behaviour should be put in place. The laws of the land should be strictly enforced equally for all, without any discrimination.

The members of the All-India Services are at the helm of administrative apparatus at the Centre, state and field level.

Their conduct sets the tone for other employees. Therefore, it is incumbent upon them to maintain the highest standards of integrity and ethical conduct at all times. They have to be judged by higher standards than others, in view of their centrality to the administration and the power, prestige and responsibility they enjoy. Any failure on their part should invite strict punishment without any delay.

There can be no effective fight against corruption without ethical and honest leadership. The role of the political leadership in this fight is as crucial, if not more, than that of the administrative leadership. Political will, firm commitment and strong support are essential to implement large-scale reforms, make meaningful progress and change the system.

In the long term, from a societal perspective, efforts must be made to mould human behaviour. Societies that emphasize right moral and ethical values, which are less unequal and discourage unbridled materialism, are likely to be less corrupt. School and parents are the most defining influence in shaping a person's values and worldview. A beginning has been made by the CVC in collaboration with the Ministry of Education and Central Board of Secondary Education to start value education in schools from primary to secondary level.

Global experience shows that rule-based liberal democracies are least prone to corruption and best positioned to fight it. Similarly, experience shows that harsh laws and stringent punishments are inadequate to control corruption. China has some of the harshest laws against corruption but continues to be ranked 66th on the Corruption Perceptions Index, 2021.[4] India is fortunate in the deepening and strengthening of its democracy with the passage of time. Its march towards a rule-based democracy where laws are uniformly applied to the rich, powerful and the ordinary is steady. There may be occasional setbacks, but the direction is clear and remains unchanged. The demand for good governance is coming from the grassroots. It is very encouraging that the public, non-governmental organizations

[4]'Corruption Perceptions Index: 2021', Transparency International, https://bit.ly/3AGiDBq. Accessed on 25 November 2022.

and community organizations are becoming vigilant and demanding accountability from the government for its actions. The citizens are no longer prepared to accept corruption as a way of life.

Growing public support and participation in the fight against corruption offers us hope. It puts pressure on thc political class. As citizens, our job is to encourage the government and its many functionaries to follow their dharma[5]. We, on our part, as Gandhi ji said, can try to be the change that we wish to see in the world.

[5]Dharma is a philosophical concept that evolved from Hinduism. The term has no exact equivalent in the English language, but loosely translated, it means 'doing your duty in a righteous way'.

3
ELECTORAL PROCESS REFORM

Stewarded by the Civil Services

N. Gopalaswami

When the Constituent Assembly (1946–49) successfully completed its work, the Constitution of India was brought into existence on 26 January 1950 and an era of electoral democracy was born. Indian leaders chose to empower the people and opted for a democratically elected government in the states and at the Centre.

The Constituent Assembly opted for universal adult franchise, a great leap of faith given the very low overall literacy level of 15 per cent, with female literacy at an abysmal 7 per cent at that time. This decision was condescendingly referred to as a 'brave thing [...] if it succeeds' by Sir Anthony Eden.[1] If only to disprove such dark forebodings, men and women responded admirably, with the country seeing regular periodic elections, hailed universally as free and fair, effecting transfer of power with an enviable smoothness, while democracy in the neighbouring countries failed to survive. Credit for that must also go to political parties and the Election Commission of India (ECI) in no mean measure. As eternal vigilance is the price of democracy, it is worth examining how far that vigil has sustained.

---

[1]Quoted from Report of the Committee on Electoral Reforms 1990 in Rajah, N.L., 'Electoral issues and the Constitution of India', *Indian Democracy: Contradictions and Reconciliations*, Aravind Sivaramakrishnan and Sudarsan Padmanabhan (eds.), Sage Publications, New Delhi, 2020.

Constitutional Provisions

The ECI was set up and a Chief Election Commissioner (CEC) took office on 25 January 1950, a day before the country became a Republic. It was a symbolic gesture, reiterating its status as an organization independent of the Executive. A separate chapter in the Constitution, Part XV, titled 'Elections' contained provisions relating to the ECI and its powers in Article 324–29, has been briefly summarized as follows:

> Article 324: Superintendence, direction and control of elections shall vest in an Election Commission.
>
> Article 325: Electoral rolls will be common for all, and there shall be no special electoral roll on grounds of religion, race, caste or sex.
>
> Article 326: Elections to the House of People and to the Legislative Assemblies of states will be on the basis of adult suffrage.
>
> Articles 327 and 328: Parliament empowered to make provision with respect to elections to Parliament and State Legislatures, but State Legislatures only in respect of their Legislatures.
>
> Article 329: Courts barred from interference in electoral matters except through an election petition.[2]

Articles 324 and 329 are of special significance. The ECI's overarching powers and responsibilities are spelt out by the first one. The last one is about courts being barred from interfering during the course of conduct of an election, helping to avoid any delay in holding elections.

Parliament enacted two procedural laws: the Representation of the People Act, 1950 and the Representation of the People Act, 1951. The 1950 Act lays down the law on the number of seats in Parliament

[2]Constitution, Part xv, Elections', https://bit.ly/3joFagi. Accessed on 23 December 2022.

and State Legislatures; delimitation or fixing the contours of each constituency; the various authorities connected with or overseeing election work and the registration of voters at the district and sub-district level; the preparation of electoral rolls, qualification and disqualification to be a voter; and on all matters connected thereto.[3]

The 1951 Act deals with all procedural issues from the time election is announced to its final completion by declaration of results and includes provisions for the qualifications and disqualifications for being a Member of Parliament (MP) or a Member of Legislative Assembly (MLA); the administrative machinery and powers to conduct elections; registration of political parties; responsibility of the candidate to declare his assets and liabilities and submission of account of election expenses; disputes, election petitions and their disposal; corrupt practices and electoral offences and disqualifications; and the rule-making powers.

While the rule-making power is with the central government, the Supreme Court has recognized plenary powers of the Election Commission under Article 324 and has declared that the Commission can make rules in any area not occupied by legislation or rules. Thus, the ECI has been given a wide ambit to enable it to effectively carry out its mandate.

The ECI, Election Management and the Many Innovations

Sukumar Sen, the first CEC of India, had a daunting task to perform in laying down every detail related to the gigantic exercise of conducting the first-ever general election. Every provision of law and rules had to be rendered into easily understandable instructions to the staff at various levels. Given the low literacy, each party's candidate was provided a symbol under the ECI's Election Symbols (Reservation and Allotment) Order 1968 and a separate box for

[3]Ramadevi, V.S., and S.K. Mendiratta, *How India Votes: Election Laws, Practice and Procedure*, Fourth Edition, LexisNexis, 2017.

the voter to recognize the candidate and deposit the ballot paper correctly. Candidate-wise boxes were continued in the second general election (1957) and thereafter, all elections had only one box with the ballot paper having the names of all candidates with their respective symbols. The first general election (1952) stretched over a period of seven months, inevitable in a country of subcontinental proportions with various climate zones. So far, 17 general elections have been held in these seven decades, and the ECI has earned a reputation for competence in conducting free and fair elections because of the strong foundation laid down by the first CEC, and continuously innovated and improved upon by his successors. Credit must also go to the bureaucracy at all levels which has been by and large neutral.

Responsibility to prepare an electoral roll of eligible voters is given to the election machinery at ground level annually—with 1 January as cut-off date—and supplemented by special revision prior to election time. Further fine-tuning has been done now with four enrolment dates every year—the first day of every quarter.

From a voter base of 173.2 million in 1951, it has reached 910 million, as of 2019.[4] The fast urbanization and consequent internal migrations posed a problem in updation at new locations and simultaneous deletion at the old ones; as well as problems in checking identity to prevent duplicate entries that increase the potential for impersonation.

It was against this background that a dynamic and no-nonsense CEC, T.N. Seshan—who was in office from 1990 to 1996—decided to make it compulsory for every voter to be given an electors' photo identity card (EPIC). Ruling parties opposed the move, ostensibly on grounds of financial constraints, but more probably because it may affect bogus voting and impersonation mischief. The CEC was firm on: 'No EPIC, no election'. The Supreme Court brokered peace by supporting the idea of EPIC but directing the central government

[4]'General Election Archive (1951–2004)', Election Commission of India, https://bit.ly/3WXU8bo. Accessed on 4 January 2023.

to provide the finance. Soon, the ECI's EPIC became much sought after as a multipurpose identity card.

The ECI approves over a dozen identity documents having a photograph but mandates that if a voter has been issued EPIC, they should invariably produce that as identity at the polling station. In Febuary 2007, the ECI had gone all out to ensure the issue of EPICs to all voters of a state that was to go to poll and so mandated that only EPICs be produced as identity. In an effort to thwart it, a few hours before the start of polling, the chief minister of the state posed a rhetorical question to the CEC, 'I have misplaced my EPIC. Will I be disallowed from voting?' But little did the surprised minister realize that an unruffled election official would open his office past midnight, make out a duplicate EPIC and deliver it to him at 2 a.m.[5] Such is the efficiency of the ECI.

In 2007, the ECI introduced an analysis of electoral rolls for their accuracy by using the information of decennial census population as a template. Any deviation between the projected population, in different age groups, as per the census and the numbers in the voters list is used to pinpoint under-enrolment or over-enrolment. The first such exercise revealed gross under-enrolment, with 60 per cent shortfall in voter registration in the age group of 18–25; and remedial steps were initiated.[6] Since then, this exercise has become a regular feature to assess the health of electoral rolls.

A further measure, Aadhaar, a biometric ID unique to every person, was launched by the Government of India (GoI) in 2009 as available to any resident, citizen or otherwise. The ECI has been keen on linking electors with their Aadhaar numbers, but civil society groups objected to it, raising privacy concerns despite the ECI's assurance that Aadhaar information kept at the back end would not be accessible to anyone, except to ECI officials. The GoI passed a legislation for linking Aadhaar with electoral rolls (in 2021), paving the way for benefits; like quicker identification and removal of duplicates; easier enrolment of

[5]I was the CEC in question and it is the conversation I had with the then CM of Punjab. (From the author's personal notes of that time.)

[6]From the author's personal note of the time.

migrants; and facilitation of remote voting for Non-Resident Indians and internal migrants (as and when considered) to follow.

Voting Goes Electronic

India adopted the conventional voting methodology of ballot papers marked by hand with pencil and later replaced by the rubber stamp. But with the voter base inching to the 400-million mark by 1980, the printing; verification to remove ballot papers with printing mistakes including duplicate serial numbers; safe storage and transport; and finally, the counting of polled ballots were all found to be time-consuming and laborious. Ballot paper size also kept increasing with growing number of contestants adding to complexity. That is when, in 1977, the ECI under CEC, S.L. Shakdhar, talked about an electronic voting machine (EVM). A prototype was subsequently readied, and the ECI started using EVMs from 1982, exercising its plenary power under Article 324. However, in 1984, the Supreme Court declared that plenary powers cannot be invoked since the law specifically mentioned ballot papers, thus ending the use of EVMs.

Eight years went by before the law got amended and rules were passed, with the parliamentary committee on EVM commending it unreservedly. But the actual use of EVMs recommenced only in 1998. In 2001, Tamil Nadu became the first big state to go the EVM way fully. That decision was challenged right up to the Supreme Court but without much success. The whole country went the EVM way—with more than a million machines kept available for 0.7 million polling stations (with 0.3 million machines being kept as spare or reserve)—in the 14th general election (2004).

The EVM had a simple design: its face mimicking the paper ballot with the rubber stamp replaced by a button, which on being pressed, emitted a 'beep' noise indicating the recording of a vote. It did not permit another vote being cast for a 15-second interval. Further, the presiding officer had to enable casting of a vote by pressing the 'release' button in the control unit. Votes were recorded in the control unit and at the counting table. The control unit would display the total number of votes polled and candidate-wise numbers.

The EVMs have found favour with voters because of the ease of operation and quickness in counting and declaration of results. Counting and announcement of results that stretched to almost 24 hours (in case of a parliament constituency in ballot paper days) gets done in just about six to eight hours now in the EVM era.

Having reduced the scope for many malpractices, the EVM became a target for attack. Initially—during the general elections of 2004—in a mild effort to frighten voters, rumours were spread that EVMs will deliver a shock if touched. The more ingenious campaigners warned that except their button, the rest would deliver a shock if touched. The ECI countered this through advertisement conveying that being battery operated, EVMs would not deliver electrical shock.[7]

Losers Target EVM: Criticism and Response

Post elections, for defeated candidates, EVMs became the one peg to hang all their disappointment and frustration. The ECI wisely decided early on that at every step of the operation relating to EVMs, transparency should be the watchword and that there should be no human intervention.

First Level Checking (FLC) and repairs are carried out two to three months prior to elections, when a mock poll is done casting 500–1,200 votes on 5 per cent of randomly selected machines. Closer to the date of the poll, machine allocation from the district to a constituency and from there to individual polling stations are also randomized through computer programs. A second mock poll is done, in the presence of contesting candidates, when machines are allocated to polling stations, with 10–20 votes polled in every machine and 1,000 votes on 5 per cent of them. A final mock poll is done in the presence of the candidates' polling agents at the polling stations just before the start of regular voting. Finally, not only the allocation of

[7]'Electronic Voting Machine', Election Commission of India, 3 April 2018, https://bit.ly/3Cl7dnt. Accessed on 4 January 2023.

EVMs is randomized through computer programs but assignment of personnel to polling stations is also randomized and buttressed; with the stipulation that the personnel posted on duty cannot belong to or be residents of the polling station area. These steps are testament to the ECI's commitment to transparency and fair play.

Notwithstanding the steps taken for transparency, losers' criticism of the machine did not wane and challenges were mounted in courts. In 2013, the Supreme Court directed the ECI to introduce Voter Verifiable Paper Trail (VVPAT) to reassure the voters of correct recording of their choice. The ECI then mandated comparing the result obtained from the EVM and VVPAT slips in one polling station per assembly constituency. Later, the Court rejected demand for comparison in 50 per cent polling stations, but increased the number to five in each constituency. The 17th general elections to Lok Sabha (2019) saw a total of 20,625 EVM–VVPAT comparisons done, with not a single instance of deviation, establishing beyond doubt the reliability of EVM.[8]

EVMs are not liked by contestants because of its accuracy and the fact that no vote gets wasted—unlike a paper ballot, which can get rejected for ambiguous marking or double/triple marking and has the potential to lead to victory or defeat with the lowest margin, namely one vote. Two such instances happened in the 2008 assembly elections: one in the state of Rajasthan and the other in Madhya Pradesh. Moreover, unlike ballot papers that can be destroyed completely by mischief mongers, EVM, even when broken up, can still give out the result as its 'chip' containing information on votes polled can be 'read' by special equipment.

EVMs come under the category of Direct Recording Systems (DRS), but are stand-alone machines, not networked, not connectable or connected to any external source, wired or wireless. While politicians indulge in blame games targeting EVMs, the common man has not fallen in that trap and has shown immense faith in the trustworthiness of EVMs and consequently, the results.

---

[8] *Presentation on EVM and VVPAT*, Election Commission of India Booklet, 2018.

Changing the Face of Elections

The CECs are chosen by the government of the day but being independent constitutional authorities, they are appointed by and report to the President of India. Since its inception, there was only one CEC, but in October 1989, two additional members were appointed as Election Commissioners and it was common knowledge that it was done because the then CEC refused to defer to the government of the day in fixing a date of election. Sure enough, two months later, the Opposition, which won the election, reverted the ECI to single-member status. There was re-enactment of this plot in October 1993, when Seshan as CEC was bent on exercising his constitutional powers to the hilt, making the political class uncomfortable. But from then on, it became a permanent feature, with the ECI becoming a three-member body.

The 1990s were important years in the history of elections in India. After the first four general elections (1952 to 1967), the Indian political scene changed considerably. Gone were old-generation leaders imbued with idealism, and pursuit of power became the obsession with electoral malpractices creeping in steadily. Booth capturing and forcible stuffing of ballot boxes, impersonation, threats and intimidation of perceived unfavourable voters, misusing state police force against the Opposition, threats to polling staff or appointing staff that would connive—all these and more were resorted to. The scene was ripe for strong action by the ECI and the tenth CEC, Seshan, was equal to the task. Apart from the introduction of EPIC, he initiated many other corrective steps, such as:

1. Appointment of senior civil servants of IAS and IPS from outside the state as independent observers to each constituency;
2. Removing officers considered as non-neutral or partisan from election duty;
3. Bringing in Central Armed Police Forces to police sensitive polling stations;
4. Claiming successfully that the CEC will initiate performance appraisal of senior officials drafted for election duty;

5. Resorting to cancellation of poll if there was report of malpractice and especially of such polling stations where more than 90 per cent of the voters had allegedly cast their votes when the overall polling had been at 60 per cent or even less;
6. Mixing of the polled ballots at the start of counting operations, preventing candidates knowing who voted for whom, to prevent post-poll violence;
7. Updation of the Model Code of Conduct and its strict implementation;
8. Asserting independence of the ECI in deciding when elections will be called.[9]

These steps made the ECI one of the most trusted institutions in the eyes of the public.

The Constitution prescribes a five-year tenure for the Legislative Assemblies and the Lower House of Parliament from the date of the first meeting. The Representation of the People Act, 1951 (Section 15) empowers the ECI to conduct an election to an Assembly or Parliament at any time not earlier than six months prior to the date of completion of its tenure. This is to ensure against any political vacuum being created by the absence of an elected body, and so the ECI is left with no scope or excuse not to conduct elections within the stipulated time. Given the regional, ethnic, linguistic and religious diversities, decision on the timing of an election is taken by the ECI after consulting the states and after ensuring that national, regional, religious festival days and other declared holidays are avoided. Since a large number of teachers are drafted for election duty, school and college examination periods are also excluded. The regional weather pattern is also factored in and the monsoon period is avoided, as it can severely affect work. Notwithstanding this exercise, sometimes, adjustment of dates become inevitable if some fine detail is overlooked, as it happened recently in the run-up to the Punjab assembly election (2022), when the ECI had to change the date of

[9]Ramadevi, V.S., and S.K. Mendiratta, *How India Votes: Election Laws, Practice and Procedure,* Fourth Edition, LexisNexis, 2017.

poll as the earlier decided date was right in the middle of a period of the traditional annual pilgrimage by a very large section of the population to a revered Guru's birthplace.[10] In an earlier instance during the elections to the Bihar assembly in October–November 2005, the ECI rescheduled polling in selected constituencies a mere week before the earlier announced poll dates, citing fresh inputs to prevent poll-day violence or mischief. Out of the 243 constituencies, poll was rescheduled in 26 selected ones in the first three phases of the originally announced four-phase election and, as a result, the polling came to be held in seven phases in all.[11]

Further, the size of the state, the number of polling sections, the overall security situations or law and order concerns are factors that decide the number of phases of poll with big states such as Uttar Pradesh, Bihar, Chhattisgarh, etc. needing multi-phase polling.

The pre-eminent position of the ECI being the final arbiter in deciding the timing of the election (in exercise of its plenary powers under Article 324) was endorsed by the apex court when, in 2002—citing delicate law and order situation and deficiencies in rehabilitation of victims of communal violence—the ECI did not agree to the Gujarat government's demand for early elections following premature dissolution of the assembly. In another incident, the ECI advanced the general elections to the Himachal Pradesh assembly (2007) because elections closer to the D-Day would prevent the snowbound areas of the state from voting with the rest of the state.

The Model Code of Conduct

The Model Code of Conduct (MCC), which lays down the dos and don'ts for the candidates and governments, is a unique feature of Indian elections. It was conceived by the political parties themselves

[10]'Press Note-Change in Election Schedule of General Election to Legislative Assembly of Punjab, 2022', Election Commission of India, 17 January 2022, https://bit.ly/3WkEHdq. Accessed on 24 December 2022.

[11]'EC Reschedules Poll in Four Bihar Constituencies', *Financial Express*, 14 October 2005, https://bit.ly/3G7iMiU. Accessed on 4 January 2023.

as they were keen on elections being fought on a level playing field, particularly to ensure that the party in power does not enjoy any undue advantages. Political parties in Kerala put together (in 1960) the code of conduct, which was implemented there initially and then other states adopted the idea too, via a committee consisting of the representatives of all major political parties. Later, parties decided to have the ECI function as the arbiter and the Commission, with Seshan as its CEC, revised and updated the document and implemented it strictly. The main features of the MCC are as follows:

1. Parties and candidates will not, by their speech or action, create ill will among communities, religious groups, etc., refrain from 'personal' criticism or private life issues and not indulge in unverified allegations.
2. No religious place shall be used as the venue for election propaganda.
3. All parties and candidates shall avoid all practices deemed as corrupt in the election law.
4. No individual's property shall be used for political propaganda or campaigning like erecting flags, pasting posters, etc., without obtaining written permission of the owner.
5. Meetings in public places and processions will be regulated by the authorities concerned strictly on 'first come, first served' basis and no special concession should be shown to the party in power.
6. Election campaigns shall not go on beyond 10 p.m. or the time specified by local law or court rulings. The use of loudspeakers shall be regulated by the police.
7. The party in power cannot announce new schemes or policy changes to favour one section or the other once the election is announced. Government ministers cannot travel at tax payers' expense for campaigning, neither use government guest houses for campaign, nor combine official tours with campaign visits.
8. The day before the day of poll shall be a campaign-free day.
9. Campaign material meant for print media and electronic media

has to be submitted for vetting by ECI officials before being released to press or visual media.[12]

The MCC implementation presents considerable challenges to the ECI as parties and candidates raise many complaints against each other and the latter has to get the response and take a decision quickly and chastise the violator if the complaint proves correct. Decisions have to be taken in a day or two, as otherwise the action loses its effect. When a violation is against any law, a criminal case is also filed against the violator. However, if it is only a propriety issue, the ECI admonishes the violator. Of late, the ECI has taken recourse to ban the violator from campaigning for a few days. The MCC implementation has become a contentious area, as many a time, complainants feel dissatisfied if their complaints are not upheld by the ECI, leading to (unfair) criticism of the ECI as being partisan.

Electoral Reforms, Politicians and Parliament

Many procedural changes that empower the elector-citizen have been ushered in because of civil society initiatives, some of which are as follows:

1. In 2003, the Association for Democratic Reforms and People's Union for Civil Liberties (PUCL) were successful in getting the Supreme Court to issue directions to candidates to file affidavits on their assets and liabilities as well as criminal cases pending against them;
2. In 2013, lawyer Ms Lily Thomas, and the NGO, Lok Prahari, successfully moved the Supreme Court to get an order that lawmakers will immediately lose their seats on being convicted—overturning as unlawful, the provision that gave them protection till pendency of appeal.
3. In 2013, the PUCL and another NGO got the Supreme Court to order the installation of a button, 'None-of-the-Above' (NOTA),

[12]Ramadevi, V.S., and S.K. Mendiratta, *How India Votes: Election Laws, Practice and Procedure*, Fourth Edition, LexisNexis, 2017, pp. 674–717.

on the EVM to enable voters not satisfied with any candidate in the fray to register their 'nay' vote.
4. S. Balaji moved the Supreme Court to issue directions to the ECI, in 2013, to regulate the announcements of 'freebies' by political parties to lure voters.

Unfortunately, the governments, in a retrograde step, tried to overturn the first two but were unsuccessful in their attempts. In sum and substance, the ECI, civil society and the Supreme Court have done far more to clean up the electoral system.

While procedural improvements can be carried out by the ECI, changes to rules and laws are Parliament's prerogative. Surprisingly, very few reforms—to be exact only six substantial ones—have been ushered in by Parliament in the last 70 years. These have been briefly listed below:

1. Powers of the ECI to adjudicate election disputes taken away from the ECI through the Nineteenth Constitutional Amendment (1966);
2. Anti-defection law to prevent party hopping by elected representatives (1985);
3. Reduction of age of eligibility to vote from 21 years to 18 years (1989);
4. Approval for EVM use (1991);
5. Approval of Electoral Trusts for funding political parties (2013) and later the Electoral Bonds Scheme (2018); and
6. Law for linking Aadhaar with Electoral Roll (2021).

Barring one (No. 3), none brought in more empowerment of the ECI/electorate or better transparency in the election processes.

Current Challenges

India is a democracy because of well run periodic elections and by sheer numbers, the largest, but are we a fair democracy? The answer can only be an unqualified 'no'. There has been palpable erosion of values in the political sphere with winning at any cost becoming the sole criterion. There is steady increase of lawmakers tainted by criminal cases—serious ones like murder, dacoity and robbery—to their 'credit'.[13]

Table 1
Members in Parliament Involved in Criminal Cases[14]

Total MPs in Lower House of Parliament: 543

Category/Year of General Election	2009	2014	2019
MPs with Criminal Cases	58%	82%	88%
MPs with Serious Criminal Cases	14%	21%	29%

Public office now seems an end in itself for the power and pelf it offers. Voters are enticed with 'freebies' offered at the cost of public exchequer and with 'cash doles' distributed by the contestants, a practice that began in Tamil Nadu in 2009, the list having expanded to household appliances, gold coins and the like. The disease has effectively spread to other parts of the southern states. Witnessed in a recent Panchayat election in Telangana were slogan-shouting women demanding 'cash' for their votes.[15]

Election law prescribes expenditure ceiling on candidates to curb money power. Elaborate instructions have been given to account for election expenditure including: video tracking of campaigns, directions to file expenditure statements at intervals during the campaign and post-poll for a final submission of expenditure figures, all theoretically foolproof. But in actual practice, candidates manage to conceal expenditures. A big loophole in the law is the lack of

[13]'Research & Reports', Association for Democratic Reforms (ADR), 29 August 2011, https://adrindia.org/research-and-reports/. Accessed on 24 December 2022.
[14]Ibid.
[15]Abraham, Bobins, 'Pay Us Money and Get Our Votes, People of Telangana's Huzurabad Constituency Tell Politicians', IndiaTimes.com, 29 October 2021, https://bit.ly/3hSOnwY. Accessed on 24 December 2022.

curbs on party expenditures. The net result has been such runaway election expenditure that only the cash-rich can contest elections.

Campaign modes have also drastically undergone changes, in keeping with the digital age, moving to online ads, SMSs, WhatsApp videos and short films, and 'paid news' (which are views paid for to masquerade as news). All of these are high cost and only those who can afford the huge spend get party tickets; the increasing financial clout of the elected representatives from election to election confirms this. Notwithstanding the ceiling prescribed for candidates on election expenditure, rules are violated with impunity with little chance of detection.

Table 2

Average Increase in Assets of 225 Re-Elected MPs[16]

Average Assets 2009–14	₹17.07 crore (₹170.7 million)
Average Assets 2014–19	₹21.94 crore (₹219.4 million)
Average Increase in Assets (Over five years)	₹4.87 crore (₹48.7 million)
Average Growth in Assets (Over five years)	29 per cent

Election campaign expenditures of political parties have gone up manifold and so have their funds. Secrecy shrouded the sources of their funds earlier and now the latest provision—political party funding through electoral bonds purchased from the Reserve Bank of India—is equally secretive, with the donor's identity kept under wraps.

Successful candidates and their parties in power recoup their 'investments' in myriad ways through rent-seeking manoeuvres. Elections and the concomitant corruption are the biggest and most pernicious canker in the body politic and needs urgent remedy.

[16] 'Research & Reports', Association for Democratic Reforms (ADR), 29 August 2011, https://bit.ly/3ZDPAsX. Accessed on 16 January 2023.

While on the one hand there is a proliferation of political parties (over 2,800 at last count), only fewer than 500 contest elections. Barring a few, most parties, even out of those known as national and state parties (which number 58), are family-run entities with hardly any inner party democracy worth mentioning. Call of civil society for a comprehensive law to regulate political parties has not elicited any response from successive governments in the last 75 years since Independence. Critical areas of electoral reforms do not seem to be a priority for political parties and governments.

We Get What We Deserve

C. Rajagopalachari (Rajaji), an eminent freedom fighter and the last Governor General of India, had the premonition to warn 100 years ago, when he said:

> We all ought to know that Swaraj will not at once or I think even for a long time to come, be better government or greater happiness for the people. Elections and their corruptions, injustice and the power and tyranny of wealth and inefficiency of administration will make a hell of life as soon as freedom is given to us.[17]

The palpable lack of political will to carry out the many reforms that are the need of the day may provide short-term advantages to politicians, but over time can lead to disaffection and loss of faith in leaders, which are potential threats to democracy and an invitation to anarchy.

George Bernard Shaw said, 'Democracy is the device that insures we shall be governed no better than we deserve.'

Citizens have to put across the message that we deserve better.

[17]Rajagopalachari, Chakravarti, *Jail Diary: A Day to Day Record of Life in Vellore Jail in 1920,* Bharatiya Vidya Bhawan, Mumbai, 1991.

4

UNCAGING THE POTENTIAL

Rebooting Human Capital

Manish Sabharwal

Our steel frame has become a steel cage. A radical reboot of our civil servant human capital regime will transform this cage to scaffolding.[1]

India has defied the odds by creating the world's largest democracy on the infertile soil of the world's most hierarchical society by overcoming our opening balance challenges of poverty, Partition, population, size, linguistic diversity and religious heterogeneity. This magnificent political accomplishment has many contributors, but the millions of civil servants Sardar Patel called 'our steel frame' are surely among them.

But why hasn't India@75 combined a vibrant political democracy with widespread economic prosperity? I make the case that our steel frame has become a steel cage. Transforming this cage into a scaffolding by India@100 requires a radical reboot of the human capital regime faced by our 25 million civil servants[2] (they would make the fiftieth largest country in the world by population). This essay details the broad contours of a new human capital regime via interventions in seven areas of: structure, staffing, training, performance management, compensation, culture and human resources (HR).

---

[1]Sabharwal, Manish, 'The Steel Frame Has Become a Cage. A $10-Trillion Economy Needs Deep Civil Service Reform', *The Indian Express*, 9 October 2019, https:// bit.ly/33kXxFz. Accessed on 4 January 2023.

[2]Author's estimate.

Context

Covid-19 has reminded us that while the total gross domestic product (GDP) matters (our global ranking is five, as of 2021), the daily lives of citizens are better served by higher per capita GDP (our global ranking is 138, as of 2021). Cultural explanations for poverty are at best, the soft bigotry of low expectations and at worst, racism; it wasn't God's will that it should take 72 years for 1.3 billion Indians to cross the GDP of 66 million Britishers. Economists remind us that there is no such thing as poor people but people in poor places—the electrician who moves from Patna to Bengaluru gets four times more salary and the same plumber who moves from Nigeria to the US gets 25 times more salary. The per capita productivity of India and Indians is sabotaged by inadequate formalization, financialization, industrialization, urbanization and human capital. The pathology is often not with individuals or firms but the fiscal, monetary and structural policy that is approved by the legislature but largely written, interpreted, practised, enforced and executed by the civil services.

India's high total GDP reflects our population, but our low per capita GDP reflects the poor productivity of our regions, cities, sectors, firms and citizens. Why has India not become a fertile habitat for formal, high-paying job creation? Why do only 50 per cent of our workers toil in factories and 42 per cent of our labour force is in agriculture?[3] Why do we only have 52 cities with more than a million people when we should have 200? Why is our bank credit to GDP stuck at a little higher than 50 per cent when prosperity requires 100 per cent? Not all of this is the fault of the civil services, but they have contributed through sins of omission and commission in making India an infertile habitat for formal, non-farm job creation. An important example of this contribution is our employer regulatory cholesterol universe—1,536 Acts that create 69,233 compliances and 6,618 filings every year.[4] Embedded in this compliance are 26,134 ways to go to jail.

---

[3]O'Neill, Aaron, 'India: Distribution of the Workforce across Economic Sectors from 2009 to 2019', Statista, 10 November 2022, https://bit.ly/2Ifz3ol. Accessed on 24 December 2022.

[4]Nair, Remya, 'Ease of Doing Business? India Still Has 1,536 Acts, 69,233 Compliances

This regulatory cholesterol may seem like a thorn in the flesh of an individual employer, but on aggregate, it is a dagger in the heart that breeds informal, sub-scale and uncompetitive enterprises that don't have the productivity to grow, pay minimum wages or afford social security.

India's 6.3 crore enterprises[5] only translate to 1.2 crore GST registrants[6], and only 70,000 of these have annual revenues of more than ₹5 crore. Compliance complexity compounds with geography, size and headcount. India's large factories and formal employment are rounding off errors in total non-farm formal employment and farm employment. The table below details the universe of employer compliance that arises from legislation but is more often than not created by the bureaucratic state:

Table 1

Gap between Compliance Required and Reported

	Acts			Compliances			Filings/Intimations		
Row Labels	**Central**	**State**	**Total**	**Central**	**State**	**Total**	**Central**	**State**	**Total**
Labour	40	423	463	937	31,605	32,542	135	2,913	3,048
Finance & Taxation	54	62	116	945	2,339	3,284	254	736	990
EHS	48	59	107	2,344	578	2,922	150	81	231
Secretarial	68	–	68	3,526	–	3,526	493	–	493
Commercial	62	127	189	2,452	4,476	6,928	121	351	472
Industry Specific	384	100	484	15,160	2,806	17,966	1,114	148	1,262
General	22	87	109	173	1,892	2,065	15	107	122
Grand Total	**678**	**858**	**1,536**	**25,537**	**43,696**	**69,233**	**2,282**	**4,336**	**6,618**

Source: TeamLease Regtech, 2020

for Firms to Follow', ThePrint, 8 July 2020, https://bit.ly/3Vvgjos. Accessed on 24 December 2022.

[5]Soni, Sandeep, 'What Will It Take for India with its 6.3 Crore MSMEs to be among Top Global Value Chains', Financial Express, 22 May 2022, https://bit.ly/3POhiyF. Accessed on 24 December 2022.

[6]'No Returns: 1.6L Entities Lose GST Registrations', *The Times of India*, 12 December 2020, https://bit.ly/3Vl4twL. Accessed on 24 December 2022.

India conducted two risky experiments after 1947. The political experiment has worked out spectacularly. India and Pakistan, born on the same night, have had very different destinies because 3 million people won a free and fair election. But the economic experiment captured by the 1955 Avadi Congress Session Resolution and the 1956 Second Five-Year Plan have ensured our labour is handicapped without capital and our capital is handicapped without labour. Mass flourishing and prosperity need all three pillars of society—private, public and non-profit—to work well and work together. Yet, our private sector has a trust deficit, the public sector has an execution deficit and our non-profit sector has a scale deficit.

In September 1984, J.R.D. Tata responded to retired Bureaucrat, P.N. Haksar's letter taunting him that businessmen were not doing enough for India's development. He wrote:

> I began my 55-year-old career as an angry young man because I couldn't stomach foreign domination... I end it as an angry old man [...] because it breaks my heart to see the continuing miserable fate of the vast majority of our people, for much of which I blame years of ill-conceived economic policies of our government [...] Instead of releasing energies and enterprises, the system of licences and controls imposed on the private sector, combined with confiscatory personal taxation, not only discouraged and penalized honest free enterprise but encouraged, and brought success and wealth, to a new breed of bribers, tax evaders, and black marketeers.[7]

Reforms over 35 years since JRD's letter—delicensing, deregulation, Aadhaar, Unified Payments Interface (UPI), inflation targeting, bankruptcy, GST, lower corporate taxes, etc.—are forcing massive changes in the structure, size, incentives and DNA of corporate India. These changes are not a passing shower but a climate change for Indian entrepreneurs. It is time for climate change in the human capital regime faced by India's civil servants.

[7]*JRD Tata: Keynote,* Rupa Publications, New Delhi, 2004.

Structure

Any organization's structure has a huge impact on its performance; what you do and how you organize yourself has a long shadow on performance, accountability and culture. The Indian state must do less so it can do more; this requires painful rationalization of the status quo. Specific interventions could include:

- **Financial decentralization**: India is too big and complex to be run from Delhi. Indira Gandhi often said that strong states lead to a weak nation. Chief Minister N.T. Rama Rao responded by saying that the central government was a conceptual myth and everything that mattered to the daily life of citizens was handled by state governments.[8] Both extremes are wrong, but we need massive budget rationalization. In 2021, the central government spent about ₹39 lakh crore and 28 state governments spent about ₹45 lakh crore, but 2.5 lakh municipalities and panchayats only spent ₹3.7 lakh crore. We have seen a massive devolution in the last few years; it is shameful that state government expenditure only crossed central expenditure in the 70th year of Independence. More money—and power—should be passed on to states and cities.
- **Central ministry rationalization**: The 58 central ministries in Delhi represent an Indian economy and society that no longer exist. Japan has eight Cabinet ministers, the US has 14 and the UK has 21. This sprawl is bad for many reasons. It diminishes accountability similar to Agatha Christie's, *Murder on the Orient Express*—if everybody did it, then nobody can be held accountable. This sprawl also sabotages the goal of ease of doing business; where you stand on an issue depends on where you sit and every ministry guards and expands its turf with vigorous energy. Many ministries should not exist: steel, Department of Heavy Enterprises, fertilizers, etc. And many ministries should

[8]Kidwai, Rasheed, 'How NTR Convinced Indira Gandhi That Strong States Did Not Mean a Weak Centre', The News Minute, 5 April 2018, https://bit.ly/3X115IP. Accessed on 4 January 2023.

be much smaller because their domain is largely in the hands of state governments, rural development, Panchayat Raj, etc. We need a rationalization after a review based on the overlap, relevance, critical mass, span of control, line of sight, etc., and also need to pass on more power to state and local governments.

- **Public sector divestment**: The case against a massive public sector is strategy (focus, resources and abilities) and history (our experience with outcomes). Here, too, the Indian state must do less so it can do more. It can never be able to competitively and commercially run a hotel or airline (Air India was bought for ₹2 crore, but ₹1.6 lakh crore was invested in the last 15 years)[9]. The new public sector undertaking (PSU) policy proposes to retain, at the most, four companies in four strategic areas. Getting to these 16 means a massively fast-tracked programme of selling 340 central companies. In parallel, the over 1,500-plus PSUs owned by various state governments must also be divested. Pending this tough but overdue divestment, all central PSUs should be taken away from line ministries. These ministries who are meant to supervise the functioning of the PSUs, have not been prudent stewards. The PSU supervision should be transferred to a holding company or a restructured DIPAM (Department of Investment and Public Asset Management).
- **Reduce top heaviness**: Most organizational structures look like pyramids, but indiscriminate and guaranteed promotions for civil servants have made their structures cylinders. They need to become Eiffel Towers with only a few people at the top and a broad base at the bottom. We should have only 25 people in Delhi with the rank of secretary to the Government of India. Every state should only have two director general of police roles.

Performance Management

All organizations struggle with setting goals and measuring progress. Economist, Charles Goodhart, believes the biggest challenge in

[9]From DIPAM, Department of Investment and Public Asset Management.

government is confusing goals and metrics. When a metric becomes a goal, it ceases to be useful. Setting and measuring goals at the individual level in government is difficult but not impossible. Any organization that does not punish its bad performers, punishes its good performers. If the *gadha* (donkey) and *ghoda* (horse) are treated equally, then the gadha celebrates and the ghoda gets frustrated. We must be careful with copying performance management systems from the private sector into government because of a different context of: infinite time horizons, complex goals, multiple objectives and a constantly changing political tone from the top. But that does not mean we cannot learn from them. Possible interventions include:

- **Ranking curves**: A court decision to no longer allow performance appraisal reports to stay confidential has created a race to the top. Almost all officers receive the top or close to the top rankings (outstanding). It is mathematically impossible for everybody to be above average and therefore the current 99 per cent outstanding rank of many civil service cadres is wrong, unfair and poisonous. But the nature of the relationship among civil servants (bosses who give tough or honest appraisals get the reputation of not being good people to work for) means that we should debate the enforcement of a forced curve with three categories[10]: Outstanding or Green (20 per cent), Good or Amber (60 per cent) and Poor or Red (20 per cent). There are several challenges with forced curves like specialized or small departments, normalization across departments, etc., but there is some experience to learn from. The Reserve Bank of India's experience with a forced curve offers some lessons.
- **Retirement thresholds:** A big challenge with indiscriminate promotions and senior post expansion is a cadre of people that are 'promotable but not postable'. They are officers who have reached higher levels but nobody wants because everyone is aware of the quality and quantity of their work. This is best

[10]A ranking system, also known as the vitality curve, forced distribution or rank and yank, grades a workforce based on the individual productivity of its members.

solved with the retirement thresholds that work well in the army; they have different ages for retirement at Colonel, Brigadier, Major General and Lieutenant general. There is no reason why this precedent cannot be replicated in government. We must acknowledge that allowing stagnating individuals—the bottom 20 per cent in five continuous evaluations—to continue in the civil services is not only a drag on performance but corrodes a culture of accountability, enthusiasm and passion. The only way to deal with this is clear triggers for early retirement. If this is too controversial, we could try to emulate models from other countries where civil service recruitment is for a fixed period of 10–20 years, after which only some people are reappointed to senior positions with shorter fixed-term contracts. This not only keeps the age profile young but also takes the emotion out of the forced early retirement for non-performers.

- **Strategic use of postings**: It is a toxic myth that governments can't manage performance because compensation is a weak tool, while postings, promotions, transfers and training are powerful currencies. Every cadre must create a confidential list of 'high performer' and 'high potential list' that is constantly reviewed by peers and used for role allocation. It is also clear that almost every branch of government has multiple departments and most cadres have a clear preference for which departments are more attractive postings.

Staffing

The staffing model of one level of entry when people are young has many advantages, but it also has many challenges. Possible interventions include:

- **Sanctioned vs actual strength:** Almost all civil services currently work with a 20–25 per cent difference between the sanctioned and actual strength gap. This is possible only with good people being overworked, non-urgent work neglected or squatting on unnecessary posts. Each situation is unique, but there are too many sanctioned posts that are not required and a cull would free up resources for other areas.

- **Specialization or technocrats**: Most people agree with the wisdom in the quip that everybody campaigns in poetry but governs in prose. This echoes a debate in leadership between generalists and specialists that is moot—any healthy organization needs both. But Indian policymaking already has generalists; they are called politicians. Politicians need assistance from technocrats with a penchant for granular details as in inch-wide, mile-deep human capital (networks, intuition, knowledge, research familiarity, judgement, experience, etc.) that comes from marinating in something for decades. This is preferred to the on the surface mile-wide, inch-deep perspective that comes from switching thought worlds every 24 months. This requires creating opportunities for cadre professionals to specialize (longer single posting and longer stays in a cluster). But this specialization must be accompanied by the goal of 20 per cent of senior roles being laterally recruited for fixed terms.
- **No staffing commercial entities:** Commercial organizations need very different skill sets than available with civil servants and no public sector organizations should have any civil servants in executive roles. As mentioned earlier, the new public sector policy envisages at most four companies in four sectors. This will need privatization or closure of more than 325 central PSUs. Pending this massive restructuring, we should shift the ownership of public sector units from line ministries to an independent holding company. The only involvement of civil servants, if any, should be at the board level of this holding company and even that should end within three years.
- **Rejig recruitment workflows:** The continuous shortage often arises because of entry-level delays. Most government cadres and departments must figure out how to reduce the time of joining from the date of the exam to within eight months and set a stretch target of six months for the future.

- **Recruit laterally for specialized functions**: Most government organizations lack specialized skills in HR, finance and technology. These horizontal functions are very important for improving the performance of government. It is overdue and urgent to create a framework to recruit a chief financial officer, chief human resources officer (CHRO) and chief technology officer with specialized skills, through an open process that encourages internal and external candidates to apply. Over time, these three functions must be staffed with people who develop specializations through compounding learning over many years and who do not rotate into other functions.
- **Selection**: The current exam pattern for officers is creating challenges in cognitive diversity (engineers are becoming the largest percentage of entrants) and gender diversity. Some services have seen a lowering in the women entrants after tests have been tweaked to become more objective, though it may be a fair point that we need more time to decide if this was correlation or causation.
- **Manpower planning**: Such planning exercises need to be done with more rigour and by incorporating the impact of technology, process improvements, restructuring the organization, etc. Currently, manpower planning exercises are often divorced from the internal and external context of the organization, cadre or service. This lack of rigour usually manifests itself in finance departments overruling budget approvals and blocking hiring, spending and staffing.

Training

The current framework needs restructuring into three clear frameworks to *prepare* (foundation or indication courses), *repair* (interventions to handle missing skills or poor performance) and *upgrade* (interventions to create new skills or prepare people for the next half of their career). We need to change how courses are chosen (demand rather than supply-driven), how people who attend courses are chosen (nomination process), how courses are evaluated (by user departments and participants) and how course attendance and performance are integrated with performance management frameworks and reports. Possible interventions include:

- Make learning continuous rather than episodic. Learning for civil servants must reflect the broader trend in the world of work where people have much longer careers. My parents had 35-year careers, my generation will have 45-year careers, but our children will have 55-year careers. This renders the key skill learning and current frameworks and infrastructure for civil servant learning, inadequate, dated and underinvested. Budget for training expenses should be about 2–4 per cent of salary expenses as a starting point.
- Make training a criterion for postings and promotions. Today, there is weak or no connectivity between a civil servant's career trajectory and attendance in specialized training courses or their performance in their courses. This lack of influence on training outcomes creates an avoidable and undesirable gap in motivation for training participants. Including training attendance and outcomes as input into postings and promotions would substantially improve their attractiveness, input and output.
- All internal training courses should include group work, final assessments and class participation weightage that translates into a single final rating (green 20 per cent, amber 60 per cent and red 20 per cent) for every attendee in every course. This rating should be included in their personnel file and embedded into the performance management framework.
- Make training aspirational through *pull* (by using training outcomes in performance management frameworks as mentioned earlier) and *push* (by making the curriculum and faculty attractive). Training currently is considered by many civil servants as a holiday, by many civil servant bosses as a way to get non-performers out of the office and by training institutes as the fulfilment of a checklist.

- Reimagine the training stack as currently devised, in terms of desirability and effectiveness, based on who is delivering:
  - Foreign (short and long courses with institutes and universities overseas)
  - External domestic (short and long courses with institutions and universities in India)
  - Internal (training institutes run and staffed by internal faculty)
- The current training needs analysis or training advisory committees, to reorient training schedules, which in most organizations are very procedural or status quo biased. Moving from the current supply-driven mindset to a demand-driven mindset will also raise the willingness of line managers to nominate their best performers.
- We must revamp the performance management framework for internal training institutes by an annual forced ranking of institutions (green 20 per cent, amber 60 per cent and red 20 per cent) and over time, the budgets and individual leadership ratings must be linked to these categorizations.
- Reimagine the training nomination process for the above stack with three nomination channels, as training nominations are currently neither consistent nor transparent. Again, where you stand on this issue depends on where you sit and we need the diversity that will come from three different vantage points:
  - By department or cluster (by the need for skills, plans or performance) for 50 per cent of the training nominations
  - By HR (for higher performers and high potentials) for 25 per cent of the training nominations
  - By individuals (based on their self-assessment of needs and aspirations) for 25 per cent of the training nominations
- Set up a digital platform to manage this training that is not only capable of delivering online learning, but also scheduling and adopting the choice-based credit system that allows individuals to keep a track of their learning and work towards qualification thresholds.
- Introduce mandatory mid-career threshold courses for all parts

of government. These courses have already been adopted for many civil services.

- Reimagine induction training (duration, structure, faculty, etc.). All services and government departments should think more systematically about their induction programmes by dividing them into four distinct phases:
    - **onboarding**: the pre-joining activities and engagements that give a feel of the organization, its processes and resources;
    - **orientation**: to provide a broad understanding of the functions and working of the organization with organizational, functional and foundational modules;
    - **induction**: to tune up the fresh entrants to perform the assigned job roles; and
    - **assimilation**: to facilitate the new joiners to imbibe the ways of working and deliver superior performance at work.
- Shift responsibility and accountability for training budgets and hours to clusters or the department, rather than embedding them in HR or overhead budgets.

Compensation

Currently, the compensation frameworks for civil servants pay too much at the bottom and too little at the top in terms of pure cash components. But a huge amount of expenditure on government servants is not captured or valued as compensation—pension, medical benefits, housing, transport, etc. Possible interventions could include:

- Moving to a cost-to-government number; the formal private sector moved to a cost-to-company concept, recognizing that there is only one pocket for government spending and accounting classifications for different employee expenses. This classification will not reduce their spending but surely reduce transparency. We need to replicate this financial prudence and transparency by moving to a cost-to-government number for each employee by monetizing benefits via creating benefit cafeteria plans that could allow civil servants to opt out of certain benefits such as housing, health, etc.

- Creating a sunset clause for non-cash benefits for government servants for housing, medical plans, pensions, etc., and converging the frameworks for these benefits between government and formal sector private employment (e.g. merge Central Government Health Scheme and Employees State Insurance, converge New Pension Scheme and Employee Provident Fund Organisation, etc).
- Freeze salaries at the bottom of civil service employees to allow formal private sector salaries to catch up for comparable levels of skills. A bulk of government employment and expenditure in education and healthcare is subject to what economist, William Baumol, identified as the cost disease—costs rise much faster than productivity. Currently, government salaries at the bottom of the pyramid not only distort labour markets by creating false benchmarks, but they eat up disproportionate amounts of government expenditure, with revenue spending crowding out capital spending.
- End cost-of-living or dearness allowance adjustments; low inflation is the biggest macroeconomic gift to an economy for investment, productivity and job creation. There is no way for private salary workers to hedge against inflation, and we must end concepts like dearness allowance for government employees to align their interests in keeping inflation low.

Culture

The old saying that culture eats strategy for breakfast is very relevant for large organizations, but that is only partly applicable in the case of civil servants because of the nature of democracy. Psychologist, Robin M. Hogarth, distinguishes between a technical problem (the rules, the goals and the players stay the same) and wicked problems (the goals, the players and the rules keep changing). Public administration is more of a wicked problem than corporate strategy, so thinking about culture over time is more difficult. But the three areas where a new 'tone-from-the-top' will greatly influence the culture of civil servants are corruption, differentiation and purpose. These are discussed in detail below:

- **Corruption**: Too many civil service leaders overlook graft among subordinates or don't question processes that breed corruption. Change needs to start with leaders at every level of government, as we all know that people don't pay attention to what you say but to what you do. We need to create accountability for ignoring corruption in your subordinates, department and domain.
- **Differentiation**: Differentiation needs a fear of falling and hope of rising. Today's culture among civil servants is to believe that working hard, knowing more and learning more is not rewarded. We must accept and create huge differentiation between people of the same age, batch and service in their later years to incentivize greater professionalism.
- **Purpose**: Most people who join the government to make a difference lose the romance of policy over time because the current HR system fails to use the intellectual, social, spiritual and impact returns that only public service can offer. Our HR systems in government need to get better at harnessing the intrinsic motivation of good officers who have joined the services to make a difference. This is hard, given the political economy of elections every five years, but it is not impossible. And it certainly is desirable.

Human Resource Capabilities

The notion that human capital management does not require more skills and investments has greatly damaged government performance and citizen satisfaction. This is not all art or common sense. The HR function has much science and process that is often practised by generalists. Most change will only stay on paper unless we create a true HR function within the government that carefully and consistently applies skills, persistence and fairness to their implementation. Possible interventions could include:

- Creating a CHRO role in every government department, cadre, organization or ministry;
- Investing in HR capabilities that could be seeded with lateral entry for a bunch of senior people in the HR function;
- Introducing external specialists to the HR committee or forming an HR advisory board;
- Setting a date for all HR interfaces with employees to be paperless, presence-less and cashless; and
- Invest in technology for analytics, personalized talent management to support postings, training and technology.

Ricardo Hausmann of Harvard University suggests that economic development is a game of scrabble.[11] The private sector provides the letters (the more letters you have, the more words you can make); the government provides the vowels. The ability of India's private sector to create new letters was handicapped under the Licence Raj, but that has changed substantially since 1991 and our companies have much higher complexity, capacity and competition. But the private sector cannot substitute for the state—if a small or weak state encouraged entrepreneurship, then Pakistan or Afghanistan would be hotbeds of venture capitalism, entrepreneurship and unicorns. The government must provide the vowels and their ability to provide these has diminished substantially over the last few decades because of a massive decline in human capital. There have been several profound announcements by governments at the state and central level which need to be backed up by measures at the bureaucratic level to ensure easy implementation. The private sector in India has come of age. It is very resilient and has displayed its intent of walking side by side the government in doing its bit for rapid and inclusive economic development. We need an enabling environment and a collaborative approach by the administration to ensure all the declared objectives are fulfilled.

---

[11]Hausmann, Ricardo, 'Secrets of Economic Growth | Ricardo Hausmann', Mossavar-Rahmani Center for Business and Government, https://bit.ly/3GDFxfZ. Accessed on 4 January 2023.

When I landed in the US for my MBA in 1994, there was a front-page article in the *Wall Street Journal* that said India is more interesting than important. I hope that the journalist is eating the newspaper in which she wrote it—what is happening in India is not once in a decade or once in a millennium but once in the lifetime of a country. But we must acknowledge our challenges. I memorized Pandit Nehru's 'tryst with destiny' speech when I was a child. But we missed that tryst with destiny. There are 300 million people in India who will never sit in the car they clean, send their kids to the school they helped build or read the newspaper they deliver. This is not a problem like cancer or climate change; this is a plumbing problem—a problem that can be fixed with the right intent. The time has come for concerted action in that direction and the results will begin to show in very short time spans.

Poet Ramdhari Singh Dinkar said, '*Kshma shobti us bhujang ko jis ke paas garal ho*' (only the strong can be kind, benevolent or generous). India has made a new appointment with its destiny of real strength that it will keep if it raises its per capita GDP by raising our levels of formalization, financialization, industrialization, urbanization and human capital. This needs many things to come together, but a more focussed, competent and energetic civil service is surely a key input. This input needs a new human capital regime for our 25 million civil servants. Government has taken the desired initiatives. The desire for reform seems to be very much prevalent. Undoubtedly, civil services still attract a very bright lot of people. The only requirement is to mould them at the initial stage itself. A larger proportion of Indian Institute of Technology-trained engineers and medically qualified entrants in the civil services indicates the attraction public policy and administration have for the youth of this country. We need to provide them the space and right environment to be able to deliver with full freedom, transparency and accountability. Thankfully, it's an idea whose time has come.

5

INNOVATION AND THE CIVIL SERVICE

Promoting a Citizen-Centric Culture

Pushpendra Rai

The last decades of the twentieth century, and the first two of the twenty-first, have seen a tremendous shift in the way the world economy operates. There has been an implosion of ideas and new areas of knowledge have been tapped. To the traditional four factors of production—land, labour, capital and entrepreneurship—a fifth one, technology, has been added. No longer is the strength and economic well-being of a nation measured in terms of availability of natural resources, manpower or strategic location. The wealth of a nation is now measured by the inventive and innovative capacity of its people and the encouragement provided by the government to develop these capacities.

In the past few decades, economic theory has been making a greater attempt to understand the importance of technology and its role in development. Sometime during this period, analysts were 'convinced that innovation is a continuous, disorderly and complex process, not a discrete event or series of linear events'.[1] The process does not start and end with the invention in the laboratory. It entails a long process of invention, innovation, commercialization and associated marketing and distribution activities. It has been acknowledged that differences in levels and availability of natural resources, labour and capital are not enough to explain economic

[1]Smith, Bruce L.R., and Claude E. Barfield (eds.), *Technology, R&D, and the Economy*, Brookings Institution Press, 1996.

disparities between countries and that technological upgradation plays an important part.

Civil servants in any country, especially developing economies, have to be mindful of such developments and ensure that the innovation element is injected in all programmes and policies of the government. While India has taken several initiatives in the past for civil service reforms, with quite a few helping to facilitate and catalyze the development process, it is imperative that civil servants, at all levels, are now sensitized to this development dimension, not only to adjust their own outlook towards innovation but also to encourage private individuals and entities to constantly upgrade methods and practices and, wherever possible, commercialize the improved product or service. The fruits of innovation and creativity are potential intellectual property (IP) assets and so appropriate mechanisms should also be in place to identify, protect and nurture those assets so as to create value and build competitiveness.

Furthermore, when we speak about innovation, we should not be confining ourselves to just the physical implementation of programmes and policies but also the manner in which they are delivered, specifically, the interface of the administration with the public. Citizen and customer centricity should be the essential ingredient in delivery processes as, no matter how well the new initiatives are conceived and designed, they will be rendered infructuous if the potential gains never reach the targeted beneficiaries. For this, feedback is key and such feedback would be reliable only if civil servants delivering the service actually experience it themselves. As the adage goes—'No one knows where the shoe pinches, but he who wears it.'

Schumacher, Intermediate Technology and Jugaad

About 50 years back, German–British statistician and economist, Ernst Friedrich Schumacher, wrote a book titled *Small Is Beautiful*[2], which grabbed the attention of the world. He encouraged developing

[2]Schumacher, E.F., *Small Is Beautiful: A Study of Economics As If People Mattered,* Blond and Briggs, London, 1973.

economies to embrace appropriate technologies, more suited to the local environment, using fewer resources and generating employment. He wrote:

> The technology of production by the masses, making use of the best of modern knowledge and experience, is conducive to decentralization, compatible with the laws of ecology, gentle in its use of scarce resources, and designed to serve the human person instead of making him the servant of machines, I have named it intermediate technology to signify that it is vastly superior to the primitive technology of bygone ages, but at the same time much simpler, cheaper and free than the super-technology of the rich.[3]

Going on to put the man at the centre of the production process, Schumacher adds, 'Man is small, and, therefore, small is beautiful.'[4]

The book reverberated around the industrialized world, also providing a spark for the development of the personal computer, as against the monster mainframe systems developed by the big companies. IBM had already entered the computer field and with its dominance in office-calculating machines, marketing expertise and sales commitment, it assumed prime position in the American computer market. By the 1960s, it was producing 70 per cent of the world's computers and 80 per cent of those were used in the United States (US).[5]

While Schumacher had questioned the basic principles of economic growth as the main concern of politics—stressing the importance of resource constraints on economic development and emphasizing that human happiness could never be achieved with the accumulation of material wealth—the main message for developing countries was to use appropriate technologies for economic activities. Subsequently, there were instances of effecting small changes to enhance productivity

---

[3]Ibid. 106–7.

[4]Ibid. 111.

[5]'IBM: American corporation', Britannica, https://bit.ly/2EhJmY7. Accessed on 26 December 2022.

and reduce drudgery of labour. The examples seen in Asia and Africa were replacing wooden bullock-cart wheels with pneumatic tyres, using bicycles to power oilseed crushing machines, etc.

However, due to its extended use, the concept of *jugaad* evolved in India and with time, was celebrated as an Indian innovation for technology upgradation. Professor Rishikesha T. Krishnan of the Indian Institute of Management Bangalore (IIMB) avers that, 'There are two main reasons why workaround *jugaad* innovations don't work—they are not scalable, and they are not aligned with the aspirations of the marketplace.'[6] Nandan Nilekani, co-founder of tech giant Infosys, calls jugaad, '[T]he result of a dysfunctional system'.[7] Consequently, while some minor incremental improvements in our processes and practices brought limited gains, we never applied ourselves into making significant changes in programme design and content, and for a long time thrived on jugaad.

The Civil Servant and Rural Development

Around the time that Schumacher's book was written, very substantial rural development programmes were being undertaken in different parts of the country. While some of them focussed on developing the rural economy, others were geared towards creating employment in slack agricultural seasons. For the hill districts of Manipur, the main schemes were Integrated Rural Development Programme and National Rural Employment Programme. The basic objective of the former was to enable identified rural poor families to augment their incomes and cross the poverty line through acquisition of credit-based productive assets. The latter sought to 'generate additional gainful employment for the unemployed and underemployed persons in rural areas, to create productive community assets for direct and continuing benefits to poverty groups, and to strengthen the rural, economic

---

[6]Srinivasan, R., 'Jugaad Innovation Not Scalable', *The Hindu BusinessLine,* 25 April 2013, https://bit.ly/3hSR2Xe. Accessed on 26 December 2022.

[7]Rao, Meghna, 'How India Plans to Turn "Jugaad" into Large Scale Innovation', *Business Standard,* 8 September 2015, https://bit.ly/3G1t58u. Accessed on 26 December 2022.

and social infrastructure to bring about a general improvement in the overall quality of life in rural areas'.[8] While the former programme was family based, the latter involved the entire community, generating employment and creating rural infrastructure.

As district officials at that time, we implemented those schemes strictly as per the templates prescribed by the Ministry of Rural Development, and very rarely did we exercise our minds in trying to adjust the formats to gain more traction in the fight against poverty. Simply because none of us were trained in thinking about innovation and effecting changes in the manner some of the programmes were implemented or technologies used. At no stage did we contemplate introducing innovative practices or encouraging the rural folks to build on the traditional practices and methods (that they had inherited over time), and to perfect them to align with current practices. Our training and behavioural patterns were not geared towards disrupting age-old traditional methods and innovating new ones.

The most popular schemes at that time were poultry, duck and piggery farming, pisciculture and minor irrigation, among others. With the benefit of hindsight, one feels that several improvements could have been introduced at that time, not only by the administration acting on its own but also inspiring and encouraging beneficiaries to innovate practices, enhancing productivity and efficiency. Innovation, in this context, does not refer to major breakthroughs emerging from years of research and development, but steady improvements in traditional practices, which increase outputs, improve productivity levels and provide higher remuneration to farmers.

For instance, in pisciculture, an innovative method was already available to culture fish.[9] It involved the distribution of fish to adjacent raceways without harming them in any way and ensuring a healthier produce. If we had applied this method in our innumerable fishery schemes, the quality of the produce would have been better and returns to farmers higher.

---

[8]*Nutrition in India,* UNSSCN, 1992, p. 148, https://bit.ly/3HeAeEv. Accessed on 6 December 2022.

[9]Raceway Culturing of Fish: US Patent Grant Number 4915059 (Issued on 4 October 1990).

Similarly, we could have dealt better with litter on poultry farms. All of us would have experienced bird excrement on a small scale. On a large scale, poultry droppings and the resulting ammonia are a problem for poultry farmers who raise flocks numbering hundreds of thousands of birds in a relatively confined enclosure. A simple invention of deodorizing[10] ensures that poultry litter—which is a source of bacteria, molds toxic residues and produces harmful gases—is treated to remove the stench and its harmful odours. While various means were used earlier, this one can be handled simply by farmers. At times, one regrets not applying this innovation in the Churachandpur district of Manipur, as it would have made the life of the people more liveable and also enabled them to use the removed litter from poultry enclosures as fertilizer. Furthermore, as hill homes were small, with little ventilation in order to stay warm, many families refused poultry farming schemes due to the proximity of the coop.

Of course, it is possible that policymakers, while formulating the schemes, would have incorporated the latest techniques, based on inputs from scientists, but incremental innovation is a dynamic concept, with improvements possible every day. Even though we did not have access to the Internet, as we do today and were hence incapable of scanning databases to look for such inventions, we did not even attempt to stay in touch with other leaders in the field or even quiz the minds of the local farmers, to explore better ways of implementing our programmes.

In most such cases, particularly in the primary sector, great innovations are based on traditional knowledge and so, a little effort to understand them would have enabled us to make significant improvements. Suzanne Scotchmer, a professor of law, economics and public policy at the University of California, Berkeley, said, 'Innovators stand on the shoulders of giants who precede them,'[11]

---

[10]'Deodorizing Litter for Poultry Farms', Patent no: 4306516A P 1980, https://bit.ly/3vdE5KS. Accessed on 26 December 2022.

[11]Scotchmer, Suzanne, 'Standing on the Shoulders of Giants: Cumulative Research and the Patent Law', *Journal of Economic Perspectives,* Vol. 5, No. 1, 1991, p. 29.

and we could have attempted to synergize traditional practices with the latest innovations to derive maximum value.

Training at the Academy

In an earlier paragraph, there was a reference to behavioural patterns. Such patterns are moulded by training methods and practices. During the Foundational Course at the Lal Bahadur Shastri National Academy of Administration, Mussoorie, as a part of classroom academics, trainees are exposed to various topics and subjects covering a broad spectrum. The curriculum includes subjects like political science, law, management & behavioural science, public administration, economics, history & culture and ICT.[12] Subsequently, during the specialized phases of the training programme for the Indian Administrative Service (IAS) officers, the curriculum includes law and legal instruments, administrative rules, procedures and programme guidelines, modern management rules and economic analysis.

There was absolutely no regular course on creativity, invention, innovation and IP. Furthermore, there is no course on the delivery of public services and on ensuring that governance becomes customer-centric. In fact, there is no training on public communication either, an aspect that has become important now due to the advent and extensive use of electronic and social media.

While we pride ourselves on our scientific temper and research infrastructure, which has developed over the past 70 years or so, little attention is paid to the practical application of the results emanating from such research and the protection of the same through the various elements of IP. It is, therefore, imperative to make changes in the academy curricula to inject a culture of creativity in the service. The syllabus should include courses, projects and case studies on invention and innovation. Furthermore, not only should the government have specialized departments dealing with science, technology and

[12] 'Foundation Course', Lal Bahadur Shastri National Academy of Administration, https://bit.ly/3I1R9dK. Accessed on 26 December 2022.

innovation but also ensure that innovation permeates through all its programmes and policies, with the performance of officers judged on their success in this regard.

Mission Karmayogi and the Imperatives of Innovation

In an effort to move in that direction, Mission Karmayogi, which was launched in September 2020, endeavours to prepare Indian civil servants for the future by making them more creative, constructive, imaginative, innovative, proactive, professional, progressive, energetic, enabling, transparent and technology-enabled. The mission draws its inspiration from the motto of the civil services, *Yogah Karmasu Kaushalam* (Excellence in action is Yoga).[13] The mission also calls for a citizen-centric approach, requiring government officials to have respectful interactions, problem-solving competencies and to undergo an attitudinal change.

This can be read along with the National Intellectual Property Rights (IPR) Policy, 2016, which seeks to 'stimulate a dynamic, vibrant and balanced intellectual property rights system in India to foster creativity and innovation, and thereby promote entrepreneurship and enhance socio-economic and cultural development'.[14] The policy stresses the need to create awareness about the importance of IPRs as a marketable financial asset and economic tool and recognizes that the '21st century belongs to the knowledge era and is driven by the

---

[13]The full verse from the Bhagavad Gita, Chapter 2, Verse 50:

buddhi-yukto jahātīha ubhe sukṛita-duṣhkṛite
tasmād yogāya yujyasva yogaḥ karmasu kauśhalam

One who prudently practises the science of work without attachment can get rid of both good and bad reactions in this life itself. Therefore, strive for Yoga, which is the art of working skilfully (in proper consciousness).
Translation from 'Bhagavad Gita, The Song of God: Commentary by Swami Mukundananda', https://bit.ly/3WqFSYR. Accessed on 26 December 2022.

[14]*National Intellectual Property Rights Policy—Creative India; Innovative India,* Government of India, Ministry of Commerce and Industry, Department for Promotion of Industry and Internal Trade, 2016, https://bit.ly/3GHhYmx. Accessed on 5 January 2023.

knowledge economy—an economy that creates, disseminates and uses knowledge to enhance its growth and development'.[15]

It is refreshing to note that civil service reforms are flagging these issues as important elements and national policies are emphasizing their importance. Intangible assets, mainly emanating from creativity and innovativeness, now comprise 90 per cent of the market value of the Standard and Poor 500.[16] While India has always laid stress on research and sharing its findings widely, rarely did we emphasize the commercialization of that research, partly due to historical reasons. Therefore, when we talk about the role of civil servants in the development process and emphasize the importance of innovation, it does not stop with the implementation of programmes in the field but also extends to the formulation of policies at the highest levels of government.

The bureaucracy at the central level, which assists in the framing of national policies, needs to be sensitized to such requirements. While our scientific institutions and laboratories have invested considerable sums of money in themselves, very rarely are they held accountable for low returns on investment in terms of generating valuable assets, which can either be deployed for public use or commercialized.

The Civil Servant as Catalytic Agent

The Second Administrative Reforms Commission, in its Twelfth Report on Citizen Centric Administration, in February 2009, had said that citizen centricity should be at the heart of governance.[17] Stressing on governance, the report said that administration had become more complex and the expectation of the citizens had gone up. It was also necessary to speed up processes and increase transparency

[15]Ibid. 1.

[16]'Intangible Asset Market Value Study', Ocean Tomo, https://bit.ly/2I5xZog. Accessed on 25 January 2023.

[17]*Citizen Centric Administration: The Heart of Governance,* Second Administrative Reforms Commission, Twelfth Report, Government of India, February 2009, https://bit.ly/3FrPf4q. Accessed on 6 December 2022.

in administration. According to feedback received by the commission, it was found that officials were not adhering to schedules; there was no proper format for meeting with the people; letters were left unanswered; there was rampant corruption; senior citizens were not respected and even reporting to higher authorities did not solve the problems.[18]

The commission had formulated a set of recommendations making it mandatory for government organizations to develop suitable mechanisms for receiving suggestions from citizens. They emphasized the setting up of suggestion boxes and to hold periodic consultations with citizens' groups. It was also recommended that deadlines be prescribed for response and resolution and information technology tools used to make the system more accessible for citizens.

The Hota Committee on Civil Service Reforms also stressed on making the civil service responsive and citizen-friendly.[19] Referring to the public office and the citizen, the report said that rarely does a telephone call by an ordinary citizen to a government office help in solving a problem. The committee recommended the setting up of toll-free phones in every government office, with the numbers given wide publicity. It was also added that the officer who received the phone call should be responsible for resolving the issue. The report noted that civil servants were surprised at the behaviour of their colleagues when they were required to deal with them after retirement and so 'it would be useful for each civil servant to be made familiar with the problems being faced by the common man in relation to government departments'.[20]

As per the report, many government departments had established information and facilitation centres for interface with the citizens, but in most cases, they were either non-functional or lacked a customer-friendly approach. The report also stated that it should be made mandatory for departments to develop their own websites

---

[18]Ibid. 6.

[19]*Committee on Civil Service Reforms: Report,* Government of India, July 2004, pp. 17–32, https://bit.ly/3XZcyKg. Accessed on 6 December 2022.

[20]Ibid. 20.

and that all documents relating to the services offered by it be made available on the website, along with the details of the officials responsible. The website should be regularly updated and a window created for accepting public grievances.

While committees and reforms commissions have repeatedly stressed on civil servants becoming customer-centric and people-friendly, the situation on the ground appears to be very different. Very rarely do you meet a person who tells you about his pleasant experience after visiting a government office. Most officials appear to be overburdened, with their tables overflowing with files and documents. Despite the increased use of computerization and many processes becoming paperless, it is still extremely cumbersome for a common man to have his issues resolved. This is despite many state governments and central administrations having dispensed with physical visit to offices and submission of paper forms, replacing them with online mechanisms. For instance, at times, when the customer is required to upload a picture on the form, he has to go through a tortuous process of obtaining the picture in the right format and adjusting it to the appropriate size. While this may not be too difficult for a millennial or an urban customer, it can become a nightmare for a rural user or a senior citizen.

There have undoubtedly been successes with some of these online processes, some going back several decades. Train reservations, for instance, which used to be a very difficult process, have become a dream with the process going online in a user-friendly and transparent manner. Earlier, planning a journey required a visit to the railway station and being subjected to obtuse, non-transparent processes. 'The major revolution of the period came from the world of computing. In particular, the Indian Railways online passenger reservation system was launched in 1985 and gradually introduced at Delhi, Madras, Bombay and Calcutta.'[21]

To some extent, such improvements also apply to paying property

[21]Baker, Joe, 'Timeline: 165 Years of History on Indian Railways', Railway Technology, 12 June 2018, https://bit.ly/2JC3RTP. Accessed on 26 December 2022.

taxes and fulfilling mutation formalities. But is that sufficient? According to a Deloitte report on customer service in the US government, 'satisfaction' is not the same as 'performance'. The report further states: 'In 2007 only 57 percent of tax returns were filed electronically. Now it's over 90 percent. No more hunting down forms in government offices or trips to the Post Office.'[22] These are seemingly small changes but matter a lot to the citizen.

David H. Maister, in his book *Managing the Professional Service Firm*, writes:

> Even if citizens perceive government customer service performance accurately, there's still a gap between performance and expectations. Citizen expectations are set by customer experience in the larger marketplace. Customer-focused business models like Uber, Amazon Prime, and Facebook, coupled with the integration of digital and mobile technologies have drastically altered customer expectations. Consumers expect to access products and services when they want them.[23]

Perception is key and more often than not, there is a wide gap between the product that is designed and implemented and the way its performance is actually experienced by customers. The only way in which civil servants can close the gap between perception and satisfaction is by actually experiencing the product or service themselves.

The Hota Committee, referred above, had remarked that after retirement, civil servants are suddenly faced with problems when dealing with government institutions. That is quite common and happens for the simple reason that their lives are fairly cocooned while in office and it is only after retirement that they experience the rigours of the clunky systems and cumbersome processes devised by them for the 'common people'.

---

[22]'Perspectives: Customer Service in Government, Insights to Action', Deloitte, https://bit.ly/3IqmcQA. Accessed on 5 January 2023.

[23]Maister, David H., *Managing the Professional Service Firm*, Free Press Paperbacks, New York, 1993, p. 71.

As a report on e-service quality says:

> Government portals in India are designed completely by IT professionals and implemented solely by the IT department. The portals thus lack clear focus on service objectives, resource commitment and citizen oriented design perspective. Additionally, as a contrast to the traditional means of interaction with the government, e-services are distant and impersonal, which create a sense of mistrust, non-reliability and dissatisfaction among citizens. Overall concern has led researchers and practitioners to work towards a generic and fundamental mission of 'citizen centricity'.[24]

Reaching the Largest Cross-Section

For services to actually become citizen-centric, civil servants have to be innovative in their approach, anticipating the needs and requirements of a broad spectrum of users (residents, businessmen, government employees, artisans, agricultural workers, etc.), encompassing diverse age profiles (baby boomers, generation X, millennials, generation Z and of course, the stubborn traditionalists). I asked the top management of a public institution how often they had tried to elicit information from their contact centre for customers. 'Never', was the response, as their needs for such purposes were met by the personal staff. After some persistence, a roster was drawn up with 250 managerial-level personnel asked to make 'cold calls' every few days to the contact centre to experience the quality of service. The management was shocked by the feedback given by the 'callers', and promptly ordered a total revamp of the centre, prioritizing issues such as friendliness, number of taps required to get simple information, unnecessary identity checks and overall reliability and stability of the system.

[24]Bhattacharya, Debjani, et al., 'E-Service Quality Model for Indian Government Portals: Citizens' Perspective', *Journal of Enterprise Information Management*, Vol. 25, No. 3, April 2012.

A government insurance company website provided a facility to download the policy after entering particulars like date of birth, password, etc. When a customer said that he was unable to download the policy for his motor car, as the website was not accepting his date of birth, he was informed that the date of birth was required only in the case of health insurance policies; but even after repeated attempts, there was no way the customer could proceed further, as the system was not geared to let anyone log in without the date of birth. Nobody in the top management was aware as customers would throw their hands up in frustration, and then meekly visit the office to obtain a copy.

In order to improve public perception of the quality of service provided by e-government, there is a need to understand user expectation; to identify issues preventing citizens and other stakeholders from using e-government services; and to understand the factors which enhance user experiences with e-government services. Therefore, it is imperative for civil servants to be innovative in assessing the associated benefits and cost for a citizen-centric service model.[25]

From time to time, such efforts have been made by various bodies, but they are very few and rather sporadic in nature. For example, after the dastardly Nirbhaya incident in Delhi in 2012, officials were asked to travel in public buses to assess the safety of women.[26] More recently, the Delhi High Court, while hearing a plea on the concreting of hundreds of trees on colony pavements ordered an official of the municipal corporation to traverse the length of the colony's footpaths on a wheelchair, without any help from anyone, to ascertain the usability of pavements (the case is still in court):

---

[25]Bertot, J.C., et al., 'Citizen-Centered E-Government Services: Benefits, Costs, and Research Needs', Proceedings of the 9th Annual International Digital Government Research Conference, 18–21 May 2008, Montreal.

[26]The 2012 Delhi gang rape and murder case involved a rape and fatal assault that occurred on 16 December 2012 in Delhi. The incident took place when a 22-year-old woman was beaten, repeatedly molested and tortured in a private bus in which she was travelling with her male friend, which led to her death after an 11-day hospitalization. The incident generated widespread coverage and was widely condemned. Her struggle and death became a symbol of women's resistance to rape around the world.

'Citizens need to be empowered and facilitated in the enjoyment of their constitutional rights, for which provision of basic civic amenities is essential, like a safe and secure neighbourhood, and tree-lined avenues and footpaths, where an endeavour of a leisurely stroll is actually a pleasurable exercise and not an obstacle dodging, harrowing experience,' said Justice Najmi Waziri.[27]

To deal with this menace, a suggestion often made is to dispense with official enclaves and make the civil servants live in different parts of the city, so that they also experience the daily trials and tribulations of the common citizenry, which subsists on the services provided by the government.

Innovative practices to deal with this problem should include the selection of the most appropriate technologies while converting to e-governance and to introduce the change only when absolutely necessary and not just for the sake of the change. Furthermore, to analyse the suitability and viability of the innovative product or service, there is a need to rigorously strike a balance between cumbersome safety procedures and convenience; ascertain wide acceptability across a wide cross section; and to make as many iterations as necessary during testing on diverse users, before actually launching it. Most importantly, it is essential to ensure that civil servants use it themselves to detect glitches and observe its actual impact and usefulness.

Making the Civil Servant the Key

The civil servant in India plays a pivotal role in the governance of national institutions and management of development policies and programmes. At the field level, the official is directly responsible for implementing schemes and projects and as he moves up the hierarchical ladder, he gets intimately involved with policymaking. The government invests heavily in the civil servant in terms of a well-structured training process. Several rounds of reforms have taken

[27]'Bhavreen Kandhari vs Gyanesh Bharti and Ors.', LiveLaw.in, 15 November 2021, https://bit.ly/3iLeDd0. Accessed on 16 January 2023.

place in the last 70-odd years, and every time, attempts are made to hone the official's skills, making him more responsive to the needs and requirements of the people.

However, a noticeable gap in the training and sensitization process has been the distance between the service and the innovative environment of the country. Since the 1980s, economists have theorized that innovation and technological advances are probably the single-most important variables in the growth process; and so the spirit of innovation has to be inculcated in the civil servant right from the initial stages and their performance assessed on contributions made in that regard.

Furthermore, innumerable reform measures have been announced to make the civil servant more sensitive to ushering in a citizen-centric environment to ensure that the system does not lose sight of the citizen, who is the ultimate beneficiary of the innovative changes made in the public delivery of products and services. The civil servant has to be fully cognizant of the problems faced in this regard and the best way to ensure that is to make the civil servant experience it himself. To this end, it is imperative to launch a mission to nurture a dynamic and effective system of innovation, promotion and initiation of innovative ways to make public delivery mechanisms more effective and citizen centric.

A mission where the civil servant is key.

6

BUREAUCRATIC CAPTURE

Safeguarding Against Benevolent Despots

Subhomoy Bhattacharjee

In the last few weeks of 2021, the Comptroller and Auditor General of India (CAG) issued a harsh audit of the Noida municipal authority. Over the past two decades, farm houses were offered for a net worth of ₹1 lakh or even less, a golf course became a backyard lane and residential colonies were created on land meant for industries. Towering above all these was the revelation that this was the first audit of Noida since it was established in 1976.[1] Yet, Noida's humungous messy affairs are hardly unique. They also provide answers to why citizens across India looking for emergency support in the Covid-19 waves could rarely depend on their municipal infrastructure.

In Maharashtra, for instance, the audit of cities such as Pune, Nagpur, Nashik and all the urban agglomerations around Mumbai have not been carried out for the past six years (2014–15 onwards). In next-door Karnataka, of the 135 urban local bodies, audit has happened only once this decade. Noida is one of the five urban entities of Uttar Pradesh, in a list that includes capital city, Lucknow Industrial Development Authority, which have not filed their annual accounts since 2005–06.

In the three layers of Indian public administration—the Centre, states and the urban-rural—the ascendant role of the bureaucracy as

[1]Jayashree E., Karup, 'CAG's Noida Report Highlights Urgent Need for City Audits to Check Massive Corruption in Land Allotment', MoneyControl, 23 December 2021, https://bit.ly/3jqsAgq. Accessed on 26 December 2022.

the dominant authority comes out most starkly in the third layer. However, the almost total dominance of the bureaucracy in the third layer has not necessarily led to an improved level of governance.

When one says dominant authority, it means the power to set policies, as opposed to the limited exercise of powers to just implement those. The bureaucratic capture of power in city and rural administration has colossal significance. India is one of the most rapidly urbanizing developing nations in the globe. A World Resources Institute analysis states that the country's urban population is estimated to reach 40 per cent by 2030, up from 28 per cent recorded in 2001. The expansion translates into a concomitant build out of the number of cities where more than a million people live. There shall be 68 cities with a million-plus population in India by 2030, almost double from the present 35 cities. 'Economic growth is the driving force behind (this) urbanization. But unfortunately this growth is largely unplanned, creating a high risk of unsustainable sprawl (sic).'[2]

Planning is out-and-out a bureaucratic responsibility but it has gotten ignored, as the evidence from audits of mega clusters like Noida and Pune shows. Instead, the bureaucracy holds the right to frame policies and decide on how a city will look, largely free from popular involvement that a democratic structure of society would have otherwise offered, if the political involvement at the decision-making stage was stronger.

The trends are manifesting themselves in the second layer—the state governments, too, as disruptive changes in the relative power equations between the permanent executive and the political overlords. We shall examine those later.

Data on Cities

As the data from audit reports and other analyst agencies show, municipal corporations of many megacities rarely have their accounts audited. It is not just small towns. Global city, Bengaluru, did not

---

[2]'Sustainable Cities', WRI India, https://bit.ly/3Vpyn3b. Accessed on 26 December 2022.

finalize its accounts for two successive years—FY17 and FY18. It isn't a surprise then, that the CAG data in FY18 shows audit of only 18 out of the 279 urban local bodies were completed. In the absence of an audit, surprising proposals—like the one from Maharashtra Chief Minister, Uddhav Thackeray, to exempt property tax in urban areas up to certain levels—can easily pass, since no one will add up the costs. In Maharashtra, accounts were not finalized for half of the 27 largest cities. Several of them, like Aurangabad, were running an arrear for four years.

Unlike the audit of central and even those of state governments, the issues which figure in the inspection of municipalities are of immediate concern to the local population. Drainage, cleaning of streets, local markets, primary schools and just about anything that dot the urban landscape is the remit of these local bodies. But who gets to check that these are up and running?

As India urbanizes massively through this decade, this lack of oversight is shocking. It was only around 2010 that the state governments for the first time allowed the CAG to audit their municipal bodies. Their support allowed the Centre to expand the scope of Section 14(2) of the CAG Act to bring municipal bodies and panchayati raj institutions under CAG audit. But the relevant changes in the state-level laws were not completed till FY12. It was only then that the national auditor picked up the books for inspection. At this rate, the citizens will be lucky to get two audits of their cities done in the two decades till 2030. The oversight shows why the National Capital Region town of Noida had run up a ₹1 trillion worth of audit queries.[3] Others are waiting to be discovered.

How do municipal officials get away with defalcations at these scales? They get the signals from their senior officers in the respective states. Former Indian Administrative Service (IAS) officer, T.R. Raghunandan, recounts one of the most brazen episodes of demonstration of this power:

---

[3]Bhattacharjee, Subhomoy, 'CAG Report on Noida Shows Why Accountability Is a Myth in India's Cities', *Business Standard*, 5 January 2022, https://bit.ly/3FTN1tJ. Accessed on 26 December 2022.

> Only in one state, Karnataka, did the government try to unseat the collector from his exalted position. In 1983, nearly a decade prior to the seventy-third and seventy-fourth Constitutional amendments, the government passed a landmark law setting up a two-tier panchayat system consisting of zilla parishads (ZP) and mandal panchayats [...]the decision that sent ripples of fear and consternation through the ranks of the IAS was the one to divest deputy commissioners (collectors) of their development responsibilities and to post officers senior to them as 'chief secretaries' of zilla parishads, answerable and accountable to the elected local body and its president. The confidential reports of chief secretaries were to be written by the ZP adhyaksha. The system (could have) resulted in a radical and fundamental shift in the power structure, both amongst politicians and bureaucrats.[4]

The revolution did not survive...'at the first opportunity, this new paradigm was done away with. In 1992, when ZP and mandal terms ended, elections were postponed and deputy commissioners were appointed as administrators of the ZPs. In a policy turnaround, officers junior to the DCs were posted as CSs, thus restoring status quo as to who was the de facto head of the district. No other state has walked this route.'[5]

Raghunandan raises a fundamental question, often not fully appreciated. He asks if the continued emasculation of the panchayats and the municipal corporations, for almost 30 years, isn't because the officers at the states and at the Centre have blocked sharing of power with the elected representatives. This is despite all political parties ostensibly being massive supporters of decentralization. No state has been able to come out of this trap.

Whether it is a city like Delhi, which has four municipal corporations or Bhubaneswar in Odisha with a single one, it is often the municipal commissioner who is the boss of the organization.

---

[4]Raghunandan, T.R., *Everything You Ever Wanted to Know about Bureaucracy But Were Afraid to Ask*, Penguin Random House India, 2019.
[5]Ibid. 24.

The top-level officers are invariably from the IAS. The method of selection of junior employees is often opaque. To correct this problem, reports from various agencies have recommended the development of a cadre of municipal employees. One of those was from the union ministry of urban development in consultation with the World Bank.[6] Naturally, the proposals have reached nowhere.

In Chandigarh, firemen have not been recruited for over a decade.[7] Nashik, in Maharashtra, has decided to fill vacancies in the corporation, paying honorarium instead of salary. Those roped in will include sanitation workers to engineers.[8] In Delhi, for instance, employees are not switched around, despite the risk that they could become too 'attached' to their posts. They stay put in the same corner, occupy their chair for decades in the same departments and never ever step beyond.

There are few exceptions though, like those from Tamil Nadu and Kerala, whose local governments are in good shape. A CAG report itself notes that accrual-based accounting system is followed in all the municipalities of Tamil Nadu.[9] In conformity with the National Municipal Accounting Manual of 2017, the state government prepared its own Municipal Accounting Manual tailored to local needs 'and not merely to coincide' with the national standards.

It is no surprise that Covid-19 got managed far better in these states than elsewhere. It was the first wave of the pandemic in 2020 which drove the Union to demand accountability from the municipal bodies. The union cabinet secretary met the municipal commissioners of the worst-affected cities. This was the first time ever that the

---

[6] *Approach towards Establishing Municipal Cadres in India*, Capacity Building for Urban Development project (CBUD), Ministry of Urban Development, Government of India and The World Bank, February 2014, https://bit.ly/3VirmBa. Accessed on 26 December 2022.

[7] Yadav, Deepak, 'Chandigarh Municipal Corporation Set to Recruit 160 Employees', *The Times of India*, 23 January 2021, https://bit.ly/3GldK40. Accessed on 26 December 2022.

[8] Pawar, Tushar, 'Nashik Municipal Corporation to Hire 500 Temporary Staff on Honorarium Basis', *The Times of India,* 16 November 2021, https://bit.ly/3jk1mba. Accessed on 26 December 2022.

[9] *Report of the Comptroller and Auditor General of India (Local Bodies) for the year ended March 2017*, Government of Tamil Nadu, 2018, p. 22, https://bit.ly/3IWBHQv. Accessed on 26 December 2022.

Centre went down to understand what the cities needed. It was also an opportunity for the Centre and states to follow up on and drastically change city governance.

As the fifteenth Finance Commission report notes, 'Typically, local governments that receive transfers to carry out spending on behalf of higher levels of government spend less efficiently than if they were responsible for raising revenue locally from taxation.'[10] Except in Tamil Nadu and Kerala, the collection of property taxes has rusted elsewhere.

The zeal to raise such tax revenue can only come when there is a periodic performance evaluation at all levels of public expenditure. The cities cheat the people by not raising property taxes and no one notices the other cheating—that of asset creation on government property, by those well connected. There is no audit of either.

Why does such a state of affairs develop? It is because the politicians in power at these bodies do not demand accountability for these steps. One way they could have is to pick up the audit reports on these corporations. There is enough fodder there for the citizens to demand response, since the issues which figure in the inspection of municipalities are of immediate concern to the local population. Just about anything that dots the urban landscape is the remit of these local bodies, including drainage, cleaning of streets, local markets and primary schools.

By letting go of their power to demand response, the political executive becomes a supporter of sorts, for the dominance of the permanent executive. The results are obvious. The public learns to develop a working relationship with the government officials at work, learns to please them or at least keep them propitiated. One of those is to demand a bribe. But the lower bureaucracy develops plenty of ways to show its clout to the public.

Here is a paragraph from the audit report of a local government. One must point out that some of the most amusing reports on how

[10]'Report of the 15th Finance Commission for 2021-26', PRS Legislative Research, https://bit.ly/3YMkgHX. Accessed on 26 December 2022.

government departments operate, tumble out from the successive audit reports of the CAG.

> District Board of Guntur leased out (April 1949) land in Mangalagiri town for a period of 99 years to the High School Committee at rupee one per year. As per the terms and conditions of lease agreement, the lessee should not make any alteration or additions to the buildings without the previous consent of the lessor. The lessee shall also not assign/underlet/part with the possession of the premises or any part thereof without obtaining the written consent of the lessor or its authorized officer. As the ownership of the land lies with ZPP, the lessee had no right to construct shops and also to levy and collect the rents from shops. However, in violation of the agreement, the lessee constructed in 1964, additional rooms in the school building. The lessee also constructed in 1992, 29 shops by dismantling the compound wall in the leased land without the consent and approval of ZPP. The ZPP, Guntur did not initiate penal action for breach of agreement. ZPP, instead, entered into (March 2000) a fresh lease agreement with the same lessee at ₹12,000 per annum for 29 shops till completion of lease period (December 2047). Accounts Officer, ZPP Guntur assessed (March 2017) the lease charges as ₹12 lakh per annum from 29 shops. This would result in loss of revenue of ₹3.56 crore for the next 30 years of lease. Action was not taken in respect of unauthorized buildings. This indicated that the ZPP had shown undue favour to the lessee.[11]

When it is not corruption but simply apathy, the results are often hilarious. Years before the Swachh Bharat Abhiyan (Clean India Mission) began, earlier governments at the Centre had dallied with similar ideas. One of those was a campaign called Nirmal Bharat Abhiyan. In Uttar Pradesh, neither the villagers nor the panchayat

[11]'Compliance Audit Paragraphs', *Audit Report on Local Bodies*, 2017, https://bit.ly/3FTORe7. Accessed on 26 December 2022.

staff believed it would work. The auditors were so furious, one of them carried a photo of a village paan shop constructed on top of a supposed latrine pit. There were other hilarious pictures. A Gram Pradhan's house had tonnes of pipes in his backyard, rusting away. Incensed audit officers posed in front of the pipes to underline how no one was interested in using the pipes to create the sewage lines.

You could write these off as insignificant instances of misdemeanour in some of India's 766 districts. Or, you could read them closely to figure out the vice-like grip local officials exercise (in almost crime-like behaviour), in district after district, for decades. They are enough to stamp a clear picture of how government works and more particularly who matters at the receiving end of the government machinery with the public. Essentially, the lack of bureaucratic accountability is on brazen display in municipal administrations.

Why has this asymmetry developed? Why has even lower-level bureaucracy in India been able to prise the politicians out of power at these levels? Why has the centre of power tipped so vastly to one side in the cities that it does not surprise anymore?

Karthik Muralidharan of the University of California, San Diego, has persuasively argued about the aspects of this problem, in a paper for India Policy Forum of National Council of Applied Economic Research. According to him, even as India's population has nearly doubled in the last 35 years from 700 million in 1980 to 1.3 billion in 2015, the total number of central and state government employees put together has barely increased (moving from 15.5 million in 1980–81 to 17.6 million in 2011–12). 'Thus, the number of government employees per capita has fallen sharply in this period and these aggregate statistics are also reflected in the paucity of front-line service delivery staff across a range of sectors in India, with several studies and reports documenting a shortage of staff,' he writes.[12]

[12]Muralidharan, Karthik, *New Approach to Public Sector Hiring in India for Improved Service Delivery,* University of California, San Diego, NBER, NCAER and J-PAL, p. 192.

On the other hand, it is relatively easy to become a politician in India than to secure a government job. In a country with low per capita income, it is thus the latter that hold the controls. This is the nub of the problem. Muralidharan also argues that the employees at the junior level are often overpaid than their qualifications warrant. The salary of the permanent government staff, especially at the non-executive level, handsomely exceeds private sector pay. He is justifiably surprised: 'Teaching is a particularly good example, where qualified candidates who get selected for permanent positions have often not spent much time actually teaching. Many ultimately find that they are simply not ready to deal with the challenges of managing a classroom. The same point also applies to anganwadi (early-childhood care) workers.'[13] He explains that this shortage leads to the Indian state doing a poor job at effectively delivering basic services to its citizens. He notes these weaknesses are apparent in almost every function of the state, including policing, water and sanitation, public health and education. He argues that the under-delivery often happens because it is understaffed and overpaid at the same time.

So, it is a powerful combination of well-paid bureaucrats, with assured tenures and years of expertise, ranged against politicians who have none of these advantages. No wonder, who often wins. The public knows this opera very well. There could have been an extenuating possibility—that of public oversight, but that battle has been effectively ceded by the politicians. At no meeting of the municipal councillors are issues of developing a cadre of employees or audit reports, whether by the CAG or the State Finance Commissions, ever discussed. In fact, in most states, the latter are not even constituted.

Even in departments where the numbers of government employees are huge, the effective results for the public are painfully slow or absent. There are nearly 65,000 sanitation workers, permanent and temporary employed by the Municipal Corporation of Delhi. By any reckoning, this is a large employee pool.

[13]Ibid. 194.

In the heart of the largest urbanization exercise in the globe, there is no public oversight or as the World Resources Institute points out—unplanned growth is the norm.

Dark Corners of States

Let us examine the same question from the point of view of the state governments. In every state, there comes a moment of reckoning when a government empties a treasury to chase a satisfying political fix. It could be a loan waiver, write-off of electricity bills or just an expenditure binge to build a city like Amaravati in Andhra Pradesh. When these crises happen, the chief minister of a state usually cuts off all ties with ministers and does a reshuffle, but not of the ministers. This reshuffle is limited to senior officers, where a bunch of tough ones are posted to key departments, like those of revenue and excise, to haul the state finances out of trouble. It happened most spectacularly in Bihar in 1999, when Lalu Prasad Yadav went to jail.

Once this powerful political leader was arraigned in the criminal cases against him, he had little time to keep a sharp eye on anything other than his court papers. The casualty was the annual licences for setting up liquor shops, which used to be carefully handed out to entrepreneurs who could pay back the government in power. The then chief minister had appointed a trusted confidant, Shivanand Tiwari, as the excise minister, but the final decisions were his. Once Lalu Prasad began his jail yatras and his wife Rabri Devi became the chief minister, a set of no-nonsense IAS officers were made departmental secretaries of excise, revenue and transport.

Ad hoc licences were abolished for all major businesses in the state. Because of these licenses, in operation since 1997–98, the state excise tax fell short of budget estimates by an average of 25 per cent each year. Losing a fourth of revenue, each year, was no chicken feed.

The trend to post tough officers to these key departments and keep politicians away deepened subsequently. When Nitish Kumar became the chief minister, he institutionalized this transition. He made the role of officers totally preponderant. A state excise minister,

Jamshed Ashraf, had to resign in 2010 after he had pointed to a possible scam of ₹500 crore in his department. Another one, Abdul Zalil Mastan, whose department wrote the prohibition bill to make Bihar liquor free in 2016 objected to the provisions of the bill.[14] One of the clauses said if liquor was found in any home, all the adult members of the family shall be jailed. It was a punitive clause, but the fact that the concerned minister had to object showed that he had little to do with the drafting. True enough, the new excise and prohibition minister in Nitish Kumar's cabinet in 2021 was Sunil Kumar, a 1987-batch Indian Police Service (IPS) officer who retired as director general of police. For nearly 25 years, the state excise department has effectively worked under the baton of officers, mostly from the police services.

The results linger for decades. If you thought Bihar was unusual, think again. In Assam, for several years, the state treasury used to be kept locked for most days every month. Another CAG audit, this time of the state treasury of Assam for the period 1999–2005, showed up not just wads of currency notes in these treasuries but also opium stored in the strongrooms of some districts.[15] Obviously, both were against the rules, but so what?

In Assam, the state government is the largest employer, so the officials manning the treasuries hold enormous power, far more than the local Members of the Legislative Assembly. By paying out or withholding salaries, they could play favourites. In many states where the state employment is the most prized, the equations change as soon as the employee enters the office. They begin to dominate the exchange with the political bosses. Most often, it happens through capricious rule setting. Intercity buses in many towns, for instance, have to earn a licence from the state, essentially the officials.

Or take another example. In Uttar Pradesh, the state has financed its four power-sector distribution companies to the tune of

[14]'Nitish Kumar Asks Excise Minister to Resign', *The Hindu,* 18 February 2010, https://bit.ly/3VKk9K8. Accessed on 4 January 2023.

[15]*Annual Review on the Working of Treasuries in Assam: 1999–2000 to 2004–05,* Accountant General (A&E), Assam, Guwahati, https://bit.ly/3Q9UNo9. Accessed on 4 January 2023.

₹1.18 trillion over 20 years since 2000–01. The net present value of these equity and long-term loans if calculated clearly will be about ₹2 trillion. The sum is 14 per cent of the state gross domestic product as on 2017–18. In return, the combined net worth of these companies, according to the auditor, is a negative ₹60,616.92 crore.[16] The state government has now decided to privatize some of these companies, but their employees are up in arms. Whose responsibility was it to advise the political executive about these costs?

Why has the bureaucracy become so pervasive? The answer paradoxically lies with the demands of citizens. In the different stages of the Covid-19 pandemic, the thrust of every state was to provide adequate masks, hospital beds and finally assured supplies of oxygen. As these were scarce, they needed to be provided efficiently but the ministers or municipal councillors were not equipped with the administrative acumen to offer the level of service, for weeks. Gradually, the space for them shrunk, with orders to just not hinder any of the work.

Just examine the range of demands emanating from the citizens, in the future. The one common refrain will be that they will demand vast scales of organization of economic activity. For instance, if the transport network in the cities has to be reordered for pedestrianization, can a non-expert deliver? Or can they harmonize safety for women at work? Or, even ensure that the local energy grid does not pack up on a hot summer night? One can add to the list, endlessly.

Relations of the Two Executives

Public policy theory, naturally, makes a detailed study of the relationship between the civil services and the political executive. One of those theories is the concept of 'political elasticity'. Developed

[16]'Audit Report on Economic Sector and Public Sector Undertakings for the year ended 31 March 2018', Table 1.7 (Year wise details of investment by the State Government and present value (PV) of the Government funds from 2000-01 to 2017–18), p. 17, https://bit.ly/3ClEONZ. Accessed on 4 January 2023.

by Herbert H. Werlin in the last century, it meant the political executive could combine hard and soft power. The combination would always keep them in control by decentralizing or delegating power when needed. It 'depends on the selection of the appropriate political hardware (including regulations and organizations) and software (officials) to create policies and practices that create respectful relationships between leaders and followers'.[17] Countries that could maintain this elasticity won in the development game, he argued. In none of the Indian states did such elasticity play out for long.

Effectively, the civil services, at the senior or at the junior level in the states, hold the key to most economic activities. The competing political groups seek to be co-opted in the delivery mechanism to secure a larger share for their caste groups. But none of them have sought to dispense with the role of who held the keys. Politicians often rail at civil servants to demonstrate that they were the ones who held the keys. Few of their constituents really believe it.

Let us assume that despite the best intentions of the Uttar Pradesh civil servant, the power sector performance worsened because no politician from any party was willing to heed good advice. If this hypothesis holds good—that political pressures keep the civil service from performing their duties to the public—it should follow that when those pressures are off, the same bureaucracy should show improved performance. Those performances should not be limited to random examples but should be visible as a general rule to the public.

As the data from the municipal corporations show and the examples from myriad state administration above them demonstrate, this has not happened. Giving unfettered or even substantial rights to the permanent executive has not improved performances. The checks and balances, introduced by the democratic structure, are the lubricants that keep the accountability of public administration going.

The safety net offered to all range of government officials could explain why some of the government delivery services are slow;

---

[17]Werlin, Herbert H., 'Linking Public Administration to Comparative Politics', *Political Science and Politics*, Vol. 33, No. 3, 2000, pp. 581–8.

it however, does not explain the usurpation of the decision-making role by those entrusted to offer those services.

Going by Werlin's argument, that the political executive could retain control when it could combine hard and soft power, the Indian political class has indubitably lost out. The permanent executive at all levels has thwarted their efforts to either decentralize or delegate power without losing control.

Checks and Balances

As the reader would have noticed by now, my assessment of the state of play in terms of the journey ahead (as the interplay between the two arms of the executive) is rather bleak.

As an intermediate stop, however, there are some suggestions which have not been put on the table, but could create some significant outcomes.

Recruitment of some senior professionals should be political. By keeping the process entirely apolitical, we have reached the current stage. This is not what the intended outcome was. One sees no reason why a political process should not be instituted. It will produce tension in the system, which is a welcome development. It is also a measure to introduce accountability in the system, if it can be also ensured that the recruits will serve coterminous with the term of the election cycle.

Since it is clear that the state administration shall not be willing to offload more powers to the third tier of governance, offering the municipal system a greater leeway in selection of officials should be an effective via media. The stakes for the political system to ensure delivery of outcome will be raised drastically.

For both state-level governance and the third tier, a salutary measure will be expansion of the pool of officers. The current practice of selecting officers to heads of state and municipal bodies is like an iron law. The officers have to be drawn from either the IAS or state civil services. This should be relaxed. A large pool of competent officers exist in:

a) central civil services;
b) professional cadres at the state; and
c) private sector.

These officers will offer the following advantage. First, they break the insularity of the system where it is easy for a chosen band of officers to make a game of the system. The lower levels of non-executives also know this and develop their game plan accordingly.

The Supreme Court has passed verdicts on ensuring governments at the state and central government level constitute central services boards which can be entrusted with the responsibility of posting appropriate officers to the right places. It has also insisted that these officers are posted for fixed tenures, so that they are not at the mercy of local politicians. This offers a very objective manner of assigning officers to jobs to which they are best suited, in a transparent method. However, neither the central government nor the state governments have constituted such civil service boards and postings continue to be done by the government in power.

Considering the complexities of modern-day administration, it has become imperative to post officers with the right aptitude in key assignments. Mere posting of officers based on their perceived loyalty to the government in power, may adversely impact efficiency and effective delivery of government programmes. Posting well-regarded officers helps in building trust with the local populace. It enables creation of a synergy of cooperation which acts as a force multiplier for government project implementation. These officers need to pay heed to audit or other observations which inspection teams have made so as to improve upon the implementation practices.

Audit reports also disseminate certain good practices that have been observed by them, in the course of audit in different states or districts. These are a repository of excellent information and need to be followed. It has often been noted that adherence to audit observations leads to an upgradation in the quality of administration when they are positively and constructively followed. In case they are ignored or stonewalled, no penalty as such can be levied, but the quality of administration suffers. In the bargain, it is the public that is the loser. It is in this context that there is need to ensure appointment of officers with the right attitude at posts which have a great deal of interaction with the public or public leaders.

It may well be asked—why should not a bank board bureau or a public enterprise selection board be developed for these posts? The central government has already instituted an appointment process that is, to quite an extent, ring-fenced from the power of the entrenched bureaucracy. This needs to be scrupulously followed in not only appointments but ensuring a fixity in tenure.

Can a similar experiment not be drawn up for some of the secretary-level positions at the state level and for all posts of municipal commissioners? The same suggestion shall be difficult to carry out, one understands, for the heads of zilla panchayats since those are held by the district magistrates. But there is room for new thoughts in respect of other posts. For those who would argue that this might open up the space for the politicians to influence the choice of incumbents, one would say that this is exactly what one should allow space for, if public administration is not to become like a benevolent despot.

7
PROTECTING INDEPENDENCE

A Reinvention of the CAG

Vinod Rai

I have often wondered what is the larger objective of having an auditor general and why the Comptroller and Auditor General of India (CAG) has been given such an exalted position in our Constitution. I wonder because, it seems no one wants to subject any department, project or newly created institution to audit by the CAG. This is true of any government whether in the Centre or in the states. However, all countries around the world have a provision to have an auditor general to oversee government's spending on behalf of Parliament. In all parliamentary democracies, such auditors general are constitutionally mandated to conduct audit of government departments and report their findings to Parliament.

In India also, the CAG has such a mandate. Considering the heightened interest of civil society in holding its government to account, we need to introspect whether the mandate is to conduct audit—prepare a report and merely place it in Parliament? Did the constitution makers conceptualize only this limited role for the CAG? With changes in governance models and standards, has the obligations of the public auditor not gone beyond the role achieved by conventional auditing methods? If the outcome of good governance is improvement in the quality of life of its citizenry, should the same not be the outcome of effective public audit?

Officials in government are vested with the authority to take decisions and exercise authority for the welfare of society and its citizens. The well-being and development of this group of citizens, who could be residing in a village, city or country, depends on the choices made by the people granted this authority. It is easier to misuse or not use this authority. In the present age, governance has assumed such critical proportions that it appears too important to be left only to government. The stakeholders in governance have expanded beyond the executive, legislature and judiciary to civil society, social organizations, media and the public. Apart from the base expanding, each new stakeholder has become very vociferous and demanding.

It is in this context that I propose to discuss the role of the public auditor.

Reinventing the CAG

What we need to introspect is whether the constitutionally mandated responsibility of the CAG, ends the moment the audit report has been placed in Parliament or is it in any way beyond this mechanical function that he performs. It would also be a good guidance to ascertain how Supreme Audit Institutions (SAI)[1] in certain other parliamentary democracies, exercise their mandate. The question that continues to repeatedly arise is whether Parliament and, in fact, the public at large, expect SAIs to be mere accountants and do arithmetic over government expenditure. If it was so, then why should constitutions worldwide appoint such high dignitaries as auditors general and give them independence from the executive and accord them a constitutional position? Evidently, what was envisioned in the Constitution was more than expecting them to be mere accountants.

The traditional role of public auditors is to conduct financial attest audit. However, the issue to debate is whether the common citizen is really concerned whether the government's financial statements are actually portrayed in the proper format. Is he not more concerned about fundamental issues such as how efficiently money collected as taxes are being expended by government on housing, healthcare, education, etc.? Hence the question: does public audit address these

[1]The generic expression for a constitutionally mandated auditor general.

issues by merely placing their audit reports in Parliament? I am raising this issue as reports placed in Parliament are routinely referred to the Public Accounts Committee (PAC). As per data put out by the Lok Sabha,[2] the PAC has met 14 times during 2019–20, 12 times during 2020–21 and 11 times during 2021–22. It is only in 2021–22 that the PAC constituted subcommittees that have had 23 meetings in all. In the earlier two years (2019–20 and 2020–21), the subcommittees barely met a couple of times.

Considering the limited number of meetings that took place, one can well assess the in-depth evaluation that they could have done of the 50-odd audit reports that the CAG submits every year. Even if we were to accept the limited number of meetings, the follow-up on the recommendations made by the committee, leaves much to be desired. Thus, besides the media headline that these reports generate on the day they are tabled in Parliament, there is no other serious remedial process that follows. Hence, public auditors need to move beyond the conventional and seek to sensitize public opinion to their audit observations, especially so in social sector audits such as rural health, primary education, water pollution, environment, sewage, solid waste disposal, drinking water, etc.

Global Trends

The global trend among other SAIs is to make government spending more transparent. In this context, legislatures in other democracies are empowering their auditors general with a mandate to hold the government financially accountable through Performance Audits of the programmes and activities of the government. In July 2004, the erstwhile General Accounting Office of the US was re-designated as the US Government Accountability Office (GAO) to reflect the agency's evolution and additional duties. Most of the agency's work today involves programme evaluations, policy analyses, legal opinions and decisions on a broad range of government programmes. At today's

[2] 'Lok Sabha', Parliament of India, https://bit.ly/3GCHRDT. Accessed on 4 January 2023.

GAO, measuring the government's performance and holding it accountable for results, is central to who they are and what they do. They continue to believe that the public deserves the facts on all aspects of government operations—from spending to policymaking. The GAO's reports and testimonies give the Congress, federal agencies and the public, timely, fact-based, non-partisan information that can improve government operations and save taxpayers billions of dollars. I reproduce below an example of how reports of the auditor general can help upgrade the quality of administration. The GAO observations in respect of 'Covid-19 Medical Surge Experiences and Related Efforts' are as follows:

> The Covid-19 pandemic has highlighted the importance of hospitals' abilities to evaluate and care for an increased volume of patients exceeding normal operating capacity, known as medical surge. All eight hospitals in the GAO's review reported multiple challenges related to staff, supplies, space or information. These are critical components for an effective medical surge response, according to the Department of Health and Human Services (HHS). All eight hospitals reported staffing challenges, such as a lack of staff to care for the increase in sick patients or staff becoming ill and unable to work, affecting hospital services. Hospitals took steps to address these challenges, such as supplementing staffing levels where possible or training staff on proper personal protective equipment use to prevent infection. Health care coalitions—groups of health care and response organizations in a defined geographic location supported by HHS funding—aided hospitals. For example, they helped coordinate patient transfers to balance hospital loads, obtain and distribute needed medical supplies, and communicate hospital needs to their states.[3]

The report highlighted the response of hospital administration to the challenge the pandemic posed.

[3]'GAO Releases Latest Study on COVID-19's Impact on Hospitals', Healthcare Purchasing News, 18 August 2022, https://bit.ly/3vgEvQq. Accessed on 27 December 2022.

The Menace of 'Freebies'

In a parliamentary democracy, it is critical that the citizens are able to hold their representatives accountable. Democratically elected representatives can only be held accountable if they, in turn, can hold accountable those who implement their decisions. An important ingredient of this accountability cycle is an independent and credible SAI capable of scrutinizing the stewardship and use of public resources. It is incumbent on the CAG to demonstrate its efficacy by appropriately responding to the concerns of citizens. It is my firm belief that it is important for the CAG to communicate and promote the value and benefits that the department can bring to democracy and accountability. An alert media and an awakened citizenry have certainly drawn attention to such accountability of those in power. It is towards this objective that the CAG should also lend weight.

A recent phenomenon observed among political parties is the declaration of granting 'freebies', if the party came to power ahead of any election. It has become the trend for each party to outdo the other in announcing the free distribution of water and power, permitting free travel for women in public transport, subsidized pilgrimages and free distribution of laptops and bicycles, among others. Considering the fact that just about all state government budgets are under stress, there is no logic to such declaration of freebies, as the party announcing does not have the faintest idea of how it will be financed. Not only are such statements grossly irresponsible, they also put a disproportionately higher burden on the taxpayer. The practice has begun to challenge the intelligence of the common man, who needs to be alerted about the regressive influence of such 'parasitical assaults' on the treasury, which will deny critical budgetary provisions for clean drinking water, primary health facilities and primary education infrastructure.

In a judgment delivered in July 2013, the Supreme Court had ruled that such announcements preceding a poll cannot be called a corrupt practice under the Representation of the People Act, 1951.[4] However, a patently unethical act to gain pre-poll advantage from the electorate, by putting burden on the exchequer, needs to be severely curbed. Time has come when amounts foregone towards such freebies should be separately highlighted by the auditor and the opportunity cost of such assaults on the budget be widely disseminated. While the auditor can neither recommend nor block such policy announcements, as they are indeed a prerogative of the duly elected government, there is a need to draw media attention to sensitize the voter to shun political parties that resort to such unfair practices. A public interest litigation (PIL) filed in January 2022, claimed that political parties arbitrarily promise freebies to lure voters. It maintained that Punjab would need ₹12,000 crore, ₹25,000 crore and ₹30,000 crore per month if Aam Aadmi Party, Shiromani Akali Dal or Congress came to power, respectively. This had to be compared with goods and services tax collection of only ₹1,400 crore, the plea in the PIL maintained.[5]

The court sought the comments of the Election Commission of India (ECI), which maintained that offering freebies before or after election is a policy decision of the party concerned and that the ECI cannot regulate state policies and decisions which may be taken by the winning party when they form the government.[6]

It is of significance that a bill had been introduced in the Rajya Sabha providing that if benefits of an already announced scheme had not been transferred to voters six months before the general elections, they should not be transferred till after the elections. However, this bill was allowed to lapse.

---

[4]Jain, Akshat, '"Freebies Not Bribes but Shake Root of Fair Polls"—What SC Said in 2013 Order It Plans to Revisit', *The Print*, 26 August 2022, https://bit.ly/3QeZ6OJ. Accessed on 4 January 2023.

[5]Tripathi, Ashish, 'PIL Filed in Supreme Court Against Freebies by Political Parties', *Deccan Herald*, 22 January 2022, https://bit.ly/3FTkuVb. Accessed on 26 December 2022.

[6]'Can't Ban Promise of Freebies by Parties, Amount to Overreach: EC to SC', *Business Standard*, 9 April 2022, https://bit.ly/3BZqdri. Accessed on 27 December 2022; 'No Power to Check Parties, Govts from Promising Freebies: ECI to SC', *The Indian Express*, 9 April 2022, https://bit.ly/3vk6SNI. Accessed on 27 December 2022.

Now as it transpires, the Election Commission does not have the power to ensure such unfair tendencies are stopped, the Rajya Sabha will not pass a bill and the Court cannot give a direction. So, should all agencies profess helplessness and allow such unsavoury practices to continue?

The Supreme Court felt that Parliament may not be able to effectively debate the issue of doing away with such 'irrational freebies', since the reality is that not a single political party wants to take away freebies.[7] The court suggested setting up a specialized body composed of persons who can 'dispassionately' examine the problem. The observations came from a bench led by former Chief Justice of India, N.V. Ramana, even as the Centre said these freebies were paving the way to an 'economic disaster' besides 'distorting the informed decision of voters'.[8] The Centre maintained that it 'substantially and in principle' supported doing away with the practice of promising freebies to voters. The court felt that Parliament would hardly debate the issue as 'not a single political party will allow freebies to be taken away'. 'We take the side of the ordinary people, the downtrodden. Their welfare has to be taken care of. We are not just looking at this as just another problem during election time […] We are looking at the national economic well-being,' Chief Justice Ramana observed.[9]

The menace of freebies has to be looked at from the standpoint that political parties and those in power in states riddled by debts, should first come out in public about where they would source the money for paying for the largesse. It seems the only way is to educate the voter and sensitize them on the long-term deleterious impact of such announcements. It is through such an education process that the CAG can analyse the adverse impact of some such announcements, in the course of their audit and highlight the findings through *Noddy*

[7]Rajagopal, Krishnadas, 'Supreme Court Calls for a Panel to Look into Freebies Issue', *The Hindu*, 3 August 2022, https://bit.ly/3VlnOxT. Accessed on 27 December 2022.
[8]Ibid.
[9]Dushyant, '7 Reasons Why SC Is Wrong About Getting into the Freebies Issue', *The Times of India*, 5 August 2022, https://bit.ly/3W2vI0x. Accessed on 27 December 2022.

book[10] type of pamphlets. This would be one attempt to step out of the ordinary and push the envelope of its mandate. This will be a change in the hitherto practised policies.

The Change Agent

The challenge is to be the change agent. The CAG's mission should be to disseminate information to create a more informed society. Audit needs to reposition itself to address this paradigm shift and introduce a threefold change.

Firstly, auditors must premise audits on the firm belief that they are as much engaged in the business of upgrading governance as any other agency in the administration. They should not subscribe to the 'We–They' concept and consider audit to be on the same side of the table as the executive. Hence, from being a bunch of fault-finders who are often wiser with hindsight, audit needs to recognize and report good practices that are observed during the course of auditing. Audit has access to government projects across states and departments. It is their responsibility to identify good practices observed in implementation of government schemes and disseminate them across the country. As models of governance evolve and newer systems to purvey government schemes are conceptualized, audit has to keep upgrading its skill sets. Working together, audit and the executive can improve the efficiency of the administration and the effectiveness of government spending. It is essential to ensure that subjective elements do not enter the implementation process. The goals are common. While the administration is the expending agency of governmental resources, audit is merely the validation agency to provide comfort not only to the legislature but to the man on the street, that monies extracted from him as tax have been most efficiently expended.

Secondly, they need to ensure a more widespread dissemination of audit observations—both positive and negative, and convert the salient observations in reports into small booklets (which are well

[10]Small booklets with photographs, briefly explaining the salient findings of any major audit—specially of the social sector.

indexed and facilitate easy understanding). The CAG had been preparing such pamphlets earlier. These had been nicknamed *Noddy* books. The books serve to educate legislators and the public about the inadequacies of policy implementation, if any. Such pamphlets should be brought back into vogue and distributed to the media, colleges, citizens' groups, non-government organizations, and the like. This would serve to sensitize public opinion of an awakened citizenry, thereby ensuring better delivery of government services.

Thirdly, in our quest for a deeper insight and a more widespread coverage of social sector issues, we must wholeheartedly support the concept of social audit. The core competence of the government auditor is limited to conducting financial and compliance audit rather than have in-depth knowledge of areas where government schemes are being implemented on the ground. In such regions, they should engage with credible citizens' groups which are working in that area, to avail of their local knowledge for a better appreciation of the efficiency in the implementation of government schemes. This will give better outreach and provide those agencies with a more credible voice in their legislatures.

These three initiatives, apart from engaging the public stakeholders in the process of accountability by moving them from the fringes to centre stage, would also help auditors in producing more rounded audit reports.

Future Challenges for Public Auditors

The challenge of technology

Though technology has no doubt made the auditing exercise easier, it cannot replace the unique skills that human intellect, judgement and leadership bring to the table. While the continued involvement of human intellect in the auditing process goes without saying, auditors need to master or improve upon, certain competencies that will ensure their continued success to advance audit quality and use them in conjunction with innovation.

With the introduction of artificial intelligence (AI), robotic process automation, blockchain technology and Internet of things (IoT), among others; it has become imperative to be vigilant and respond to the technological innovations to continuously improve auditing procedures. Automation is raising concerns among professionals about their job security. Hence, the importance of upskilling and training audit teams in a range of areas, including data and technology, in order to thrive in this new environment and create a niche for oneself.

For all the technical acumen, compliance knowledge and numerical exactitude auditing demands, at its core, is also very much a business of people—of dealing with different organizations manned by skilled professionals or administrators. For the successful auditor, exceptional people skills are a must. Empathy, for example, allows an auditor to better understand the client's perspective as the audit operation progresses. The capacity to provide a sympathetic ear and shore up soft skills are of paramount importance and irrespective of professional and technological developments, these skills will never lose their importance.

Digital auditing

A new generation of emerging digital assets could use AI, data analytics or blockchain at the back end. It is therefore offering more diverse opportunities for possible uses. As digital assets become more mainstream, companies will find many interesting choices that can transform their businesses digitally.

Accounting and auditing teams have to be equipped to deal with digital assets, such as cryptocurrency, in a financial statement. The challenge for them would be to decipher whether to audit it as cash, financial instruments or anything else and hence, the need for qualified digital auditors.

The evolving regulatory ecosystem is becoming more complex because of new technologies and is seeing chief financial officers (CFOs) and their teams embracing online platforms that allow them to monitor audit progress in real time, from any location in the world. The evolution is helping professionals to ensure that authentic and relevant audit methodologies are applied consistently at each and every location.

With digital auditing, CFOs can now identify outliers with greater confidence and analyse shifts and patterns to close in on potential issues in advance, instead of noticing them too late, or even worse, missing them altogether. This approach can transform conversations with audit committees and regulators from simple speculations to more confident and better factual conclusions. Riding the near-constant streams of data analytics, digital auditing can help professionals look at data from multiple perspectives, derive key insights and share them with their teams. The new norm will be that of using remote, continuous or forward-looking reporting; and the national auditor and his professional skills have to be continuously upgraded to meet these challenges.

Growing need for sustainability reporting

It is becoming increasingly clear that sustainability reporting will continue to dominate decision-making among investors, regulators and government organizations. The declarations, post the COP-26 meeting,[11] have further emphasized these factors. Notwithstanding differences in scope and motivation, all stakeholders share a common message—there is an urgent need to improve the consistency and comparability in sustainability reporting. A set of comparable and consistent standards will allow organizations to build public trust through greater transparency of their sustainability initiatives, which will be helpful to investors (and an even broader audience) in a context in which society is demanding initiatives to combat climate change.

Large institutional investors, as well as increasing number of companies and central banks demand better disclosure of climate risks and sustainability indicators. Prudential regulators are starting to incorporate climate analyses into stress tests, and regulatory stress testing of banks and insurers increasingly includes estimates

---

[11]The November 2021 Conference of Parties (COP26) for the UN Climate Change Conference, hosted by the UK in partnership with Italy, in Glasgow, UK.

of climate change impacts. Regulators' involvement in sustainability reporting is influenced by their governments' public policy positions. Consequently, regulators' views of sustainability reporting are more prominent in most jurisdictions around the world.

In response to public policy initiatives to tackle climate change, organizations will need to adapt their business models to become compatible with net-zero carbon-emission targets that major jurisdictions have set in line with financial markets that are evolving to a net-zero world. Policymakers also expect that, in their reporting, companies may have to consider global public policy initiatives relating to climate change. Auditors will have to play a major role in providing assurance if sustainability reporting were to be standardized and the information provided required such assurance. Developed and emerging economies can no longer ignore this aspect and auditing companies, including the public auditor, will have to maintain their focus on such sustainability reporting skills.

Building trust in society

The auditing of government and public entities has a positive impact on trust in society. It focusses the minds of the custodians of the public purse to use public resources effectively, as they know that after audit scrutiny, the public will be aware of their actions. Such awareness thus, supports desirable values and underpins the accountability mechanism leading to efficient decision-making. Once the citizens are sensitized to such findings, they get empowered to hold the custodian of the public purse accountable.

It will be very convenient to remain in a state of lethargic non-performance with complicated rules, fear of investigations and time-consuming procedures as an alibi. However, given a little imagination, innovation and initiative, the challenge of enabling and empowering the poor and marginalized is within the realms of possibility. All it requires is a simple innovation of processes, a slight tweaking of the rules, sensitization of the people who work for the scheme (and for whom the scheme works) and insistence on transparency. Thus, it is very important for the CAG to ensure that the credibility and integrity of the department remains of paramount importance.

By the very nature of its functions, the public auditor has a contrarian proclivity. It looks at all issues placed before it with a certain predisposition, viz. a questioning or suspicious bearing. This feeling is reciprocated, though not very openly, by the entity that they seek to audit. Thus, it provides all an excellent gambit if a chink is observed in the armour of the auditor. This chink can be in its independence or impartiality, its professional competence or its integrity. Any attempt to ensure the credibility of the institution must ensure the strict adherence to these factors.

Conflict of interest

As distinct from private sector audit—where the auditor's agreed task is specified in an engagement letter—in public audit, the audited entity does not have a client kind of relationship with the CAG. The CAG is at liberty to discharge his mandate freely and impartially, taking management views into consideration in forming audit opinions, conclusions and recommendations; but owing no responsibility to the management of the audited entity for the scope or nature of the audits undertaken. The SAI should not participate in the management or operations of an audited entity. Audit personnel should not become members of management committees. Any SAI personnel having such affiliations with the management of an audited entity, which may be conducive to a lessening of objectivity, should not be assigned to audit that entity.

The integrity of auditors establishes trust and thus, provides the basis for reliance on their judgement. Auditors have a duty to adhere to high standards of behaviour in the course of their work and in their relationships with the staff of audited entities. In order to sustain public confidence, the conduct of auditors should be above suspicion and reproach. Integrity requires auditors to observe both the form and the spirit of auditing and ethical standards. Integrity also requires auditors to observe the principles of independence and objectivity; maintain irreproachable standards of professional conduct; exercise due diligence; discharge their duties responsibly; make decisions with the public interest in mind; and apply absolute honesty in carrying out their work and in handling the resources of the SAI.

Professional competence

The need for a professional workforce is a prerequisite for any well-managed organization. The Indian Audit and Accounts Department is no exception to this rule. There is no doubt that the capabilities of the officials and staff are on par with the best in the auditing world. They are the pillars on which the institution of SAI, India, is built. The CAG has always attached great significance to the professional development of its human resources. The initial training of its auditors and the mid-career training have always ensured that auditors continuously keep upgrading their skills. It is in recognition of their professional competence that the audit of specialized institutions such as the International Atomic Energy Agency (Vienna, Austria) and the World Intellectual Property Organization (Geneva, Switzerland) was entrusted to the CAG of India. This is besides the audit of United Nations (UN) agencies such as the World Health Organization, Food and Agriculture Organization and the main UN headquarters. In keeping with this legacy, auditors have to ensure that they continuously upgrade their skills to build a strong hold on the overall business and administrative environment, as well as a strong grasp on accounting standards and regulations. They need to be able to understand complex and highly technical processes, document them and identify associated risks.

Making Scrutiny by the PAC More Effective

The PAC is decidedly the most important committee of Parliament. It has a very critical and pivotal role to play in ensuring that the trust between government and the citizen is maintained and accountability in government spending is ensured. The citizen looks up to the PAC to bring about transparency and accountability in government dealings.

An effective PAC must hold departments to account by ensuring organizations correct deficiencies and implement the auditor general's recommendations, in accordance with the legislature's intentions. It should promote a non-partisan and bias-free environment. The role of PAC is to determine if government departments are fulfilling their mandate and implementing government policies; and expending monies passed by the legislature for the purpose it was intended.

The PAC has an excellent track record in holding government departments to account, especially when the CAG's observations have found major inadequacies. However, the PAC cannot reasonably call each department or entity every year. Therefore, it must be free to select the entities of high public interest without interference from others. In this endeavour, it should be guided and advised by the CAG. To facilitate greater and more in-depth examination of audit reports, it would be worthwhile to constitute subcommittees on thematic or geographical basis, such that more departments can be called for examination. This would ensure accountability and help upgrade the quality of government spending. Such subcommittees had been constituted earlier, but the practice has not been consistent. It should be formalized.

In-camera PAC meetings with the CAG would be advantageous to sensitize members to the nuances of the report under discussion and that of the department to be examined. Such meetings would enable members to discuss matters of audit significance and identify the most critical and outstanding recommendations from past reports. This is a practice found in many jurisdictions. Meeting regularly with the CAG would also help PAC members become aware of all information available to assist with their oversight process and to understand their unique responsibilities. In fact, it would be of great assistance to the members if PAC could formalize an internship programme to help provide reliable research support, free from partisanship and government interference. It should also have a formal process to follow up on recommendations made by the auditor general.

It would also be of immense benefit to the members, the PAC

secretariat and departments to be examined, if the committee could have a fixed meeting schedule. A preset meeting schedule would allow time for members to plan meetings, gather information and undertake research in order to effectively hold entities to account. It would even allow entities time to prepare to appear before the PAC.

Suggestions have also been made to have a common digital platform of the PAC of Parliament and the state legislatures to monitor the execution of their recommendations. There is also a need to have a committee of PAC chairpersons which should have a comprehensive discussion on the working of the PACs and brainstorm on the manner in which the working of such committees can be more effective.

There has also been considerable debate on whether the PAC could post transcripts and have online hearings as is done in Parliament. For no particular reason, these have not been permitted. It would be worthwhile to allow a live telecast of PAC meetings for citizens to see for themselves how discussions are held.

The Three Foundations of the CAG

In the final analysis, independence, objectivity and impartiality of the public auditor will constitute the bedrock of its credibility.

The auditor has been granted independence from the legislature and the executive. While the audit reports are placed in the legislature, there is no manner of oversighting that the legislature can do to the public auditor. It also follows that independence from the audited entity and any outside interest groups is a sine qua non for auditors. They have to be independent, impartial and also ensure that they appear to be so. Independence of mind and appearance is necessary to enable the auditor to express a conclusion—and be seen to express a conclusion—without bias, conflict of interest or undue influence of others. Objectivity and impartiality have to be the hallmark and their reports need to be accurate. Conclusions in opinions and reports should be based exclusively on evidence obtained and replies received from the audited entity and assembled in accordance with the auditing standards.

In taking the initiative as mentioned above, the institution will be subjected to scrutiny. This entails that it practises objectivity and transparency in the conduct of audits. It must ensure the organization maintains a zero tolerance of lack of probity and its human capital—the auditors—remain professionally outstanding and are equipped with the latest trends in public auditing. It is imperative that they are objective and trustworthy, as they deserve trust if they are judged as credible, competent, independent and can be held accountable for their operations. The CAG's utmost priority is to strive for service excellence and quality within a self-defined code of ethics and morality.

8

TRANSPARENCY IN ADMINISTRATION

An Insider's Perspective

Satyananda Mishra

India is a very big country. It has a very large population, about 1.4 billion. Its diversity is staggering: numerous castes, many religions, close to two dozen languages and many more dialects; and finally, vast economic, educational and social disparities. To administer such a country, a very large civil service is an obvious requirement. India inherited the civil service from the British when they left in 1947. In the last 75 years, much has changed, including the complexion of the service, as should be expected.

One thing has not changed though. The civil service continues to be permanent in India. This is constitutionally mandated. Article 311 of the constitution of India clearly mentions that the state cannot remove from service any civil servant (or a member of the military) without following the due process of law. The due process is long, dilatory and heavily weighted in favour of the accused civil servant and, therefore, practically, not many civil servants, especially those from the higher services are dismissed from service for misconduct or poor performance, and everyone retires only on superannuation. Service conditions do not include any incentive for more than expected standards of performance or disincentive for poor or non-performance. Nearly everyone gets promoted to the higher ranks or scales of pay, more or less, automatically and for the members of the All-India Services (Indian Administrative Service [IAS], Indian Police Service [IPS] and Indian Forest Service [IFS]), on time scale. Permanence of tenure and career promotion has been the most defining differentiators between the civil service and careers in other sectors of India's economy. A very large number of young men and women get attracted to civil service at all levels, among other reasons, for the security it offers.

Permanence is good for the civil servants. It protects them from the vagaries of regular change in the political executive due to elections every five years, at all levels of governance. They can take independent decisions or give free opinions on issues before them without the fear of any punishment or loss of job. However, it has also worked to the detriment of the system and the citizen at large. Secure in the belief that they are there till their superannuation at the age of 60—and that there is an almost assured channel for career advancement for nearly all—the civil servants have, by and large, not invested in acquiring new skills or knowledge, nor have been held strictly accountable for delivering outcomes. There is a pervasive feeling of self-assurance that, come what may, their job is secure.

Much of the ills in India's administration can be attributed to the permanence of its civil servants. There is simply no incentive to do better, improve systems and make the government more accountable to the people. Civil servants have framed most service rules to further strengthen the permanence already granted by the Indian constitution and have come out with assured promotion policies, from time to time. Permanence of tenure and lack of strict accountability are two of the most noticeable hallmarks of the Indian civil service.

Some Attributes

India has rarely debated if the civil service should continue to be permanent; it is almost taken for granted that, like several other features in India's constitution, permanent civil service is part of its basic structure. In the absence of any rigorous appraisal system in place, nearly everyone is promoted to the highest level in his class. For example, age permitting, all members of the IAS, IPS and IFS end up at the top of the scale or close to it. Even every Indian Foreign Service officer, gets to the top of his scale by the time he retires. It is unbelievable but true that everyone is rated good enough to be promoted along the ladder, till he reaches the top. Numerous additional posts are created by way of cadre restructuring to make such promotions possible. At one time, the office of the secretary to the Government of India had a principal private secretary, a private secretary, one or two private assistants, a stenographer and some peons. In the IFS, states have a principal chief conservator of forest (PCCF), one chief wildlife warden, one or more additional PCCFs, conservator of forests (CFs), additional CFs etc., in cascading order. In some states like Haryana, there are neither forests nor wildlife of any consequence, but all these posts are still there, solely to provide promotion to new batches of officers. State secretariats and police headquarters are replete with countless additional chief secretaries and special director generals, respectively. All other central services, including the foreign service, are no different. Permanence of civil service has played havoc with all principles of human resource management. Since there is no other form of incentive for exceptional achievements or disincentive for subpar performance, promotions have been deemed the least that civil servants deserve. Citizens have very little awareness of this and, therefore, accept the regular promotions of senior civil servants as normal.

Besides its permanence, the Indian civil service has a few more distinct attributes, such as high degree of opacity in the decision-making process, unclear key result areas and accountability matrix, lack of professionalism and inherent suspicion for the citizen. Under the Constitution, the executive is accountable to the legislature. The civil servants are too protected and shielded for any in-depth interrogation by the legislators or the citizen. In a manner of speaking, most often, the civil servants do not have to explain to anyone the exact reason why they decide one way or the other.

First reform of civil service, therefore, should be by way of revisiting the provisions of the Constitution and removing the permanent character of the civil service or, at least, making it qualified. Promotions and continuation in service should be strictly based on periodic tests and interviews by the same Union Public Service

Commission (UPSC) that recruits the senior civil servants in the first place. Independent appraisal by specially appointed committees with public representation should be taken into account, alongside the in-service appraisal by superiors, for considering promotion to the next higher position. Needless to say, those failing the tests and appraisal standards must be asked to leave.

The Technological Paradigm Shift

Independent India has made a few attempts to reform the civil service by setting up successive civil service reform commissions for this purpose. However, the governments have not brought about any substantive reforms based on the recommendations of these commissions. Technology has ushered in unintended reforms and brought greater efficiency and transparency, often. If one looks back at the last 75 years, one notices that most of the changes and improvements in governance have come from technological inventions forcing the hands of the civil servants. The Green Revolution in the 1960s and 1970s, which relieved India from its chronic food shortages, was triggered and made possible primarily because of the breakthrough in seeds of wheat and rice and judicious application of chemical fertilizers. Extension services to take the technology to the farmers were mediated through civil servants surely, but the primary factor that unleashed unprecedented productivity in agriculture was the genetic improvements brought about by scientists in laboratories in diverse countries across the world, including India.

Travelling by train, for example, is ubiquitous in India and reserving berths in trains was a nightmare for decades until computerized reservation became possible. Similar was the case with telephones. Getting a phone connection and being able to put through a long-distance call was fraught with many impediments and could be overcome either by bribery or influence. All that became a thing of the past the moment mobile phones appeared on the scene. Getting a copy of a sale document or a court order or any such day-to-day essential record was so difficult for many that a parallel industry of middlemen had grown everywhere around respective government offices. The digitization of most of these records and processes, and the online application system have vastly simplified lives of people, as they can get the copies of all essential records almost instantly. As can be easily seen, this has become possible by eliminating active civil service agents from these processes and substituting them with machines and computers.

Legitimacy and Transparency

Citizens perceive the government, even after 75 years of Independence, as largely opaque, unfriendly and difficult to relate to. This is nothing unique to India, but the distance that separates the citizens from the government is far more here than in many other democracies. Suspicion of the citizens and secrecy of government functioning came as inheritance from the colonial past. It has persisted because it adds to the mystique of the government and the public servants, who would probably prefer the opacity. Several attempts have been made to bridge the gap with some degree of success, but citizens are still wary of the civil servants in particular and the government in general. The folklore around this persistence of disbelief—in what the ministers or civil servants promise or say—is proof of the strange relationship that exists between majority of the citizens and the public servants, which include the political executive and legislators.

Generations of Indians have grown up with this indelible impression about the government and its employees as corrupt and arbitrary. The effect of this on democracy as a form of government has been enormous, although this fact is seldom acknowledged or discussed in the press or in academia. This erosion of trust of the citizens in the public servants at large, has progressively chipped away much of the legitimacy any government must enjoy to be effective. Restoration of legitimacy, from time to time, through general elections has not repaired the loss of public trust sufficiently. This manifests frequently in popular culture, literature, films and social media as well as in social unrest and protests against the governments.

Therefore, many have argued that inviting the citizens to have a deep look into the decision-making process in the government and, thus, making them party to decision-making (even if in a manner of speaking) would bridge the trust gap and increase the government's legitimacy. This process would also enhance accountability of the public servants.

Right to Information

The genesis of the movement for right to information (RTI) in the 1990s was rooted in this belief. If citizens can freely access all information held by various public authorities in India, they would understand the rationale of the decision-making process and judge for themselves, if the process followed by the authority concerned had been fair and just. This would result in citizen oversight on what is going on inside the government and, thus, demolish the walls separating the two and keep the public servants on their toes.

The RTI Act of 2005 was the first serious attempt made by the government of the day—under severe pressure from the civil society—to make a dent to the state of opacity that has always shrouded the government and its working, from top to bottom. This right derives from the Constitution, in which, Article 19 guarantees freedom of speech and expression. The right to know how the government and its myriad institutions decide is considered an integral precondition of the freedom of speech and expression. Since RTI activists had drafted this piece of legislation, it is very simple and straightforward in its language and architecture. The scheme of seeking and getting information from various public authorities is so simple that even the most common citizen can ask for and get almost all kinds of information, with a few exceptions.

The intent of the law is very clear from the Preamble: it is to achieve the twin goals of strengthening democracy through enhancing transparency in the functioning of the government and to contain corruption.

> Whereas the Constitution of India has established democratic Republic;
> And whereas democracy requires an informed citizenry and transparency of information which are vital to its functioning and also to contain corruption and to hold Governments and their instrumentalities accountable to the governed;
> And whereas revelation of information in actual practice is likely to conflict with other public interests including efficient operations of the Governments, optimum use of limited fiscal resources and the preservation of confidentiality of sensitive information;
> And whereas it is necessary to harmonise these conflicting interests while preserving the paramountcy of the democratic ideal;
> Now, therefore, it is expedient to provide for furnishing certain information to citizens who desire to have it.[1]

The Indian constitution provides for a three-tier government system: a central government; each state has a government of its own; and at the sub-state level, there is what is known as rural and urban local bodies, democratically elected local governments, spread from the village level to the district level. The first two governments existed during the colonial time before 1947. The third tier was introduced later through amendments to the Constitution.

All these governments share common architecture and procedures of governance and secrecy defines most of their working. The experience of the citizens in dealing with the government agencies and civil servants is, mostly, that of a supplicant rather than that of the owner of the government. This relationship, cemented over decades, even before India became independent, generates mistrust in the public towards the government and the civil servants; and lack of accountability among the civil servants towards their customers, namely, the citizens. The objective of the RTI Act was, in the end,

[1]'The Right to Information Act, 2005', Right to Information, Government of India, 15 June 2005, https://bit.ly/3PvztZR. Accessed on 15 December 2022.

to diminish the trust deficit and enhance citizen experience and convenience.

This law is unique among such laws anywhere in the world, in the sense that it offers near total access to the citizens to get any information they want from all public authorities, except a few. Implemented truthfully, it has the potential to reform the way the government has worked until now, as nothing can be hidden from the public gaze. The free disclosure of office files showing the entire decision-making process, in any particular case, would deter the corrupt officials and political executives, like the ministers, from compelling the civil servants from recording partisan views in writing—out of fear that, ultimately, the citizens would get to know. The civil servants would feel empowered, as they can freely express their views in official files, the RTI acting like a shield against unholy pressure from vested interests, inside and outside the government. Thus, the quality of decision-making would improve, corruption would be contained and delivery of services streamlined.

In the first few years of its implementation, very large sections of the civil society quickly adopted this law and made use of it. Though no very credible surveys exist, RTI has reduced opacity in decision-making to some extent and inculcated a sense of accountability in the civil servants. Many government departments and public authorities have amended and simplified their internal decision-making processes to bring those in line with the RTI. As mandated in the law (Section 4 of the RTI Act), all public authorities have had to publish, in their respective websites, large details of the rules and regulations they follow. Ease of doing business has become a buzzword, as also, the smooth delivery of services. Many state governments have in the meantime enacted complementary laws for making delivery of service also a citizen right. This has further brought about reforms in the way the government departments have been working. Of course, increasing use of digital technology in government offices, also mandated in the RTI Act, has helped in this process of enhancing transparency.

The old adage 'eternal vigilance is the price of liberty' applies in the case of RTI or, for that matter, to any such citizen right conceded by the state, statutorily or constitutionally. In the case of RTI, since the access to information is entirely dependent on the willingness of the public authority (that is the sole holder of the information) and its information dispensing civil servants—in spite of the clear legal provisions—the citizens are always at the mercy of the state. The state appoints the information officer and the appellate authorities at the public authority level, who decide if the information is to be disclosed.

The RTI Act has fixed a strict timeline of 30 days for disclosing the desired information or the denial thereof. However, the experience has been that tens of thousands of appeals are pending for decision in information commissions and most of them are progressively interpreting the provisions of the law in favour of the public authorities. The appointment of information commissioners, both at the central and state levels, is increasingly being made as an act of patronage by the state rather than based on competence and impartiality of the individuals concerned. There is now a widespread feeling that the RTI is losing steam as a tool of citizen empowerment and, to that extent, as a means of reforms of the governmental processes.

Amendment to the RTI Act

The amendment of the RTI Act in 2019 reduced the status of the information commissioners from that of a central election commissioner (and indirectly that of a Supreme Court judge), to that of a secretary to Government of India or the chief secretary of a state; and also reduced their tenure to three years from the original five years. This has weakened the information commissions. In a government set-up, the respect that statutory or constitutional appointees command, is dependent upon the status that is accorded to such appointees. Thus, the message implicit in these amendments is clear: information commissions are not as important as the Election Commission of India (ECI) or the Supreme Court and, indirectly,

RTI is not such a great right to be protected by an empowered body.

It is widely believed that much of corruption in the government is due to the nexus between big business and political parties. Elections have become very costly and the political parties need continuous funding for them. Public contribution to political parties is negligible, so the parties approach businesses for funds. Businesses and industries provide funds to political parties, clearly expecting that if the respective parties come to power, they would take decisions favourable to them.

In the last two decades, large-scale scandals indicting governments of gross wrongdoing to favour particular industries or businesses have rocked the Indian state. Allocation of coal blocks and a spectrum for wireless telephone to industries are two such cases, that led to prolonged agitation against the central government of the day. They were some of the main reasons for the defeat of the government in the general election that followed in 2014. Civil society organizations, the ECI, independent researchers and political observers are unanimous in their view that the electoral funding needs urgent reform and political parties need to be far more transparent in the management of their finances. No amount of nudging has really persuaded the political parties to adopt transparent ways of collecting funds.

The ECI did not require, until recently, that political parties should disclose the details of the donors of less than ₹20,000 each. For example, a major political party had never disclosed the details of even a single donor claiming that it had not received any funding larger than ₹20,000 from a single source during the two decades or more of its existence.[2] Such is the degree of cynicism and callousness that drives most political parties. When the RTI Act was enacted in 2005, many citizens felt that the political parties would be automatically treated as public authorities and disclose all manners of information. But very soon, it became clear that the political parties were in no mood to bring themselves under the RTI Act

---

[2]Tripathi, Ashish, 'Anonymous Donors "Run" Political Parties in India, Congress Tops the List', *The Times of India,* 10 September 2012, https://bit.ly/3WCFuXf. Accessed on 2 January 2023.

or disclose any information, much less the details of their donors.

It is against this background that some citizens approached six major political parties in 2013, including the Indian National Congress, Bharatiya Janata Party, Communist Party of India (Marxist), etc., seeking various information under the RTI.[3] The political parties claimed that they did not come under the definition of public authority as provided in the RTI Act and refused to disclose any information. Eventually, this matter came up before the Central Information Commission (CIC) in a complaint. The CIC, after extensive hearing in the matter, ruled in 2013 that the political parties were public authorities within the meaning of the term as defined in the RTI Act and, hence, must disclose information to the complainants. This order was widely hailed in the country as a landmark judgment, as it widened the remit of the transparency law beyond the government and extended it to private organizations that received substantial financial benefits from the state. In the case of political parties, among other benefits, by way of total exemption from paying any income tax.

As expected, the political parties appealed against this order to the High Court. The order remains unimplemented till today, with superior courts not deciding clearly if they agree with the CIC's order or not.[4] Citizens have no knowledge of the donors who provide funds to the political parties. Allegations fly thick and fast during election time against the political parties in power, for it is they who are likely to receive the maximum funding from private donors. Since government decisions—both in the domain of policy and implementation—can bring rich dividends to some and deprive others of such benefits, accusations of large-scale political funding for return of favours are commonly made, always not without basis. An order by a statutory authority that could have brought far-reaching

[3]Chhokar, Jagdeep S., 'Saying "Political Parties Need Not Reveal Funding Sources" Kills the Spirit of RTI Act', *The Wire,* 25 December 2020, https://bit.ly/3ImHYER. Accessed on 4 January 2023.

[4]Jebaraj, Priscilla, 'Political Parties Yet to Comply with RTI Act', *The Hindu,* 21 March 2019, https://bit.ly/3vz12bE. Accessed on 2 January 2023.

transparency to the conduct of elections in the country and pierced the opacity shrouding the business–political party relationship, remains unimplemented with impunity. If implemented, this would be a salutary governance reform and free the civil servants from huge pressure from extra-constitutional forces in taking free decisions (in many cases involving commercial policy and award of contracts and other public goods to private parties).

It is also very pertinent to draw attention to certain recent developments in India, to get an idea of the forces at work that impact the civil services strongly and for the better. One is the increasing use of social media like Facebook, WhatsApp, Twitter and Instagram by very large sections of the population. Today, India has nearly 1.18 billion mobile connections, 700 million Internet users and 600 million smartphones, which are increasing at the rate of 25 million per quarter.[5] With this level of digital penetration, flow of information among people is too wide and fast for the government authorities to be able to withhold information of public importance for long. Interrogation of the government and its decision-making process is increasing and since the governments have to seek re-election every five years, they cannot afford to brazen it out for long and need to share facts with the citizens.

India has historically had a very intrusive and pervasive government that touches or seeks to impact a wide spectrum of people's lives. Laws, rules, regulations, welfare and development schemes and programmes are an everyday presence in the lives of a very large percentage of its citizens. Therefore, the popular reaction to any major lapse on the part of the government, in any of these areas, is being noticed more aggressively by the people and reflected in the electoral outcomes. Consequently, there is a lot of pressure these days from the political executive on the civil servants to simplify and deliver.

[5]Abbas, Muntazir, 'India's Growing Data Usage, Smartphone Adoption to Boost Digital India Initiatives: Top Bureaucrat', *The Economic Times,* 26 October 2021, https://bit.ly/3WBOcVP. Accessed on 4 January 2023.

Delivery of Services

Elimination of the agency of civil servants in delivery of many of the services to the citizens has, to some extent, freed people from the rent-seeking stranglehold the former had over the latter for a long time. By way of many welfare measures, the governments disburse a wide variety of subsidies and grants to large sections of citizens. Much of these grants did not reach the intended beneficiaries as corrupt intermediaries, including government employees, siphoned off much of it.

With a view to stemming this leakage, governments have progressively resorted to direct benefit transfers (DBT). Beneficiaries of such grants and subsidies are compelled to open bank accounts linked to their unique identity numbers (Aadhaar). A very large number of beneficiaries, hundreds of millions, access their bank accounts these days through their cell phones and use payment gateways for various transactions. Consequently, there is a very little human interface and the grants reach the beneficiaries without any rent-seeking.

The RTI had triggered a wave of transparency in the working of the public authorities. The introduction of DBT and a host of other accompanying measures, as stated earlier, are the indirect contribution of this movement. This is an act of substantial reform in the way the government had always worked. From old age and widow pensions to scholarships for students, financial assistance to small farmers and payment of minimum support price for agricultural products—all such payments are now automatic and is not mediated either through civil servants or any public intermediaries at any level. This has plugged large-scale leakage of government funds and delivered all the subsidies and financial support in the hands of the intended beneficiaries.

Ease of Doing Business

Many old laws and rules have been repealed. Self-certification of various documents for use in courts and government offices has been introduced in place of attestation by gazetted government officers.

Most applications for services, ranging from ration card, electricity connection, land records, approval of building plans, etc., are now made online. Some of these initiatives have made the life of citizens slightly better. More systemic changes are needed. For example, three to four levels for decision-making in the government (if not more), have been one of the primary reasons for the pervasive red tape. These levels need to be reduced without diluting the rigour of scrutiny. But reduction in levels would inevitably result in reducing the manpower in the government, a prospect not politically acceptable in a country with a serious unemployment problem.

Governments have invested little in training and retraining of the civil servants at all levels. In fact, except for very senior levels in civil services, the cutting-edge-level civil servants are hardly trained in their careers that are three decades long or more. Their knowledge becomes jaded and out of tune with the times and precedent becomes the sole guiding light for decision-making. Recruitment of the right personnel has always been a serious problem and continues to be so, even now. This is partly due to political interference in the recruitment process at several levels and also because the quality of education (both general and technical), has hardly improved and there is always a paucity of candidates with the right fit.

In a big country as India, with much colonial and feudal baggage and all manners of diversity, designing and maintaining a civil service suitable for most and sufficiently agile to change with the times is not easy. Civil service reforms, attempted periodically through commissions, have made very little impact. It is only through the introduction of disruptive technologies and deepening of democracy, that whatever reforms one sees around in these decades have been possible. To build trust and better acceptability among citizens, civil servants, especially the upper echelons (viz. IAS and IPS), should unreservedly accept the RTI, both as a citizen right and a tool for greater transparency. They also need to adopt newer technologies so that their own legitimacy and that of democratic institutions, increases. Finally, the time has come to examine if the civil service should continue to enjoy the degree of permanence as it does now.

From Permanence to Progress

Modern administration has become very complex. The citizen has become very demanding and would like to hold his government to account. He is seeking transparency. It is the obligation of those in power to provide transparency and thereby ensure the accountability of those in authority. Modern-day civil servants need to be trained from the very initial stages and moulded to be able to meet the aspirations of the public. The use of technology; easy delivery of services; ensuring transparency in administration; and affording the citizen the right to be informed of the government's decision-making process has become a sine qua non of good governance and needs to be imbibed by all in administration. The government has initiated Mission Karmayogi, a much-desired module for capacity building of civil servants. Along with the newer techniques to ensure a tech-savvy administrator, government must also ensure an interference-free working environment where objective, impartial and balanced decision-making is feasible. Posting civil servants mainly on the assurance of their loyalty to the government in power, may reap desired dividends in the short run but will definitely impact the efficiency of effective delivery of services. Political parties need to recognize that as civil society matures, the ability to garner votes merely on caste or religious denominations will decline and the quality of administration, development and delivery of services will become the prevailing norm.

While recent trends in posting officers have revealed a preference for loyalty at the levels of all governments, any amount of capacity building will not obliterate the deleterious effects of relying merely on this factor. The need is for innovative, agile and out-of-the-box thinking which is dynamically aligned to the efficient delivery of government policy programmes. Modern-day bureaucrats are capable of providing such service and it would do much harm to their initiative and dynamism if selections are made on consideration other than efficiency or aptitude. The country has been losing rank in the ease of doing business or transparency factors and there is a need to retrieve the situation to ensure rapid and inclusive economic development.

I continue to be very optimistic about the future of Indian civil services. India is a country of the young. Aspirations run high. Technology is revolutionizing the flow of information. The government at all levels must be sensitive to these changes. Walls separating the citizens from the administration must go or become sufficiently transparent. A very accountable, competent and humane civil service alone will survive. These imperatives for survival would enhance the pace of reform of the civil service in the years to come.

9

A THREE-LAYERED PARADIGM

Possibilities for a New-Age Civil Service

S. Ramadorai

Civil services reform is a long-standing endeavour. Indian civil services, referred to as India's 'steel frame', has contributed immensely to the country's growth and development; amidst a volatile social order in a fledging nation post-Independence, divided by language, ethnicity, caste, class and many others.

However, the ramifications of global changes are being felt by the government in the form of increasing citizen expectations for better governance through effective service delivery, transparency, accountability and rule of law. It is time we redefined and re-established our expectations for a new-age civil service. A twenty-first century civil service should be one that is defined by meritocracy and values, where the country's best talent contributes to nation-building, while ensuring that world-class services and opportunities reach the citizenry. Integrity, objectivity, impartiality and compassion will be indispensable components of this new order of governance, which not only commands the confidence and respect of citizens but also is revered and valued by the ministers.

The Indian civil services is a median layer between the political class and the people of this country. To me, all three layers constitute a complete system. From a system change prospective, I believe that any change to the Indian civil services, unless complemented by changes to the other two layers, would most probably yield mixed results. However, keeping in mind the scope of this article, I will focus on changes within the Indian civil services, rather than worrying about the external environment over which we have limited control. I am optimistic about the fact that as society progresses, our political system will show more signs of maturity and the citizens will be more aware of their rights and responsibilities—a change that would enable them to participate in governance and engage meaningfully with people in the administration. Repealing Indian civil services is not an option. So, a forward-thinking approach, without dwelling much in the past should be considered and changes should be implemented in a time-bound manner to yield maximum results.

Taking these realities into consideration, the focus should be on recruitment, training and management of the civil services that form the foundational components of the system and are interrelated in a way where one cannot succeed without the other.

Recruitment

Skilled and motivated personnel are arguably the most important asset and determinant of an effective government. As the custodian of recruitment for civil services, the Union Public Service Commission (UPSC), as an institution, has made the country proud with its robust image of reliability and for maintaining the highest standards of probity over the years. However, the developments in various fields of activity, the growth of technology and the need for continuous improvement in the functioning of the civil services calls for taking a fresh look at the processes of recruitment and training. There should be openness to consider changes required to make the recruitment process more efficient and effective.

To improve the overall framework for recruitment and training in the civil services, we can look at the following areas.

Mainstreaming lateral entry

India has experimented with the lateral entry system at a very small scale and it is time to expand and mainstream the system to bring in more experts from the private sector, academia, non-governmental organizations (NGOs) and the public sector. This would fulfil the twin purpose of bringing in a wider diversity of perspectives, skills and experiences in the civil services and speedily addressing the problem of shortage of civil servants at the Centre.

However, we need to be mindful of the fact that the efforts that go into attracting new experts from outside the civil services to bring in the 'missing' skills carries the risk of remaining unfulfilled when those people struggle once inside the establishment. The way things are done in the civil services, be it decision-making, execution of processes or culture, is legacy-driven with very limited scope for flexibility and adaptation. Thus, a robust policy framework is essential, along with efforts to help external appointees find their way within the government through training, mentorship and orientation.

Transforming the recruitment process

Today, many job interviews are unstructured conversations and for the most part, hiring managers are still using their intuition or judgement to choose candidates. The results, however, yield hit-or-miss outcomes. This is why more private sector organizations are exploring the use of predictive analytics and augmented decision-making to find the right new candidates, such as systems using artificial intelligence (AI) and behavioural science. While this may seem futuristic for many government agencies, the capabilities are rapidly evolving in the private sector and could readily be applied to building specialized public sector workforces.

On the other hand, establishing a new norm where the interviewing panelists get to spend considerable time with the candidates, instead of the existing limited-duration question and answer sessions, to assess different facets of the candidate's personality, can be a welcome change. The process can be made metrics-driven through the inclusion of psychometric tests that will provide a clearer understanding of the attitude and aptitude of the incoming pool of civil servants.

Making civil services a career option after 12th

Initiating a 10+2 entry model has a lot of potential to set a new precedent. Young people who have just come out of secondary education are more trainable. They have a mindset that helps them absorb learning more readily as they do not have a baggage of prior experience. This allows an opportunity to develop a workforce of young people specifically trained to meet the needs and get aligned to the vision, mission and values of civil services. There could be separate four-year degree programmes for the services which should include subjects that prepare the candidates for entry into the civil services, with the ability to handle specialized departments and respond to complex challenges.

Attracting and retaining civil servants

The race is on to recruit the next generation of civil servants. It is no secret that today's young and emerging professionals are raising the bar in their pursuit of meaningful, purpose-led, socially conscious roles and careers that ideally will allow them to have an impact in driving positive social change. Governments, as an employer, can typically meet this emerging workforce's preference for meaningful and purpose-led work that it highly values. Right value propositions should be highlighted in future recruitment efforts, proclaiming the civil services as a prime environment for young people who truly want to 'make a difference' by enabling social change. Governments should be proactive in attracting and retaining the next generation of civil servants, introducing critical new skills and ultimately reshaping their workforces to align with the demands of a digital and sustainable society.

Training and Capability Building

The term 'capability' could be a better alternative to the term 'capacity' because more often than not, the latter is misused by practitioners as they have conversations about quantity rather than quality. In this case, I would define capability as a product of the interaction between the skills, experiences and methods of an individual; and the culture, structures and processes of the organization they work in. Capability building will come from learning and embedding 'enabling routines'.

Learning-by-doing and learning-before-doing are the main ways in which organizations learn and create knowledge and capability, with the former usually being more important.

Experience is just as important; people need to practise what they have learned. Partner alliances can be developed, wherein talent is fed through the partner's pipeline to practise new skills and put to use their newly acquired knowledge.

Leaders at different levels of the government need to identify the strengths and weaknesses of their teams and then mitigate the gaps, if any, by suggesting and eventually implementing the appropriate changes.

Skilling, reskilling and upskilling

The shelf life of skills is becoming short and dispensable amid new technology disruptions and evolving organizational priorities. Thus, skilling, reskilling and upskilling the existing talent pool will be critical in overcoming talent shortages and enhancing the quality of public services.

Currently, there are various training programmes in the civil services, but there is tremendous scope for improvement in them. While there could be some general training programmes, other programmes should be in tune with the needs of the departments, employees and the roles they are expected to play.

To make the training effective, there should be a listing of the various posts in the civil services along with role descriptions. This will, for instance, bring out the difference between the role of a deputy secretary in the health department and the person holding the same post in the home department. Also, while the roles of district collectors may look similar, at the ground level, the expectations from them change according to the needs of the district and demography. The role and work of the district collector of Mumbai is different from that of Bhupalpally, which is one of the aspirational districts in Telangana. So, apart from a general training, a specialized training that takes into consideration the needs of the districts or the departments will help in orientation of the officials posted there.

Emphasis must be laid on the skill development of the personnel at various levels. These will include, but are not limited to communication (internal and external) skills, noting skills, drafting skills, technology literacy and adeptness, problem-solving skills, systemic thinking and comprehension of the nuances of the departments and ministries where the personnel are posted.

A public-sector skill development council could be set up, which will benefit not only the civil services staff but also the employees of various public sector organizations. Such a council shall design skill development programmes, some of which shall be compulsory for all civil servants to complete periodically and should also have modules for additional qualification. Such qualifications could be considered assets at the time of promotion or should be incentivized through other means.

As the chairman of National Skill Development Corporation (NSDC), my focus was to involve the industry in the skilling process that was primarily aimed at jobs in the private sector. There are currently 37 Sector Skill Councils (SSCs) operational, with more than 600 corporate representatives on their governing councils.

The SSCs developed a competency framework and created over 2,000 Qualification Packs (QPs) and National Occupational Standards (NOS) mapped to every job role in different industries, leading to an outcome-driven skill development programme. A similar exercise may be carried out in the civil services to make it more effective by enhancing the management skills and performance levels of the personnel.

Developing domain specialization

All civil servants undoubtedly become specialists in general administration, as they are trained heavily in law. The civil servants are expected to handle departments, of which, they often do not have enough knowledge. As a result, the decisions end up being merely administrative, often lacking the understanding of the nuances of the subject. This is not to undermine the intellectual capacity of those posted in various departments, but those with specialized qualification and knowledge of the subject will be in a better position to carry out the responsibilities they are entrusted with. The days of generalists are over in most organizations globally and in India. This is the age of specialization. The private sector has upgraded management by entrusting specialists to relevant assignments, as it enables optimal performance by individuals and their departments.

Letting young civil servants develop a specialization of their choice after they finish their field stint can be a positive step towards this. This will help flatten the steep learning curve that many civil servants have to go through.

Deputation to private companies, etc.

To expand the scope of continuous learning for the civil servants, the government can introduce deputation to private organizations (micro, small, medium and large) and non-governmental and grassroots organizations; so that they can learn modern management practices, innovations and best practices, and acquire domain knowledge. In many countries, such as the United States (US) and France, we have seen practices of civil servants being permitted to work in the private sector as well as in other non-government institutions while retaining a lien in government. The deputation should not be as observers or as overseers, but as learners, where the civil servants work as employees.

Mentoring

Mentoring junior officers by senior civil servants or retired civil servants with impeccable credentials could be institutionalized and given more importance. This will help young officers during their formative years in service. I believe that most mentees select their mentors and not the other way round. The mentees have to believe that when they share anything, they share as equals and that their professional well-being is protected—that they will not be ridiculed or their confidentiality breached. A person who intends to be a mentor has to create that comfort zone.

Here is an example from my mentoring journey. Whenever I

was travelling, I would often take along a junior colleague to meet a client. I ensured the junior had a chance to speak and then afterwards, I would give them feedback and say, 'You could have done this', or 'You could have done that'. Similarly, if I observed somebody giving a pitch or a talk, I would meet the person afterwards or send an e-mail to say 'well done' or coach the person on how they could have done better. Along the same lines, senior civil servants may take keen interest in mentoring young officers and this practice will go a long way in building a mentor–mentee culture where the mentees benefit from the wealth of experience of their mentors.

Building institutional memory through knowledge management systems

There is an enormous amount of knowledge that is being created every day in the life of a civil servant as well as in the department where the civil servant works. While some of it gets translated into procedures and policies, a significant amount of it remains uncaptured. Over time, much of this institutional knowledge goes away as people take on new jobs, relocate or retire. With the coexistence of physical and digital records, the management of this functional and experiential knowledge has become all the more complex, offering very little scope for knowledge capture, retention, integration and retrieval.

An explicit strategy is required to maintain institutional memory. As part of the strategy, we must identify the entire gamut of things that is expected of every civil servant while working in a team, so that implicit assumptions and experiences are converted to explicit expectations and records. For instance, a civil servant enabling an induction process for new entrants can include the functional and experiential knowledge of a relevant field of study into the onboarding process of new team members; similarly another civil servant handling training and capability building can capture scenario-specific experiences in the refresher courses and so on.

Technology must be used to create a process and an integrated platform through which different teams across locations continually capture and curate institutional knowledge—making it a living and evolving body of valuable information that is accessible to everyone in the civil services ecosystem.

Institutional knowledge management using technology is an evolving discipline and Tata Consultancy Services (TCS) has been an early adopter. They developed a web-based enterprise-wide knowledge management system known as Knowmax, which focusses on building reusable knowledge assets across horizontal, vertical and geographical domains and it acts as a central knowledge bank for all projects being executed by TCS, resulting in significant time and effort optimization.

Digitization, E-Governance and Whole-of-Government or Whole-of-Society Approach

Today's challenges call for an agile approach that enables incorporation or removal of players as the shared mission between Union and state governments evolves, along with the support of technology that facilitates seamless collaboration and communication.

Now more than ever, India needs an adaptable and flexible whole-of-government or whole-of-society methodology to address the challenges facing the nation. Our success with CoWIN, Direct Benefit Transfers (DBT), Swachh Bharat Mission or Passport Seva makes a strong case for this approach to be adopted rapidly.

Perhaps, my experience at TCS in the late 1990s makes me a strong advocate of the whole-of-government approach. When I took over as the CEO of TCS in 1996, I needed to know the total number of employees by location, technology skills, hiring projections, the number of projects being worked upon and their status. But when I asked for these numbers, I often got vague estimates or I would be told that they would come back later with an answer. On some occasions, I got no answer at all. When I did get an answer, it was often too late and when I cross-checked the figures, I would invariably end up with conflicting numbers.

It became obvious that our information management systems were inadequate. They were fragmented because they had been developed at different times by individual departments and business units using disparate technologies. Moving data between them often involved a loss of accuracy, integrity and timeliness, which was just not acceptable.

We needed to create a single unified system—the digital backbone for 'One TCS'. This led to the evolution of Ultimatix—a state-of-the-art system at that time that enabled us to bring together on one platform, data about: projects, clients, employees, prospects and capturing relationships between them on a real-time basis. The transition to Ultimatix helped in addressing the digitization requirements of a fast-growing business, enhanced efficiency multifold and enabled the company to move forward to the next level of growth.

A similar exercise across all levels of the government may be carried out to reap the benefits of digital technologies in public service delivery. We should automate every major touchpoint between the government, citizens and businesses immediately. However, end-to-end digitalization will require massive process reengineering and integration. The exercise may seem expensive at the time of creation, but it will give long-term benefits, including saving of time, cost and improvement in efficiency of all departments.

An increasing number of activities at all levels, be it in the public or private sector, is becoming virtual with every passing day and no organization can afford to be left out. This is true of governments and, in turn, civil services. But while using information technology (IT) to deliver services, governments have to ensure that no section of the society is left out of the virtual services due to barriers in access to technology.

While we work towards these goals, it is essential that we bridge the digital divide in the country, which is not merely between the urban and rural population but also within the haves and have-nots. It is due to the imbalance between the availability of access in terms of resources on one hand and the absence of skills required to be part of the digital world. Coupled with this is the erratic internet connectivity.

Among those technologically challenged are not merely the recipients of services, but also the service-givers in the form of civil servants and personnel of various departments, up to the local self-government. Therefore, it is necessary, primarily for the civil services personnel to be trained in the use of IT at various levels of governance. Once the civil servants are able to map the usability of IT in the discharge of their roles and responsibilities to society, they will be in a better position to use IT in governance. One measure that could be adopted is the establishment of a coordinating authority in the form of a chief information officer or equivalent at the national level.

The whole-of-government approach can be an efficient pathway towards achieving the United Nations's Sustainable Development Goals (SDGs) in areas of education, health, energy, infrastructure etc. If we are to achieve the 2030 Agenda, we must focus on building new partnerships and strengthening the existing ones for better outcomes and greater impact.

For example, partnerships at NSDC led to the creation of a vibrant skilling ecosystem in the country. NOS/QP were created to reflect both the Indian realities as well as the aspirations of youth. In terms of outcomes and impact, NSDC has trained more than 32.5 million people since its establishment in 2008, of which 9.1 million trainees received direct job placements. This could be achieved by building partnerships with over 600 training partners and creating a robust network of 11,000+ training centres spread over 600 districts across the country.

Private and Institutional Involvement

India has a nimble private sector, a growing start-up ecosystem and a vibrant civil society that was non-existent in the previous decades. The private sector, start-ups and the NGOs can become an equal partner of the government. There are instances where the public administration has partnered with NGOs, civil societies and private sector to advance large-scale social change through effective policy implementation, but those are still outliers and not the norm.

Following the economic reforms of the 1990s and the subsequent globalization, there have been several opportunities where public–private partnerships (PPP) have been successful. The PPP model that was implemented to roll out the Indian Passport Seva has numerous takeaways for an efficient and effective public–private collaboration. India's rapidly expanding middle class and its rising economy had led to a growing demand for passport services. This put a massive strain on the Ministry of External Affairs's limited infrastructure, obsolete legacy systems and inadequate human resources. Citizens had to deal with inconvenient and cumbersome processes, a limited number of passport offices and endless delays. Traditional manual processes led to inefficiency and made the passport service delivery process prone to errors and inordinate delays. As part of this mammoth transformation, multiple stakeholders were integrated, processes reengineered for faster throughput and change management administered for officials at various levels. The high quality of services delivered from the state-of-the-art Passport Seva Kendras, where TCS staff work together with ministry officials, has been recognized globally.

A focus on affordable technology to allow equal access is imperative for inclusive development. Technology-enabled development in sectors such as health and education will go a long way in ensuring equitable development; and civil servants can play an integral role in its implementation.

Collaboration with academic institutions will also be critical in generating insights based on deep research and in promoting original thinking. Every department of the government can identify a few academic institutions to collaborate on interdisciplinary and multidisciplinary areas of research. Funds must be set aside, agenda for research must be set and time-bound research outputs must be used for making effective public policy implementation frameworks and impact evaluation.

It is time we made such PPP models a norm within the ambit of civil services, so that we can enhance efficiency and improve impact of the various citizen-centric programmes. This calls for a streamlined collaboration framework where there is scope for seamless replication of successful use cases to achieve scale and speed in project implementation.

Towards a Sustainable Future

The governments at every level and in all regions of the world are beginning to recognize that action needs to be taken quickly to address the huge economic, social and environmental challenges that the planet and people are facing and to move towards a sustainable future. While much of the responsibility for advancing sustainability might appear to fall on the shoulders of the private sector, the government has a crucial role to play in facilitating the transition to an economy that is much more energy-efficient, less damaging to the environment, promotes frugal consumption and ensures fair distribution of resources. For example, public procurement is an important instigator in facilitating the desired behavioural shift in business and is relevant to a wide variety of important environmental issues, such as highway construction, power generation, transportation, etc.

As India surges into its projected growth trajectory, green growth strategies are needed to promote sustainable growth and to break the pattern of environmental degradation and natural resource depletion. We need the civil servants, given their access to both the political leadership and the citizens, to communicate the need for change and a strategy to get from here to there.

Sustainable Development Goals

India has made noticeable improvements in key social indicators for education and health since Independence, mainly as a result of large-scale government programmes, such as mid-day meal scheme and National Health Mission. The country also halved its poverty rate and enjoyed strong improvements in many human development outcomes.

However, India has been ranked 121 out of 163 on the 2022 Global Index of Sustainable Development Goals,[1] adopted as a part of the 2030 Agenda signed by 193 United Nations member states

[1]'Rankings: The overall performance of all 193 UN Member States', Sustainable Development Report, https://bit.ly/3IX9rO2. Accessed on 18 January 2023.

in 2015. The Covid-19 pandemic has reversed the course of poverty reduction, at least temporarily. The economic slowdown caused by the pandemic is believed to have a significant detrimental impact on poor and vulnerable households. The informal sector, where the vast majority of India's labour force is employed, has been particularly affected. As in most countries, the pandemic has exacerbated vulnerabilities for traditionally excluded groups, such as the elderly, women, persons with disabilities and migrants.

Going forward, there is a need to adopt new models to deal with the various complex social challenges with speed and scale through technology-led information-enabled social investment; and measurable collaborative projects with the participation of local communities, civil societies, social enterprises, corporates and governments.

The future agenda must include better governance, better social services and high-quality independent institutions that promote and protect dignity, equality, sustainability, social justice and human rights for all. Our primary focus for SDGs should be to ensure that no one is left behind.

Focus on Citizen Centricity

The citizens are at the core of good governance. When governments deliver services based on the needs of the people they serve, they can boost public satisfaction and develop enduring trust between the citizens and the government. Citizens are the very purpose of the existence of the civil services. Citizen-centric governance should be participative, transparent, inclusive, responsive and accountable to the people. These set of foundational values need to be cascaded down to the last person in the civil services, so that values are internalized, followed and practised as a part of the organization's culture.

With growing social awareness among the citizens, there is a need for expanding the scope of dialoguing between the civil servants and the citizens. It is necessary to create channels of communication and participation that will bring in greater openness in the local governance, make officials more connected with the grassroots and improve scope for better understanding of problems. There is a need to focus on the outcomes of citizen-centric governance indicators such as Right to Service Act, Right to Information, Citizen's Charter, Grievances Redressal Mechanism and e-governance.

Digital transformation in governments is resulting in an ever-increasing number of ways in which civil servants can interact with citizens to identify problems and capture their inputs on an ongoing basis. For instance, social media can enable policy discussions and debates to overcome geographical and time-related barriers.

Public sector innovation is another aspect that demands consideration. Human-centred design principles that emphasize how people interact with systems and processes need to be adopted while formulating and implementing initiatives. Participative approaches must be included throughout the lifecycle of a project, so that inputs from citizens are captured in an ongoing basis.

Diversity and Inclusion

The significance of women's equal representation in governance and leadership has been well-recognized across the world. When women take leadership roles in public administration, governments become more responsive and accountable. It has also been noted that women's participation in public administration improves the quality of services delivered, as well as enhances the trust and public confidence that people bestow on the state organizations. In our country, deep-seated historic, cultural and socio-economic impediments have prevented an equitable distribution of opportunities—where women have been deprived of their seat at the decision-making table across different organizations and sectors. The Indian Administrative Service (IAS) has been no different in this regard.

The private sector is not doing well either, despite a lot of efforts made by many corporate leaders. I feel it takes sustained efforts over a very long period of time for one to see the kind of results that we all wish to see. Early on, after I took over as CEO of TCS, on one occasion, my human resources (HR) head decided to meet a

US client to try and find out why TCS had lost a particular project. The client told him that their employees had felt threatened by our proposal team—it was an 'all-male Indian team' while their workforce was all American and of equal gender. It was a lesson in the value of diversity and inclusion and that is when we started hiring local people and stepped up the hiring of women in all geographies. This is a case study with lessons to emulate for every organizational set-up that is keen on improving its gender ratio.

In India, we already have supportive laws, policies and regulations to further the cause of gender equity and equality. The challenge of attaining gender parity is highly complex and cannot be solved by policies alone. We need community-level shift in attitudes that hold women back. We already have an enabling legislative framework; what we need is for people to be more invested in the cause of women's equality and convene the partnerships that are likely to accelerate progress.

An overhaul in attitude and induction of a collaboration model within the civil services framework, to promote the cause of women's representation, can be a positive step in the direction of enhancing women's participation in civil services.

Presently, there is a scarcity of data and analysis on the existence and efficacy of policies that promote women's equal participation and involvement in decision-making in government on a local, regional and national level. Through the integration of technology, more measured approaches can be introduced to assess the efficacy of policies on the ground based on quantitative parameters. Hybrid work environment in the space of public administration has the potential to enhance women's involvement in civil services.

We also need to look at creating more public awareness about women's participation in nation-building. There are way fewer women taking up the civil services exams every year as against the number of men, primarily because most families in the country still give more weightage to their daughter's marriage than her financial independence or self-esteem. Efforts have to be made to collaborate with social media platforms and media channels, so that, a positive and encouraging outlook towards women's career and education can be propagated and conservative and limiting social practices that hinder women's growth can be dispelled. An enabling framework can be created in collaboration with schools and colleges, through which female students are nudged towards public administration at an early age.

The Start of a Journey

As society evolves and becomes more connected and aware, demanding more accountability and better governance—and as new initiatives get launched on both mission and standard mode, in congruence with the technological advancements—there is a need to strengthen the civil services personnel on aspects such as: emotional intelligence, ethical values, empathy, communication, learnability and the ability to work in a collaborative environment.

The subject of civil services reforms has a huge scope and it could not be possible to discuss everything within the scope of just one article. However, it is not to suggest that issues, such as political influence, frequent transfers and posting, tenure and performance evaluation are any less important than the topics discussed in this article.

We need to understand that the process of reforms is a journey and not a one-time event. The country right now is at a critical juncture and there is a need to address multiple challenges with equal priority—be it the growing disparity between the haves and have-nots; inequities in access to healthcare; education employment opportunities and social justice; more pandemics and diseases; climate disasters and so on. This calls for a bold and decisive civil services and resurgence of new and independent institutions to shape a better society going forward. As we set goals for the centenary of India's independence, we must continue our journey with concerted efforts—constantly improving and adapting—but not losing focus.

10

A MINDSET OF SERVICE

Towards A Collaborative Effort

Naina Lal Kidwai

The civil services, particularly the All-India Services, have always commanded considerable respect from the people of India.

The twenty-first century has witnessed a significant expansion of the civil services processes and responsibilities. Recruitment has become more competitive, and training norms and procedures more rigorous and stringent. There is a greater emphasis now on performance management practices. Effective management of public resources has necessitated open, transparent and accountable systems of delivery. The appointment of India's first Lokpal is a clear demonstration that India is second to none in making its public administration clean and fair. Clearly, accountability levels in government today are far higher than they were ever in the past.

On the one hand, the Indian Administrative Service (IAS) is referred to as the 'Steel Frame of Governance', with neutrality and anonymity as its core character attributes. On the other hand, there is the growing perception that it has failed to deliver on its promise and has accordingly invited criticism, including from the prime minister of India.[1]

In this context, it is time the country implements civil services reforms rather than blaming the bureaucracy for all the ills facing the

[1]Gupta, Shishir, 'Behind PM Modi's Stinging Critique of the IAS, a Jan Meeting Holds the Clue', *Hindustan Times,* 17 February 2021, https://bit.ly/3W13Edn. Accessed on 8 December 2022.

nation. It should start from recruitment itself and then be expanded to cover induction and other specialized trainings with a view to creating a cadre of accomplished civil servants who can then deliver on what falls within their remit. Civil servants (IAS) must possess the necessary knowledge or skills to perform specific functions. However, they cannot be expected to and will never be experts in everything and hence, the need to collaborate with partners for better delivery of social services on the ground.

Collaboration

Civil service reform aims at strengthening administrative capacity to perform core government functions. One of these functions is to forge collaboration and adopt a multi-stakeholder approach to achieve the good governance outcomes. I have attempted to highlight some success stories to strengthen my arguments for collaboration and 'multi-stakeholderism' as weighed against a go-it-alone approach. Recording these success stories hopefully also encourages replication and scaling up across the country.

It needs to be underscored at the outset that collaboration is not an end in itself; rather, it is a means of delivering better results for the public by meeting their needs in a seamless way. Its other benefits include saving money, reducing duplication and promoting innovation. The idea of 'joining up', collaborating and working across departmental and other public bodies to meet government's objectives needs greater emphasis now more than ever before in view of the growing complexities. Cases of good convergence between line departments leading to the attainment of collective outcomes for the Swachh Bharat Mission (SBM) are relevant.

An example is the National Rural Livelihoods Mission (NRLM) and SBM-Gramin convergence in several blocks of Ranchi and West Singhbhum districts, in Jharkhand, during SBM-Gramin Phase I. Village Organizations (VOs) formed under NRLM have played a leading role in the construction of individual household latrines (IHHLs) in the villages of these blocks of Jharkhand with funding support from the mission. These VOs were instituted by the Jharkhand State Livelihood Promotion Society (JSLPS) with active support of Village Water and Sanitation Committees (VWSCs). Effective convergence between SBM-Gramin and the VOs accelerated the construction of toilets in these blocks. For starters, to equip VO members, VWSC, Block Development Officer, UNICEF, Public Health Engineering Department and JSLPS field staff collaborated to organize a one-day triggering exercise-cum-orientation programme. In addition, five-day duration mason trainings were organized by the VWSCs with support from UNICEF at the block level.

Notwithstanding the different roles played by each of the organizations, they actively participated in the triggering exercises and follow-up activities carried out subsequently. Their dedication towards the SBM-Gramin campaign motivated VWSCs and VOs to put in place all possible efforts to ensure the success of the mission. Prior to this training, the village communities had no experience of constructing toilets or maintaining them. In fact, it was a first-hand experience for the VO members to undertake IHHL construction work under SBM-Gramin. They also had to deal with procurement of material from multiple vendors in these districts while recruiting masons from neighbouring villages. In areas that lacked manpower, the VO members took the lead and provided *Shramdaan*, or voluntary service, to construct toilets. The village community and Panchayati Raj Institution members actively supported the efforts of the VOs by providing all necessary guidance and inputs to accomplish the targets.

Experience gained from this activity of building individual toilets motivated members of the VOs to promote toilet usage. The success of this case led to the development of a model for convergence for SBM, as well as for other schemes with VO as a viable platform. It also built up a healthy competition between VWSCs and VOs; and the blocks worked towards their open defecation free (ODF) targets with renewed vigour and speed.

Another great example, in an activity which usually does not have any well-known women participation, is that of Jharkhand's trained women masons (or rani mistries, as they are popularly called). These pioneers in masonry work were instrumental in building over 15 lakh toilets in a single year (2018–19) and the state was declared ODF (rural) much ahead of the national cut-off date of 2 October 2019.[2]

The rani mistry training drive in the state was meant to solve a problem associated with the stymied progress of the SBM campaign in the state in 2017 and 2018. The conventional strategy of routing work and funds through the local administrations to village panchayats and mukhiyas was not yielding results quickly enough. The raj mistries (male masons) were not showing any interest in the work either. The then SBM Secretary, Government of Jharkhand, Ms Aradhana Patnaik adopted a different strategy to capitalize on the potential of the state's 1.5 lakh women self-help groups (SHGs).[3] This was a well-calculated move towards a hitherto unexplored gender activity.

It was a request from a woman in Gumla district that triggered the mass training of women through the SHGs—and the rest is history. This movement, the first of its kind, emerged as a mammoth uprising of female interest and skill motivation, thereby transforming into a typical example of multi-stakeholder coalition engagement with convergence between different centrally and state-sponsored schemes (NRLM, SBM, rural and urban development, etc.), to create community-based livelihood opportunities benefitting every partner in the coalition. It was a grassroots-level movement that gained traction and fervour from among the women themselves. They had neither been encouraged nor permitted to display their skills in this activity, and once given the opportunity transformed the challenge to a tangible asset-creation movement. Many of these women have not let the opportunity go by and have already graduated to home construction, getting absorbed as trained masons to undertake construction both under rural and urban housing schemes.

There are several other successful models of convergence and multi-stakeholderism which have proven to be hugely successful models of

---

[2]'Rani Mistris', Vajiram & Ravi, 16 December 2018, https://bit.ly/3QavPF7. Accessed on 4 January 2023.

[3]Jebaraj, Priscilla, 'Rani Mistris Score Swachh Goal', *The Hindu*, 16 December 2018, https://bit.ly/3Glb7z6. Accessed on 27 December 2022.

government–stakeholder collaboration and I would therefore recommend a 'best practices' compilation that can then be used as a module for training the civil services cadre.

Accessibility

It has been our experience that inaccessibility contributes, albeit incorrectly, towards building public perception regarding the importance and invincibility of civil servants. This is a trait from the days of the British raj, when high government officials maintained a distance from the hoi polloi merely to keep up a myth of the administration being aloof, impersonal and thus impartial. An easy-to-access approach can and has, dramatically changed that perception. Our work at the India Sanitation Coalition in water and sanitation endorsed this view. It has not only demonstrated the willingness of the administration to work closely with and among the public, but seems to be convinced of the tremendous benefit that the public derives from such an approach.

I am convinced that civil servants' relative isolation and inaccessibility had entrenched their attitudes and traditions and not left them open to new thinking and change. Can there be a 'bulldozer blade' that can be effectively used for clearing this barrier during this proposed reformative process? The answer is yes and there is evidence to strengthen the argument.

Jharkhand was interesting from multiple standpoints when Phase I of the Swachh Bharat was implemented in the state between 2014 and 2019. One of the key points of interest was 'Jal Sahiya'. Under SBM-Gramin, jal sahiyas, or members of the community charged with effectively implementing the scheme, were playing an important role, both in triggering the village for adopting the right kind of sanitation behaviour and construction of toilet post the triggering. Only once the construction of toilets for a community was achieved, would the sahiyas continue to work with the community—to ensure that the behaviour to always use the toilet and not defecate in the open was sustained to give the community its ODF status.

These women leaders who were nominated and trained by the Gram Panchayats were an important connecting link between the community and elective members of the panchayat. Being women, they were a very important factor in persuading the village womenfolk on the need to change their lifestyle and begin using newly constructed toilets. The toilets were seen as symbols of women having gained in *izzat*, or respect—in being able to perform their ablutions behind closed doors and at a time of their choosing, rather than waiting for darkness to fall before they could step out—and thereby also a status in the family or village community. The feedback of the women leaders on how well the programme had been implemented was considered as being unbiased, for they were not only considered as being apolitical but also as not a part of the local administration.

The incumbent government bureaucracy in Jharkhand grabbed the success stories and appropriately made use of their unique disposition. The women leaders were provided complete accessibility for them to reach out to the senior-most officials at the helm of the programme, via WhatsApp or voice call, with critical assessments. This helped with the monitoring, evaluation, learning and enabled timely action as rural Jharkhand achieved its ODF status.

I am pleased to share a research study which establishes that jal sahiyas are an important cadre at the grassroots level, for drinking water service delivery too, as they are often seen actively engaged in activities related to the implementation of the Jal Jeevan Mission (JJM).

Community Management of Rural Water Supply

Community Water Plus, a research project, investigated 20 case studies of successful community-managed rural water supply programmes across 17 states in India. Besides the resource implications of the programme, the study provided insights into the kind and quantum of support that was required to be extended to communities, leading to improvement in water supply to rural households. In Jharkhand, the community was represented by the VWSC, where jal sahiya, the female lead of the community, played a vital role. Exemplifying the public–community partnership, the drinking water and sanitation department within the government of Jharkhand provided technical and financial support (which included substantial financial subsidies for operational expenses), while VWSCs undertook the job of operation and maintenance. The assessment indicated that the majority of consumers in the villages that were included in the study received acceptable service levels, which established the effectiveness of the service provision.

The cadre of jal sahiyas was unique to the state of Jharkhand. It was created with a view to building a strong democratic set-up in which these women community leaders were expected to play a big role, especially around the implementation of water, sanitation and hygiene (WASH) programmes.

The drinking water and sanitation department that implements both SBM and JJM in the state, appointed over 32,000 jal sahiyas for the effective implementation of various WASH programmes in far-flung areas of the state, in 2012.

With adequate training and support, these community leaders over a period, not only became champions of WASH ensuring better services for their villages but also earned performance incentives and honoraria, becoming to a certain extent, financially self-sufficient.

Specialization in a Digital Age

Governance is becoming increasingly technologically enabled and specialized. Our work at the India Sanitation Coalition during SBM-Gramin Phase I, showed the importance of the ability of the mission directors and principal secretaries to understand and interpret big data, to intervene and provide impetus to the programme.

Ambitious missions with tight timelines need big data with high velocity to attain big results. Data, when properly sourced, structured and analysed, can provide the much-needed evidence enabling decisions and actions. Improved operational efficiency, optimal resource targeting and improved decision-making are the advantages of big data. Successful programmes invest substantially in big data to generate insights and evidence for action.

As sanitation was a low-priority area and not much was invested in it until 2015, it was deprived of any structured data till that year. The SBM, aimed at making India ODF, generated interest among all stakeholders. Leading the implementation of SBM, the Department of Drinking Water and Sanitation (DDWS) at the Union Ministry of Jal Shakti made substantial investment in the space, over the years, to generate data needed for big sanitation results and outcomes.

There was a requirement of expertise which demanded specialized skills. The DDWS then had the advantage of a leadership whose ability to make good judgements and take quick decisions, made all the difference. Besides, the then secretary of DDWS was supported by a technical team, external to the government bureaucracy, which provided a technical understanding of the programme; including the necessity to collate and analyse data. Ideally, one would expect part of the bureaucracy itself to have that specialized skill to handle the emerging technicalities before being able to strategize, plan and implement.

Before I set out my recommendations around specialized skills for the Indian civil services cadre, let me just put together a piece of evidence on how the DDWS used a multipronged strategy to generate and use data for programme and management decisions. Three key pillars helped build and use big data in the sanitation sector to achieve collective outcomes.

Volume of data: The sector adopted a systematic approach to generate the requisite volume of data that could provide insights on a fast-moving sanitation mission to support action. In addition to collection and analysis of data at the local levels, it initiated major data collection interventions to build big data on sanitation. The commissioning of Baseline Survey (which covered all the households in rural India), three rounds of National Annual Rural Sanitation Survey (NARSS) that covered over three lakh households and three rounds of Swachh Survekshan Grameen (SSG) that covered over 25,000 villages and over one lakh public places. Direct feedback from over 50 million citizens on the programme contributed to building the big data needed in the sanitation sector.

Data on status of sanitation in rural areas is now available for over 160 million households spread across 0.6 million villages.[4] This data provides information on the socio-economic status of households, their location and whether they have access to a toilet. This is well structured and presented in relevant modules in the Integrated Management Information System of the SBM so that all state, district and local governments can use it for planning and monitoring.

Variety of data: For the first time now, we have structured data on various dimensions of the programme—social, behavioural, technical, financial and geospatial. There is data for over a 100 million households on the type or technology of toilets built, which helps one understand the safety of toilets, faecal sludge management challenges and other dimensions of the toilet technology. Government is effectively using this data now to design future interventions related to solid and liquid waste management (SLWM), including the management of faecal sludge in rural areas aligned with the goals and objectives of Phase II of the rural mission. Besides, there is real-time data now on the incentive money being paid to households for building and using their toilets and the amounts that remain to be paid. This has supported budgetary forecast and financial planning and accountability in the sanitation sector.

Geotagging of sanitation assets and infrastructure was seriously pursued too. Over 90 per cent of the toilets built during SBM Phase I were geotagged, so one could locate these toilets using their geo coordinates. This promoted accountability on the part of the programme managers and duty bearers, besides providing credibility to the claims made under the Swachh Bharat programme.

More interestingly, the sanitation sector, for the first time, could claim to have primary data on the use of the toilets. NARSS

[4]'SBM 2.0 IMIS App Reports', Swachh Bharat Mission(G) Phase-II, https://bit.ly/3ZaarUl. Accessed on 4 January 2023.

scientifically captured these usage trends over a three-year period to provide useful insights on the usage pattern. This is now central to the planning and management of the mission aimed at the sustainability of the Swachh Bharat outcomes.

Velocity of data: Managers need data in time to intervene and provide impetus to programme results and outcomes. The programme invested in creating a management dashboard which presented analysis and trends using the high velocity data[5]. A dedicated team of data professionals working across the development blocks of India never let the velocity slow down. Two independent national surveys, that I mentioned above, helped maintain the velocity and provided data on various parameters that the programme needed to achieve the desired results.

Investment in big data provides commensurate operational effectiveness and big results. But do we have a cadre of officials with enough specialized knowledge and skill to appreciate that first and then, adapt it to the programme which is headed by them? As India forges ahead on its digitalization journey, the inclusion of the basics of data science in existing induction curriculum and on the job training becomes necessary.

Engagement with Civil Society Organizations

In a globalized world, the welfare role of the state is perhaps shrinking. That space is occupied by Civil Society Organizations (CSOs). The government alone can't reach out to the masses and deliver. CSOs plug in the gaps left by the government and partners government to ensure the success and durability of programmes.

About 3.3 million CSOs work in India, with the majority being rural and small. India has a CSO for every 400 people. Civil servants' engagement with CSOs would help in the process of delivering the services, which have not been reaching remote areas besides assisting

[5]Velocity refers to the speed with which data is generated. High velocity data is generated with such a pace that it requires distinct (distributed) processing techniques. An example of a data that is generated with high velocity would be Twitter messages or Facebook posts.

the government to achieve its development objectives. It would also help citizens voice their aspirations, concerns and alternatives for consideration by policymakers; and enhance the accountability and transparency of government and local government programmes.

I would like to quote from our experiences with the Global Sanitation Fund Programme (GSF), which had supported the low-income states of India, in implementing the SBM-Gramin between 2014 and 2017.

The programme aimed at improved planning, implementation and partnerships and relationships within a designated framework. It was premised on a bottom-up approach where CSOs would not just audit the implementation outcomes, but also support the government in planning and implementing the programme.

In 2014, the GSF-supported programme in India helped close to 380,000 poor and marginalized people across the villages of Bihar, Jharkhand and Assam realize access to improved toilets.[6] Studies revealed that from the onset of the programme to December 2014, more than 4,800 villages were onboarded for collective action and about 2.7 million people were approached with basic, yet critical, hygiene messages. About 10,000 people were trained on improving their sanitation and hygiene situation. GSF has been successful in augmenting the capacity of partners and more than 10,000 people were involved in the delivery of services. The GSF initiative reached 1.1 million in remote areas and helped provide improved toilets. Each of these were designed and implemented with local interventions. By this using local know-how the GSF sent out a strong message of using innovative practices at different locations. The programme has helped strengthen local institutions through the intervention process and by targeted capacity building. It has successfully demonstrated lessons to enable local approaches to reach scale. These results encouraged and strengthened state-level institutions to adapt and scale-up similar interventions state-wide.

---

[6]*Global Sanitation Fund: Progress Report 2014,* Global Sanitation Fund, https://bit.ly/3vjKBzF. Accessed on 28 December 2022.

The programme is designed to respond to fundamental challenges in the rural sanitation sector. It is consistent with the core principles espoused by the Government of India's community-led total sanitation (CLTS) programme, 'Nirmal Bharat Abhiyaan'.

GSF served to build the capacities of state and district programme officers besides that of the sub-grantees, who the fund supported from its resources. What was achieved through this engagement was improved delivery on the part of each stakeholder and a strengthened relationship between the state and district governments, leading to improved outcomes in these GSF-intervened states and districts.

What I wish to highlight here is that the said engagement was productive because the buy-in from the decision-makers in these states was never a challenge. There were these conscientious and upright officials who led the mission from the front. They were willing to partner and were comfortable dealing with any critique of the programme if they knew the sources were trustworthy. CSOs and the interventions, like GSF, were trusted in these places and partnered with.

Later, what these states saw is now history. Jharkhand stood first in the Swachh Sundar Shauchalaya, with five of its districts among the top-10 districts in the country, according to the results declared by Union Ministry of Jal Shakti in 2019. Giridih emerged as the topmost district in the country; East Singhbhum secured fourth position; Saraikela sixth; Koderma seventh and Lohardaga district in ninth position. East Singhbhum topped among seven specially mentioned districts, in constructing clean and beautiful toilets under the SBM across the country.[7]

I therefore strongly recommend the compilation of these 'islands of excellence' in programme implementation and analytics. These real-life examples and modules enable the government to undertake actions to increase the scalability of its programmes and not reinvent the wheel each time.

---

[7]'Jharkhand Comes First in Cleanest Toilet Competition', *Hindustan Times,* 26 June 2019, https://bit.ly/3Vx4lKK. Accessed on 28 December 2022.

Engagement with Corporates

Arun Maira, former member of the Planning Commission, has written, 'The government's job is not to make a profit. It is to improve the world for everyone. "Making profit is easy, changing the world is hard," was the poignant statement of a business management student at an international conference on business responsibility.'[8]

There are several good examples of corporate partnerships, the Zila Swachh Bharat Prerak (ZSBP) initiative being one of them. A milestone partnership between Tata Trusts and DDWS, the programme put India's rural sanitation coverage on a fast track by putting young professionals on the ground to achieve the objectives of SBM-Gramin. A major output indicator of the mission was the sanitation coverage. ZSBPs acted as the eyes and ears of the district magistrates (DMs) in the sanitation space, with ZSBPs providing boots on the ground and focus. From 39 per cent at the launch of the mission, the sanitation coverage of rural India rose to a commendable 98 per cent in 2018–19, over double of where it had started from. Two independent surveys—one by the National Sample Survey Organization in 2016 and the other by the Quality Council of India in 2017—had identified the usage of toilets at 95 per cent and 91 per cent, respectively. As an outcome, over 540,000 villages and 585 districts had been declared ODF, across 27 states and Union Territories. ZSBPs played a pivotal role during that period.[9]

Another example is ITC's Health & Sanitation Programme, which aims to build awareness on the critical link between sanitation and health so that families could come forward with the interest in building toilets for themselves. For maximum impact, campaigns were customized for different groups—men, women, children and community leaders.

---

[8]Chandrasekhar, K.M., and K. Jayakumar, 'Corporate Management Isn't What Civil Service Needs: Administrative Reforms Can Only Be Delivered by Change in Executive Goals, Not Change in Personnel', *The Times of India,* 30 July 2021, https://bit.ly/3VGCvg6. Accessed on 8 December 2022.

[9]'Swachh Bharat Mission Well on Track to Achieve ODF India', Press Information Bureau, 9 January 2019, https://bit.ly/3YhF5ei. Accessed on 8 December 2022.

Community groups—generally women's SHGs—were formed and they carried out most of the activities: identifying potential households, providing information and building awareness, managing funds, supervising construction, following up on usage, etc. Families got a loan through the group to build the toilet, but they did bear part of the cost. In fact, their financial stake fostered a strong sense of ownership and encouraged regular repayments.

Through joint efforts by the government/bureaucracy and corporates, we can effect transformational changes, helping us achieve our Sustainable Development Goals (SDG) commitments.

Mindset Reform among Civil Servants

In all the experiences that have been highlighted above, I have tried to illustrate the effective delivery of government initiatives and programmes, designed to bring benefit to the community at large and the poor and underprivileged in particular. The programmes illustrate the accessibility, openness and willingness of the ground-level administration to partner with CSOs in support of and for more effective delivery of projects designed for any targeted group. The need for better collection of data, its analysis and its credibility can hardly be underscored. The success stories enumerated above indicate to the criticality of such databases. Nevertheless, what stands out for recognition is the partnering of district administrators with CSOs. Such partnering cannot be left only to individual administrators who have the requisite mindset. It is the need of the hour and hence, such moulding of young civil servants needs to be built into the training modules itself.

The need of the hour is not mere 'buy-in' by these officials into civil society-sponsored programmes but the openness and willingness to partner with them on a long-term basis, on a 'shoulder-to-shoulder' mode. In instances where administrators have demonstrated such willingness at the higher levels in the district, the close collaboration of other officials engaged in delivery of government-sponsored schemes has become that much more easy and effective. Hence, in the capacity-building process, as a part of Mission Karmayogi, this aspect needs to be factored in. It will definitely ensure better-targeted and leakage-free delivery of government programmes.

In the final analysis, the political element in a parliamentary democracy cannot be ignored. The relationship between the bureaucracy and political executive is another area of concern that needs to be dealt with. It is an issue that is both complex and sensitive in a democracy like ours. It is not always that political interference at the ground level is detrimental to ongoing schemes. There are however, elements that attempt to push themselves in, more often to gain public acclaim than to gain access to government funds. Where seasoned and mature administrators have been able to effectively handle such political associations, the progress has been smooth. The relationship has to be of trust and willingness to partner from both sides. Delivery of government programmes and good administration does not in any way require the subjugating of the bureaucracy to the political executive. A civil service, by its definition, is permanent and meant to be objective. Its allegiance is not so much to the party in power but to be accountable to declared policies and programmes of the government. The need of the hour is to give priority to efficiency and impartiality and abhor the tendency of the political executive to prefer loyalty over efficiency. The need is to serve the Indian people with efficient delivery of good governance and government announced projects.

To serve India and her people is paramount.

11

FROM INCREMENTAL TO EXPONENTIAL

Reimagining Civil Services in India's Amrit Kaal

Sanjeev Chopra

The Civil Services Examination (CSE) conducted by the Union Public Service Commission (UPSC) draws over a million aspirants each year, thereby making it one of the toughest examinations anywhere in the world. But if clearing the examination is tough for the candidates, the challenge for the government is perhaps greater. Inducting such bright people into a complex ecosystem in which rules, roles, expectations, reputation, rewards and career progression are dependent on a range of factors—many of which are not in the control of the officer—requires newer ways of motivating officers to retain their optimism, as well as passion for excellence.

This essay goes on to examine the genesis of the common civil services examination, the establishment of the Lal Bahadur Shastri National Academy of Administration (LBSNAA) for the development of an esprit de corps—a feeling of 'one for all, and all for one'—among all services and the evolution of a training pedagogy that worked satisfactorily till the economic reforms of the 1990s. It takes up the recommendations of the Administrative Reforms Commission (ARC)[1], with regard to specialization and the introduction of mid-career training programmes (to enable

[1]The ARCs are committees appointed by the Government of India to review the public administration system of India. Two such committees have been appointed, the first under Morarji Desai in 1966 who later became the prime minster and the second was headed by the then Union Minister, Veerappa Moily.

officers to make the transition from field functionaries to governance professionals after the first 10 years of their services).

In his review of civil services training, the current Prime Minister (PM) wanted LBSNAA to be at the forefront of a future-ready Atmanirbhar Bharat in the Amrit Kaal[2] of India's independence. This called for a quantum leap in the country's growth trajectory 'from the incremental to the exponential'. This was the context in which the PM announced the National Programme for Civil Services Capacity Building (NPCSCB)—Mission Karmayogi (MK)—in August 2020, aimed at 'making him [the civil servant] more creative, constructive, imaginative, innovative, proactive, professional, progressive, energetic, enabling, transparent and technology-enabled'.[3] He tasked the civil services with achieving the target of a $5 trillion economy by 2025 and a $40 trillion economy by 2047. Finally, we examine whether it is time for a separate examination for different services, keeping in view the attitude and the aptitude of the aspirants.

PM, CM and DM

Till the turn of the century, the saying in the Hindi heartland, in popular parlance, was that there were only three authorities in the country: the PM, the CM (chief minister) and the DM (district magistrate). Within their respective domains, they exercised abundant power, authority and patronage. Becoming the PM or the CM could take several years in the rough and tumble of politics, but the key to becoming the DM (or Superintendent of Police) in of one the 700-odd districts in the country lay in cracking the CSE conducted

[2]The term was first used by the Prime Minister in 2021 during the Vigilance Week. He said: 'We are celebrating Azadi Ka Amrit Mahotsav. In the next 25 years, during "Amrit Kaal", the nation will move forward towards attaining resolutions made for Atma Nirbhar Bharat. Today we're working to strengthen "good governance", "pro-people pro-active governance".' ('Budget 2022: What does "Amrit Kaal" mean?' ET NOW, 1 February 2022, https://bit.ly/3X5CJOj. Accessed on 28 December 2022.)

[3]'Cabinet Approves "Mission Karmayogi"-National Programme for Civil Services Capacity Building (NPCSCB)', PIB, Delhi, 2 September 2020, https://bit.ly/3uV6tRH. Accessed on 16 December 2022.

by the UPSC, which over 2017–21, drew over a million aspirants each year, thereby making it one of the toughest examinations anywhere in the world.[4]

The question is—can the extant system of recruitment and training keep pace with the resolve of the political leadership to make India a $40 trillion economy by 2047? Will interventions like Aarambh and MK motivate officers to adopt 'lifelong learning' as an imperative? Will Indian Administrative Service (IAS) officers take the lead in acquiring skills relevant to their evolving roles and motivate others to do the same? Or will they resist the effort with clever procrastination?

The CSE

The CSE selects officers not just for the IAS, but also for the Indian Police Service (IPS) and 14 Group A services, including the Indian Foreign Service and five Group B services. Based on their merit, category and preference, they are allotted to different services. After the initial foundation training at LBSNAA, they are sent to their respective academies for professional training, while the IAS officers stay back for theirs.

The genesis of the common exam can be traced back to the meeting of the Premiers of the then 11 provinces[5] of India with Sardar Vallabhbhai Patel, the Home Member in the Interim Cabinet, in October 1946. After Independence, Pandit Jawaharlal Nehru wanted to induct foreign service officers directly, but this was opposed by the Home Department, which argued that all top positions in the government, including the superior central services, should be filled

---

[4]Less than half take the preliminary (qualifying exam) and the vast drop in numbers is on account of the limitation on the number of attempts. As such, if the preparation for the prelims is not up to the mark, aspirants avoid taking the exam, as it counts as an attempt, whereas filling of the form is not. Of these half-a-million candidates, just about 10,000 qualify for the mains exam. One-fourth of them will make it to the interview stage and of 800-odd candidates who get the offer letter from UPSC, about one-fifth will be appointed in the IAS.

[5]Assam, Bengal, Bihar, Bombay, Central Provinces, Madras, Northwest Frontier Province, Orissa, Punjab, Sindh and United Provinces.

in through a public examination. For a fledgling nation, it was the best decision in the context of the times.

As training institutions for different services were dispersed,[6] it was not until 1960 that all those selected by the UPSC were brought together for the Foundation Course (FC) at the National Academy of Administration (NAA), as LBSNAA was then called. Home Minster G.B. Pant said in his Lok Sabha speech of 15 April 1958:

> We have, since the achievement of Independence, made earnest efforts to bring about a suitable change in the outlook and approach of our services. We propose to set up a National Academy of training so that the services, wherever they may function, whether as Administrative officers, or as Accountants or as Revenue officers, might imbibe the true spirit, and discharge their duties in a manner which will raise their efficiency and establish concord between them and the public completely.[7]

This was a clear departure from the colonial-era practice of training Indian Civil Service (ICS), Central Services and Indian Police officers in their respective training academies with little or no interaction. With the establishment of the NAA, officers of the Indian Forest Service, Indian Economic Service and the Indian Statistical Service were also brought together for the FC.

Members of Team India

The objective of this FC was to help officers make the transition from being brilliant individuals to becoming members of Team India. It was about the development of an esprit de corps for the entire batch across services, so that over their service career, they could know their cohort, preferably by first names and have a positive recall of shared moments of learning, adventuring and trekking across the

---

[6]For example, the training of police officers was at Mt Abu in Rajasthan.

[7]Saroha, Sakshi, 'Glorious Journey of LBSNAA from Delhi and Shimla to Mussoorie', *The Indian Express*, 26 April 2022, https://bit.ly/3I33JcQ. Accessed on 28 December 2022.

Himalayas, taking part in theatre festivals and general comradeship.

All this made perfect sense till the early 1990s, when government departments interacted primarily with each other, the Planning Commission and public sector undertakings (PSUs). All services were (and continue to be) eligible for a central deputation under the Central Staffing Scheme (CSS), as all departments and ministries were doing almost the same kind of work—implementing legislation assigned to them as per the Rules of Business, preparing the annual budget and the minister's address to Parliament, which also outlined the government policy in the sector. Ministries oversaw the implementation of programmes as varied as the Border Area Development programme under the Ministry of Home Affairs (MHA) or the Jawahar Rozgar Yojana, the precursor to Mahatma Gandhi National Rural Employment Guarantee Act (MGNREGA) under the rural development ministry. Thus, if an officer knew the fundamentals—norms for release of funds, review of programmes and appraisal for the Planning Commission—they could make a transition from one government department to another, both in the state and the central government, for the essential task was that of 'administration'. The task of 'visioning' was outsourced to the experts of the Planning Commission, which of course held consultation meetings with officers from the state and central government. But in the final analysis, the entire plan budget was their remit.

To illustrate: till the aviation sector opened, the Ministry of Civil Aviation dealt with Air India (then a PSU) and the Airports Authority of India. However, post-liberalization, the ministry has been dealing not just with the aviation regulator and the International Airport Authority of India (IAAI) but also with private airlines, as well as the airports in the public–private partnership mode. Such an example can be extrapolated for every ministry, including the defence ministry as the government moves towards indigenization of manufacture and possibly also looking at export markets.

The Changing Profile of a District Officer

It must however be placed on record that the Academy, too, was taking incremental steps to update the content and format of training, especially as the role of the DM also underwent a change. Prior to the 1973 Criminal Procedure Code (CrPC) amendment, the DM was the presiding judge in criminal trials. As collectors, DMs were also the heads of the revenue administration and land revenue was a significant contributor to state's resource mobilization efforts. However, by the early 1970s, many state governments started giving remissions on land revenue and few state governments were willing to take over lands for land revenue defaults. As tenants secured rights, government was more concerned with land reforms, strengthening co-operatives and making provision for irrigation. Then came the 73rd and 74th Constitutional Amendments, which authorized state governments to transfer funds, functions and functionaries of 29 departments to panchayats in rural areas and municipal bodies in urban areas.

While this may have 'diluted' the power of the DM, it did not dent the salience of the IAS as a service for municipal commissioners and chief development officers (CDOs). COOs are also drawn from the successful candidates of the CSE exam. The DM continues to perform a miscellany of tasks—from law and order to land management to protocol functions, general coordination and conduct of elections.

Over the years, the academic component of the professional phases was strengthened with the establishment of research centres on a range of development interventions—from land reforms to co-operatives, urban affairs, gender, disaster management and policy systems. By the mid-1980s, there was a change in the training pedagogy: greater emphasis on syndicate work, case studies, village visits, exposure to PSUs and leading non-governmental organizations (NGOs). In the 1990s, the National Dairy Development Board stepped in to develop case studies on co-operatives and rural development interventions. A land reform unit was established to study the impact of land reforms and officers were expected to carry out the socio-economic survey of a village in their district training.

FC in the Time of Amrit Kaal

However, as we enter the Amrit Kaal of India's Independence centenary (2022–47), the design and structure of training of civil servants must reflect the aspirations of a new India. One must mention here that the 'people of India' are now young, literate, ambitious and entrepreneurial with an median age of 28.7 years[8] and are no longer dependent principally on agriculture. They are willing to skill themselves and migrate to newer pastures, especially urban areas, in search of meaningful employment and professionally satisfying careers.

In fact, the Aarambh immersion was conceptualized from 2019 as a flagship component of the FC. Aarambh, literally 'the beginning', was a programme to dismantle the artificial barriers between technology, human resource and the environment. It was designed to be in sync with an India in which technology was the driving force in all domains—from agriculture to health, school education and urban mobility. Anchoring Aarambh at the Statue of Unity was also symbolic of the connect Sardar Patel had with the civil services.

LBSNAA and the World Bank

Aarambh was not just about incremental interventions in a particular field; it was to be the exponential game changer. LBSNAA faculty worked with the World Bank and the Department of Personnel and Training to curate a programme which drew thought leaders who have impacted polity, academia, technology and governance. In one of the keynotes at the first Aarambh (2019), World Bank Group President, David Malpass, spoke on the need to balance a high growth trajectory with equity.

> India has been a development success story. This country cut extreme poverty in half within a generation, and is transforming itself into one of the world's fast-growing standouts. The goal

[8]'India Population Distribution in 2021, by Age', GlobalData, https://bit.ly/3i9mFvS. Accessed on 4 January 2023.

> of becoming a $5 trillion economy by 2025 is both worthy, and achievable with strong economic reforms. […] Yet to stay in the forefront, India's civil service needs to shift from a focus on enforcing compliance […] to finding ways to ensure high quality services and regulation. […] You will need skills in communications and negotiations, and to work across units and ministerial boundaries to address the complex challenges that you will face in your careers.[9]

The second Aarambh (2020), structured the foundation course with focus on the related themes of *Ek Bharat—Shresth Bharat:* Cultural and economic diversity oneness as India's unique strength; *Atmanirbhar Bharat*: in Energy, Health and public systems for Black Swan events; and *Naveen Bharat*: Research & Innovation in Education, Industry and Administration.

'Moving towards a sustainable Five trillion-dollar economy' was the theme for the third Aarambh held at Statue of Unity on 11 and 12 January 2022. The programme had to be rescheduled and curtailed because of Omicron but could be seen as a continuum of the earlier programmes. The other themes included drivers and constraints to growth; strengthening the infrastructure pipeline; scaling up investments in the private sector; new education policy and skilling; and a holistic social protection infrastructure.

A Future-Ready India

The political executive was sending out three related, but nuanced messages. First, that all civil services should be trained together and develop professional skills—both for their domains, as well as for envisioning a 'future-ready' India. Second, that the IAS must hone specialist skills in specific sectors and not take up positions for which they are not professionally trained. Third, while the government, through MK, was willing to provide professional as well as financial

---

[9]'Strengthening Indian Civil Service towards Efficient Service Delivery', The World Bank, 28 October 2019, https://bit.ly/3V7LENA. Accessed on 16 December 2022.

assistance for improving competencies, the onus of acquiring these vested with the officers themselves. Although not stated explicitly, it is also clear that the government will not hesitate to induct lateral entrants into roles that members of the civil service are found wanting.

This brings us to the unique and special training needs for the IAS. Unlike other services, the IAS has two distinct, though interrelated roles. The first is about administering districts, which is essentially a 'hands-on' implementation role. This is, what one may call the DM-type role and in this, would be included the tenure as a subdivisional officer, community development officer, additional district magistrate, municipal commissioner, etc.

The second role begins after the first decade, when officers serve directorates, departments and ministries—both in the state government as well as at the Centre. The former is the remit of the 18-month professional phase(s), including the year-long district training, while the Mid-Career Training Programmes (MCTPs) and MK address the second.

This training of being an effective field functionary commences immediately after the FC with a series of attachments, from defence establishments to large infrastructure projects in public–private partnership mode. This is followed by Phase I, in which academic inputs are given on law, public administration, management, economics and information technology skills with district administration as the focus. This is followed by a year-long attachment with a DM in the state cadre, followed by another six weeks of experience sharing at the Academy with their peers and immediate seniors. Officers also carry out assignments and action research projects which are evaluated by a panel comprising external experts and internal faculty. Since 2015, the academic councils of Jawaharlal Nehru University and LBSNAA have worked together to make the syllabi practical and relevant.

Also, from 2015, on completion of their Phase II training at LBSNAA, the Department of Personnel and Training has been offering officers a three-month attachment as assistant secretary in one of the departments or ministries of the Government of India. Officers study the actual implementation, monitoring and review of policies and programmes of the Indian government implemented at the district and sub-district levels, before they are sent out to the states for their first field posting.

Everything under the Sun!

One critique of the IAS is that unlike every other service selected through the CSE, this is a generalist service which spends the first 10 to 12 years in doing everything under the sun in the districts as well as municipal corporations. In fact, on this there is no disagreement that officers with good coordination, communication and negotiation skills are required to run districts as varied as Mokokchung in Nagaland to Patiala in Punjab. These are also the years when they implement programmes and understand the complexity involved in rolling out a wide variety of interventions—from Kisan Credit Cards for financial inclusion of all farmers to polio eradication campaign, as well as the MGNREGA and the Rashtriya Krishi Vikas Yojana. Thus, due to the wide gamut of roles performed, any IAS officer would better appreciate the manner in which rural programmes provide diverse benefits, such as the positive impact of rural roads on agro-marketing and food processing; of functional toilets, sanitary pads and bicycles for girls on women's education and health, etc.

However, DMs have gone on to do some remarkable innovations—from making airports in the public–private partnership mode to leveraging corporate social responsibility and District Mineral Foundation funds for upgrading infrastructure in rural schools and primary health centres. Often, officers find one or two sectors more interesting than others and this is how specialization begins or ought to begin.

From Field Administrators to Policy Professionals

After a decade in the field, officers participate in the MCTPs, which facilitate their transition to becoming governance professionals in a couple of selected domains and continue with this specialization over the next two decades of their service. During this period they must serve both at the Centre and the state, thereby fulfilling the important task of bringing in knowledge from their state to the policy initiatives at the Centre. The second ARC had recommended eight broad areas of specialization: economic management; industrial development; agricultural and rural development; health; education and social sector; personnel management including training and human resources; financial matters and national security.

The MCTPs are now designed to keep these broad specializations in mind. During my tenure as the director of LBSNAA, academic inputs were divided into general and sectoral, such that while one or two sessions were common to all the participants, officers were expected to choose one of the specialization areas mentioned above for an in-depth dive or immersion. This in turn, was linked to their preferences in their annual appraisal forms. The roll out of MK, will form the basis of the new and upgraded human resource management objective of government. It is in this context that one must understand the new MK, which recognizes that to contribute significantly to their departments and ministries, officers should always be ahead of the learning curve.

Meanwhile, it is important that governments ensure IAS officers are not posted in areas outside of their specialization—and certainly not to non-cadre posts in corporations, development boards and apex federations—for it detracts them from their core functions and competencies, besides demoralizing the officers in these organizations. Why should an IAS officer be the chief executive editor or managing director of a Food Corporation of India or the National Agricultural Cooperative Marketing Federation or the National Horticulture Board or the Jute Corporation of India?

From Rules to Roles: Mission Karmayogi

By 2021, India had become the sixth-largest economy in the world, besides being the second-largest producer of steel and mobile phones and third in the production of electricity. More significantly, it had improved its ranking in the Ease of Doing Business from 142 in 2014 to 63 in 2021 and was striving to improve this position with a slew of investment-friendly policies. It had also pipped China in terms of growth. All this called for a new architecture of governance—one in which the civil service reimagined its role as a facilitator and co-creator, rather than as a controller and regulator. The focus had to shift from rules which were 'limiting the scope for action' to roles which empowered the officer to ensure effective delivery of the tasks at hand.

This had three direct implications for the IAS. The first was that 'the context is more important than the text'.[10] The second: 'rules' are not sacrosanct. They can be recast. Rules are milestones, not goalposts. They are a means to an end, not an end in themselves. Thus, attested copies and documents have been replaced by self-certification. This simple intervention has not only saved time and resources but also given 'dignity' to the individual who is now responsible for whatever they affirm. And last but not least, if an officer cannot fit into the earmarked role, they can, and will be replaced by one who can—either from within the system, or through a lateral entry[11] if a person for this role is not available from within the system.

This was the context in which the Prime Minister announced MK in August 2020. It was felt that empowered with specific role competencies, the civil servant would be able to ensure efficient service delivery of the highest quality standards.

Framework of Roles, Activities and Competencies (FRAC)

Ever since its announcement, MK has been discussed in almost every newspaper, TV channel, social media as well as in academic

[10]Address by Cabinet Secretary Rajiv Gauba at the LBS National Academy of Administration to the Induction Training Program of the IAS (March 2020).

[11]Lateral entry refers to the induction of private sector specialists in government departments. The chosen candidates will be appointed on a contract basis for a period of three years. The deputation validity can be extended up to five years based on the candidate's performance. The selection is made by the UPSC.

journals connected with governance, public administration and political economy. From the numerous reports, commentaries and editorials available in the public domain, including the websites of Department of Personnel and Training (DoPT), LBSNAA, the Institute of Secretariat Training and Management and the World Bank, the following key points emerge—the focus is on 'how and now'; stakeholder engagement; FRAC; comprehensive coverage of all employees with committed resources; and the establishment of an Integrated Government Online Training (iGOT) platform linked to the human resource management portal.

Unlike the earlier ARCs, which were excellent in intent and purpose and listed the dos and don'ts, MK gives equal, if not more emphasis on the 'how', with the caveat that the change must begin now. Clear timelines have been drawn up and displayed on the website of the DoPT so that each stakeholder is aware of what is expected. The six interconnected strands include strengthening existing institutions; refreshing policy detailing competencies that are required for each role and activity related to each position; creating a strong push for a culture of life-long learning among civil services; strategic human resource intervention; and continuous performance analysis. This is followed by the Stakeholder Engagement Plan (SEP), which provides a detailed overview starting from stakeholder identification and their engagement in the project to identification of roles and responsibilities of stakeholders; besides a grievance mechanism to address any issues that may crop up in the process of implementation. The idea is that every employee must feel empowered, involved and responsible.

However, the real driving force behind MK is FRAC. This involves mapping of three constructs—roles, activities and competencies, supported by knowledge resources—for each individual position within all government ministries, departments and organizations (MDOs). Before identifying requisite competencies, an organization will also have to question the logic and rationale of its own existence. Why is it doing what it is currently doing? Is there any duplication of effort, or redundancy on account of technology? This was best done in-house, with reform champions taking up the gauntlet of questioning the logic of the rules they were implementing—the very rules which gave them power, discretion and authority. In fact, the FRAC will give an officer greater clarity about the role, as well as the resources that are required to ensure effective delivery. Officers will also be able to ensure that those who work with them also receive the required competency sets.

The emphasis on every employee is indeed a salient feature of the MK. Unlike earlier interventions restricted to the leaders, MK extends to all the 4.6 million employees of the Government of India in the first instance, with possibility of extending it to all state governments, zilla panchayats, municipal and public bodies in the next phase. A transformation at this scale had never been envisaged earlier and it is the most comprehensive learning experiment for government employees ever. It is also important to note that a sum of ₹510.86 crore has been committed to MK for five years (2020–21 to 2024–25).[12] The expenditure is partly funded by multilateral assistance to the tune of $50 million.

The iGOT Karmayogi

Underpinning all this is the iGOT Karmayogi, a Special Purpose Vehicle under Section 8 of the Companies Act, 2013. More than anything else, it gives the individual a greater ownership of their own learning and it offers 'democratization', choice and flexibility with regard to time, space and pace. It will offer to the junior-most civil servant access to the same knowledge resources as to those in the highest echelons. It will also encourage them to self-assess the progress through independent proctored assessments. The subject expert group will curate the best of digital e-learning content for each of the roles identified by the MDOs. The LBSNAA has been able to shift a lot of its FC syllabi to the iGOT, thereby giving more time for Aarambh and other innovative projects.

---

[12]Javaid, Afra, 'What Is "Mission Karmayogi" and Why Does the Union Cabinet Approved It?' Jagran Josh, 3 September 2020, https://bit.ly/3G6SfT2. Accessed on 4 January 2023.

Civil servants will have to take online courses and be evaluated on their performances in each course across their service span.

Along with the online courses, important professional milestones like confirmation after probation, deployment, work assignment and notification of vacancies, among others, will also be integrated on the platform. Political discretion in postings will be reduced as postings will depend on the performance as outlined in their annual performance appraisal reports (APARs), besides performance in both online and offline training programmes. Officers will also get an opportunity to become trainers and mentors—in their chosen field of specialization and offer programmes on the iGOT—which will also help them in their professional growth trajectory. The intent over time is to do more independent workplace assessments of performance, which is aimed to bring more accountability and ensure a real-time improvement in the services provided.

The Annual Health of Civil Services Report (AHCSR)

Another initiative that links to all that has been said above is the AHCSR, which will be anchored in the Capacity Building Commission[13]. Not only will the report feature the highlights from the departments and ministries based on their performance indicators, but it also encourages individuals to list innovations and best practices done by them at their workplaces which have the potential and possibility of a scale up. This is in addition to the acknowledgment of the work under the PM's Awards for Excellence in Public Administration.

---

[13]Constituted on 1 April 2021 by the Government of India, the Capacity Building Commission has been mandated to drive standardization and harmonization across the Indian civil services landscape. As the custodian of civil services capacity building reforms, the commission's role is central to the overall institutional framework of MK.

The Future of the CSE

Before closing, one must stir the hornet's nest by asking if we should continue with a common examination to recruit officers for such a range of job profiles. A step towards specialized assessments had been taken by the Railways as the recruitment to IRTS, IRAS and IRPS[14] was delinked from the CSE. Earlier in 2012, the parliamentary standing committee on MHA had asked the government to consider a separate examination for the IPS, and in fact, a limited departmental examination for IPS was held, but the result was withheld on account of litigation. Would it not make sense if the preliminary examination and the compulsory papers were common to all services, but service-specific papers introduced for the IAS, IPS, Indian Forest Service and Revenue Services with focus on public policy and governance; criminal law and internal security issues; international affairs; and tax policy respectively? There are certainly pros and cons for this suggestion, but it is high time these issues were discussed, not just from the point of view of the convenience of the aspirants, but also from the point of view of attitudes, attributes and skill sets (as outlined in the FRAC exercise conducted by the MDOs). The Capacity Building Commission may like to address this issue by engaging in a multi-stakeholder consultation so that India gets the governance professionals it deserves in the Amrit Kaal, and beyond.

---

[14]Indian railways traffic service/accounts service/personnel service.

12

PARTICIPATIVE GOVERNANCE

Citizen-Administration Partnership

Kiran Mazumdar-Shaw

It is well accepted that models of governance at the national and sub-national level have to undergo changes if government organizations are firm in their conviction that a 'citizen-centric approach', dedicated to upgrading the welfare of a people dwelling in a city, town or village, is to be ensured. The civil services and the Indian Administrative Service (IAS) officers in particular, come more into contact with the common man at the grassroots level. It is this group of persons who now need to shed the 'distanced and aloof' image, which was a hallmark of the British legacy and don the role of 'facilitators' who work side by side with citizens' organizations to fully release the benefit of government projects and schemes. A mindset change is thus called for to 'handhold' citizens' initiatives for a better standard of living.[1]

Besides the requirement for a multi-sectoral approach to policy framing with a greater participation of the public, it has become more critical to have a multi-department and organization approach in the implementation to ensure that targeted beneficiaries do derive the benefit of schemes devised by government. In this multi-organization approach, a collaborative approach with citizens' groups also providing inputs has reaped rich dividends. However, such a collaborative

[1]Chopra, Sanjeev, 'Indian Civil Servants Are Expected to be Karma Yogis. But Look at Ground Reality First', *The Print,* 7 December 2021, https://bit.ly/3VZ7DHb. Accessed on 4 January 2023.

approach requires a mindset change in the bureaucrat and this has to come about at the early stages of the training itself. We proceed to discuss the benefits of such a participative and collaborative effort in Bengaluru city, which has decidedly improved the ease of living in the city. It is our experience that where administration has adopted an open and participative approach, development has been faster and more permanent.

In this effort, the role and importance of technology and digitization can hardly be ignored. Administrators and citizens alike have to be tech-savvy to deliver benefits which are leakage proof, reach the targeted population and are efficiently delivered within the shortest time span. The government at the state and municipal levels have done much to ensure that the maximum benefits of technological development can be derived with least interference by humans, thereby ensuring a distortion-free delivery of service.

A Citizens' Collective

Bengaluru has witnessed several public participation initiatives, over the years, in collaboration with government, all working towards reforms, improving city administration, citizen service delivery and governance. In the past, platforms have been created by the government for key civic organizations in the city to provide their suggestions for short-term and long-term plans for Bengaluru. But in such instances, the moment the new government is elected, these platforms disintegrate and much of the advocacy work has to start all over again.

However, this is one city where there are several civil society organizations with actively engaged citizen members trying to find solutions for several urban problems that impact the quality of life of citizens—such as universal healthcare; solid waste management; urban transportation; affordable housing; education; water and sewerage; safety and security; and other infrastructures. The city has been at the forefront of public–private collaborations, citizen report cards, creating coalition with non-governmental organizations and civic society forums. These civic groups have played an important role in pressing for micro policy reforms, demanding and mobilizing better services, monitoring actual provision, pushing for greater accountability from service providers and engaging in mass campaigns to create citizen awareness on several issues.

The Bangalore Political Action Committee (B.PAC), established in 2013, is one civic organization that has existed now for over eight years, seen three different governments from different political parties, but has managed to establish itself as a non-partisan, forward thinking, credible organization keenly working to improve the quality of life of citizens of Bengaluru.

The role of civil servants has become increasingly complex, with the need to manage and balance diverse demands from citizens. The role of the civil servant has to therefore, shift from being an administrator to being more consultative, participatory but impartial in nature, looking at technology and innovation-driven solutions to the urban problems faced by the city. The civil servant, more than ever, needs to have a team that has deep understanding and expertise of the domain issues of urban planning, environment, water, waste management, etc. with a good understanding of technology and the vision to use digital tools and open data for innovation in service delivery and better governance. These officials can play an influential role in achieving positive outcomes through coalition and collaboration, such as improvement in efficiency levels of service delivery, equity in service delivery, institutional reforms and policy changes that suits the growing demand of citizenry.[2]

An important prerequisite for such partnerships and reforms to be effective is to ensure that citizens and Resident Welfare Associations are equipped with knowledge, skills and the confidence to play an active role in public dialogue, consultation and local decision-making.

---

[2]Ravindra, Adikeshavalu, 'An Assessment of the Impact of Bangalore Citizen Report Cards on the Performance of Public Agencies: ECD Working Paper Series 12', The World Bank Operations Evaluations Department, June 2004, https://bit.ly/3kFZIRP. Accessed on 27 January 2023.

Case Studies: B.PAC and Others

Prior to the constitution of B.PAC, Bengaluru city had seen few groups or organizations working with government. A few were constituted by government in association with corporates such as the Bangalore Agenda Task Force in 1999 and Agenda for Bengaluru Infrastructure and Development Taskforce, constituted in 2010, among several others.

Each of these groups or institutions had a vision and some focus areas and have contributed to participatory governance in its own way. Several of the works undertaken through these forums have fostered increased civic activism, public awareness on key issues and resulted in some improvement in quality of services in select areas. Some of these successes are being replicated in other Indian cities as well.

As the B.PAC website describes:

> Bangalore Political Action Committee (B.PAC) is a non-partisan citizen's group that aims to improve governance in Bengaluru and to enhance the quality of life of every Bengalurean. B.PAC is specifically targeting good governance practices, integrity and transparency in all arms of the government, improving the quality of infrastructure in the city and identification as well as support of strong candidates for public office at all levels. Ultimately, creating a safer city where the rule of law is ensured for its residents as highlighted in B.PAC's Bengaluru charter and agenda.[3]

B.PAC has worked resolutely on a number of policy interventions in the mobility space. Transport accounts for 23 per cent of global energy-related greenhouse gas (GHG) emissions today and for 34 per cent of the 2050 urban GHG abatement potential.[4] Transport is also a major contributor to air pollution, accounting for around half of the current global nitrogen oxide (NOx) emissions. E-mobility

---

[3]B.PAC, https://bit.ly/3HbPCQn. Accessed on 3 January 2023.

[4]*Transport, Energy and CO_2: Moving Toward Sustainability*, International Energy Agency, https://bit.ly/3Qb0TEL. Accessed on 4 January 2023.

is one of the best solutions for reduction in air and noise pollution and elimination of emissions. Electrification is the most flexible, energy-efficient and sustainable way to decarbonize the economy.

Recognizing the power of electrification in reducing GHG emissions, we worked with the Carnegie Institute and were the first state in the country to come up with an electric vehicle (EV) policy—the Karnataka Electric Vehicle and Energy Storage Policy, 2017.

Five years on, while there has been some progress on infrastructure creation like charging stations, the number of private EV vehicles on the road and the number of EV buses inducted into the fleet—both are marginal and the current pace is not sufficient to meet our 2030 goals. We realize that even if we are able to influence policy as citizens, we still need to have a road map to achieve the goals and need to work alongside the government to develop a granular plan with annual targets and be constantly vigilant with regard to on-ground progress on implementation against policy. This work is ongoing.

Officers should be strategic in their approach looking at the larger vision of decarbonization and must have intermediate goals—from policy to implementation—to monitor progress. They should lay out the long-term objectives and devise a road map to achieve it with participation from citizen's groups and give out periodic report cards with progress metrics.

Post-trauma investigative and trial procedures

We created a complete toolkit for schools, including a model template for child protection policy and procedures for child abuse reporting; media interaction; redressal mechanism for child protection-related issues; post-trauma childcare; at all times emphasizing protection of the child's privacy. The work that we collectively achieved was very far-reaching in its thinking, and it was really commendable that the state incorporated all our suggestions in the policy.

We were also the first state in the country to provide in-camera hearings for Protection of Children from Sexual Offences Act (POCSO) cases so that children do not have to be present in the courtroom along with other common criminals, which is very intimidating. This special court was implemented in full consultation with various civic groups working in the area of child safety.

We were able to implement swift action, great collaborative working between all concerned civic groups and great coordination with all stakeholders such as schools, parent groups, etc.

Bengaluru Metropolitan Land Transport Authority (BMLTA) Bill

Bengaluru has been ranked as the tenth-most congested city in the world, with its residents losing up to five days in a year to traffic congestion.[5] Exponential vehicular ownership, coupled with a slacking public transport network, has contributed to unsustainable mobility in the city with multiplicity of agencies like the Bengaluru Metropolitan Transport Corporation, Bengaluru Metro Rail Corporation Limited (BMRCL), Karnataka Rail Infrastructure Corporation, Bengaluru Development Authority, Transport Department, Regional Transport Office, Bruhat Bengaluru Mahanagara Palike (BBMP), etc. working in silos under different legislations. With no single local authority to plan, design and regulate transport services, citizens lose out on a commuter-centric, seamless mobility experience.

A historic step towards city transportation has been made possible by the Karnataka assembly by passing the BMLTA Bill to ensure seamless urban mobility. The BMLTA will be a unified transportation agency that unites several government agencies and develops initiatives like the common mobility card and multi-modal transportation hubs. Again, this particular project has had a long chequered 14-year history. It required concerted citizen pressure to ensure that the individual transport providers lobby does not get its way in maintaining its dominance in each mode of transportation. This institutional framework is to have a unified well-designed mobility plan with opportunities for enhanced multi-modal integration and increased use of public transport such as buses, trains and metros and consequently,

[5]'TomTom Traffic Index Ranking 2021', TomTom, https://bit.ly/3iQmF48. Accessed on 8 December 2022.

lead to a reduction in traffic congestion and improved air quality in the city.

This issue has been going in and out of cold storage since 2006. The concept has seen multiple forms over the years and B.PAC, once again, renewed the dialogue with government back in 2017.

Following are the high-level summary of roles and responsibilities of an overarching agency like the BMLTA:

- Plan: Serve as the statutory organization in charge of setting up a unified vision for the city's transport and mobility; and developing the city's transportation and mobility plans and their subsequent effects on commute times and mobility patterns.
- Convene: Convene all agencies and relevant stakeholders delivering mobility services in the city; and sign off on transport and mobility projects in the Bangalore Metropolitan Area (BMA) and align all such projects with the unified transport and mobility vision for the city. Importantly, such an agency will also serve as a platform for a participatory visioning of the city through wider and more active public consultation.
- Coordinate: Coordinate with the various line agencies to ensure that all of their projects adhere to its vision of the city and its transportation needs.

This was a very complex project. There was great consensus across citizen groups, but individual transport service providers feared loss of autonomy and the project kept getting stalled for years. A bold political will was required to push the project. The passing of the Bill provides a remarkable example of government–private participation in policy formulation, designed to benefit the common man.

Unclogging the City

Bengaluru is the fastest-growing metropolitan city in the country. It is struggling with all the challenges of an overburdened and unsustainable transport network. The infrastructural support structures have not kept pace with the unprecedented growth in economic development and that has resulted in a gridlocked transportation network. It requires completely reimagining mobility in the next decade, away from proliferation of private vehicles, to single-minded focus on investing in public mobility infrastructure at scale rather than small incremental investments that are currently made.

Private vehicle registration has increased by 350 per cent between 2007 and 2022 (2.1 million to 10 million). On an average, the city witnesses approximately 10–11 million trips every day, out of which 3–3.5 million are on Bengaluru Metropolitan Transport Corporation buses, 450,000–500,000 trips are by metro and about 150,000–200,000 trips are on suburban rail. A large portion of daily trips in the city are through privately owned vehicles, autorickshaws, cabs and shared mobility services.[6]

As a result, the city's share of public transport lies at an abysmal 48 per cent, whereas cities like Mumbai and Kolkata are at 80 per cent and they have continuously been investing in public mobility infrastructure. Considering the narrow and fully built-up environment, buses will continue to play a major role in public transportation in the city.

This was an argument that we projected to the earlier government and they even announced a big investment for buses in the budget. However, with the change in the complexion in government, this advocacy has to be re-established. The current leadership does not fully grasp the narrative yet and the alignment between investment and public transport outcome sadly remains unappreciated.

In such a scenario, in the last three years (2019–22), there has been marginal net addition to the fleet of 6,500 buses in the city. The government is traditionally used to investing in road infrastructure, but without buses, this only incentivizes greater private transport usage. With the unfortunate Covid-19 situation, public transport was the biggest casualty. Ridership in public transport has fallen drastically.

---

[6]Kidiyoor, Suchit, 'Bengaluru's Number of Vehicles Doubles in a Decade, But BMTC Fleet Size Remains Stagnant', *The Hindu,* 21 May 2022, https://bit.ly/3id6ptW. Accessed on 4 January 2023.

Instead of boldly combating this shift—with higher investments in buses, increased frequency, improvement in real-time information availability and incentivization of public transport—the government has once again become hesitant. It is clear that our work on shifting the narrative in favour of public mobility and investing in public transport will be a long-drawn-out intervention.

Officers need to be able to focus on the bigger picture and the outcome for which they are working in the medium to long term. If they had defined the priority as driving a behavioural shift towards public transport, then the immediate knee-jerk reaction of low consumer uptake of bus services would not have been a deterrent. The approach should have been to say, 'How can I incentivize in the short-run greater usage of bus services to achieve a paradigm shift in mobility based on public transport from 48 per cent to 80 per cent?'

Another aspect of improving the flow of traffic is the state of the roads. City roads development and maintenance is a hotly debated topic in all urban clusters in India. Every road in Bengaluru was an example of chaos of traffic, broken footpaths, hanging cables, clogged drains, overflowing sewage, and haphazard street lights, transformers and telecom fixtures. Patchwork and piecemeal repairs, with poor quality design and construction, result in repeated digging and fixing of the same road over and over again. Such unsystematic and haphazard short-term fixes are a drain on city finances, while doing little to improve the quality of the road thereby, inconveniencing commuters.

Once again, this needed a paradigm shift in re-imagining the design of our road infrastructure by creating a hierarchy of use. Tender SURE (specifications for urban roads execution) represented this paradigm shift in road design. The fundamental issue that needed to gain acceptance here was that we needed uniform urban road design and standard specifications to be adopted in development and maintenance of city roads. This leads to poor carriageway for commuters, adding to vehicular congestion and fatalities. Now, all urban road tenders in the city of Bengaluru by default has Tender SURE.

Despite the parameters for the Tender SURE project being cleared by a high court-appointed Technical Advisory Committee (TAC), it continued to face criticism from road users and elected representatives alike, who were accustomed to having roads widened to make way for motorized traffic. The concept of uniform carriage width and wide footpaths facilitating pedestrian movement was unheard of previously.

Therefore, even after the first contract for St. Marks Road was awarded, the transport minister and Bangalore in-charge minister made a site inspection amid huge citizen activist pressure and announced that the state government would go back to the drawing board and redesign the project by reducing the footpath width.

The St. Marks Road pilot was successfully completed, being managed by Jana Urban Space and its co-founder, Swati Ramanathan, who steadfastly maintained that the current roads would see three times the expenditure over a 10-year-period as compared to Tender SURE roads.

Today, after many trials and tribulations, Tender SURE roads have been accepted as the standard and the city has over 100 km of well-designed roads under various stages of completion. It has taken over 10 years and intervention by multiple civil society organizations before this could be mainstreamed. The project has now become a showcase for other cities to come, experience and emulate how to build city roads, keeping the pedestrian as the highest on the hierarchy.[7]

Courage of conviction was very important for this project. It was executed and mainstreamed amid great adversity with court intervention, with large sections of civil society, media and contractors all shooting down the project because they had not experienced something like this before. We were able to convince the key political leadership and the bureaucracy that this was the right thing to do after we had exhausted all logical consensus-building steps, including getting a court order. Educating citizens on futuristic projects is a critical element for success and speed in executing

[7]Krishnan, Rishikesha, 'Will B.PAC and iSPIRT Transform Urban Politics & the Software Product Industry Respectively?', iSpirt, 11 February 2013, https://bit.ly/3WI5Nvq. Accessed on 4 January 2023.

projects. This is also a very significant example of how there is need for government officials to follow a more accessible and participative approach, since the entire initiative has saved millions for the corporation and become a great convenience for the commuting public. The authorities need to recognize that there is no 'We–They' relationship with the public. Both are on the same side and engaged in uplifting the welfare of the citizen.

Cleaning Up the City

During the construction of the metro line, garbage and debris used to be dumped all along the line. Several meetings with BMRCL officials requesting for clean-up did not yield results. Finally, B.PAC filed a case with Lokayukta on 'Dumping of debris and garbage on Metro Medians'.

In March 2015, Team B.PAC filed a complaint to the Lokayukta with nearly 800 photographs of debris and garbage that was strewn all along the metro medians and surrounding the metro stations. B.PAC relentlessly pursued the public interest case with Lokayukta through 2015. At each hearing, both BBMP and BMRCL refused to acknowledge the existence of garbage and each organization would say it was not the other's responsibility to clean up. During the fourth hearing of the complaint on debris and garbage under the Namma Metro Line, B.PAC further submitted over a hundred photographs showing evidence of debris, construction waste and garbage still lying in the median of Namma Metro despite Upa Lokayukta's previous order to BBMP to clean the mess.

Finally, the Upa Lokayukta ordered a joint site inspection by BBMP commissioner and BMRCL chief and their respective teams, in his presence. BMRCL officials who were present were directed by Upa Lokayukta to work out a plan along with BBMP officials and submit an action taken report within a month along with photographic evidence. He also directed BMRCL officials to submit a compliance report ensuring that drinking water and toilet facilities were made available in all metro stations, with emphasis on the convenience for differently abled passengers.

The impact of this action is that 56 km median of operating Namma Metro is free of garbage and debris and sapling plantation has been made mandatory by BMRCL.

Both the BMRCL and BBMP chiefs refused to attend four hearings and sent only their junior officers. Both organizations refused to accept that there was a problem. Because of B.PAC's dogged persistence and an Upa Lokayukta, who took this matter very seriously and summoned the chiefs for a site visit, we were able to get a solution. If the BMRCL and BBMP leadership had the humility to acknowledge the problem and agreed to clean up, we would not have had to go to Lokayukta for this matter. This is a matter for civil servants to reflect upon. This has been an exceedingly significant development as it illustrates how recalcitrance on the part of senior echelons in BMRCL and BBMP created an avoidable delay. Had they been forthcoming on B.PAC's request, so much effort and time could have been saved.

This learning is significant, as it points to the non-participative or not-so-constructive mindset of the officials. It is this mindset, that needs to be changed for them to function hand in hand with citizens' groups. Such an approach will be a win-win development for all.

During the Covid-19 pandemic, B.PAC and its trained civic leaders from its incubator programme 'B.CLIP', collaborated with the government as Covid-19 warriors in delivering the required food, medicines, medical infrastructure and other assistance, created awareness and assisted in providing healthcare services. The government had created a list of hospitals and required healthcare equipment in different hospitals. Civil society organizations such as B.PAC and others worked with corporate social responsibility partners, embassies, etc. to direct aid in cash or kind (equipment, food, medicines) to the identified beneficiary organization. Such collaborative work between multiple stakeholders during crisis ensured that all the support that various organizations were willing to give was channelled to the right beneficiaries. Our grassroots connect provided the much-needed reassurance to donors that their support was going to the people who needed it most, on a timely basis, without worrying about leakage along the way.

During the period of extreme crisis when lives were at stake, Bengaluru put its best foot forward when government, civil society organizations, corporates and citizens worked most collaboratively to provide the best response possible.

Another example of our collaboration with local government is working towards the Swachh Bharat Mission. While the process is slow, effective source segregation of household waste is bringing awareness and advocacy with civic and residential associations in association with municipal authority. Bengaluru generates nearly 5,000 tonnes of waste, of which about 1,800 tonnes is generated by bulk waste generators, daily.[8] Various civic groups in the city are engaged in working with the government in finding local technology and systemic solutions to tackle the waste menace. While there are many technology solutions being deployed elsewhere in the world, our waste character has such a high moisture content that all technologies may not work. Segregation and creating awareness about segregation is a first and very important step.

Over the years, civil society has played a very big role in pushing source segregation to about 40 per cent. Removing organic waste and having two or three more levels of segregation such as plastic and paper; medical and hazardous; and bottles and cans improve value recovery significantly. Civil society has had a big role to play in policy development, wet waste processing at household level, waste-processing centres and dry waste collection at ward level. Over time, the value chain for these waste materials has been built. Government and civil society organizations need to continue creating awareness and improving the segregation percentage year after year.

Transforming IAS Skill Sets

A number of the issues that we have discussed in the previous section are a result of rapid unplanned urbanization without a citizen-centric

[8]'In-Situ Composting for Bulk Waste Generators in Bengaluru to Become Mandatory', *The Hindu*, 18 March 2022, https://bit.ly/3GD2LCQ. Accessed on 4 January 2023.

vision of delivery of various services. It is devoid of the vision for futuristic thinking to build the physical, infrastructural, technological and peoples' capacity that is necessary to meet the requirements of the next 20 years and find solutions to meet current and future challenges. In the first 60 years since Independence, the large focus of the central and state governments was on improving rural infrastructure and livelihoods. Urbanization and its concomitant challenges commanded low priority in national political discourse.

As economic development and job opportunities led to large-scale migration from rural areas to cities, especially in a city like Bengaluru—which is rapidly closing the population gap with Mumbai and Delhi—it has totally failed to keep pace with the demands of urbanization and economic progress. While this problem is faced by other cities as well, Bengaluru's problem is exacerbated in that, it is one of the fastest-growing cities in the world (not just in the country). Therefore, a one-size-fits-all approach will not work. The city's infrastructure development has to be viewed very differently from Mumbai or Delhi.

Both the political leadership and the civil service leadership lack the grand vision that can cater to such hyper growth. Investments decisions on infrastructure are always incremental and therefore, the city is always playing catch-up, whether it is on issues related to mobility, roads, waste management, environment or health. In fact, most of the new ideas are coming up from various citizen groups and not out of a detailed planning exercise by the government. All the examples cited above and many more that are in the works are all demands from citizens. The generalist, administrative role played by the civil services is clearly not sufficient to meet the complex service requirements of today. The city must rapidly build strong urban planning capacity and a cadre of technocrats who have deep domain knowledge on areas such as transportation engineering, transportation economics, EV technology and water technologies, among others. Large outlays in infrastructure require innovative funding methods. Clearly, we need financial experts who can manage these large budgets and capital outlays and who have the knowledge and expertise to drive efficiencies in operating costs. Since we are dealing with large amounts of data, which can be used very effectively for decision-making, the leadership must have a good understanding of technology and how it can be leveraged to deliver services at the population scale. The civil services leadership must also have a strategic mindset that can drive bold, new innovative solutions to solve problems. This has become a necessity, since they will have to align their thinking and planning capabilities to the best that is available in the country, for the synergy that will drive speedy development efforts.

Further, several services are provided by vendors, so the government needs to build strong capacity in outcome-driven contracting and outsourcing, with strong monitoring systems to review progress. This is the area where the role of technology and specialization will play a predominant part. Externally, the civil services leadership needs to have the ability to build strong networks and capacity to manage multi-stakeholder demands. The approach has to be more consultative with citizens. They must view themselves as providers of citizen services rather than merely an administrator or a regulator.

Cities experience tremendous pressure in terms of management and operation of urban systems as well as service delivery. Significant changes are taking place in the governance of Indian cities—one of the important developments being the proliferation of various forms of networks and partnership with civil society. Many urban reforms such as partnerships with public–private and civil society organizations are introduced to improve quality of governance and service delivery. Privatization, decentralization, restructuring of departments and administrative procedures, laws and regulations, social audit, e-governance, citizen charter, redressal of grievances, transparency and sound personnel policies constituted major strategies of urban governance reform.

Many urban local bodies introduced innovations to improve billing and collection, rationalization of service charges, simplifications of tax assessment system, computerization of services and improved accounting and fiscal management systems.

To address the aforestated challenges and work with citizens aspiration and growing needs, administrative officials have to be equipped with skills and the wherewithal to make the service delivery job truly participatory in approach.

Civil service officials leading various functions have a vital role to play towards citizen-centric delivery of services. With increasing digitalization of the economy, technology-led intervention for effective public service delivery is the way forward. A citizen-centric approach in city administration and governance is what the urban citizens are expecting from civic officials. It is towards building this kind of capability and mindset that institutions engaged in the training of administrators need to be geared. It is sincerely hoped that initiatives such as Mission Karmayogi undertaken by the government will fulfil this inadequacy and help in creating 'people-friendly' bureaucrats who will play the role of 'facilitators' more than 'regulators'.

13

REFORMING THE REFORMERS

Accountability for Results in Public Administration

Prajapati Trivedi

In 2013, the Performance Monitoring and Evaluation System (PMES) of the Government of India covered 80 departments in the central government and 800 responsibility centres (subordinate offices, attached offices and autonomous bodies) under these departments.[1] Seventeen states of the Indian Union, cutting across political lines, were at various stages of implementing the PMES and it was also hailed and adopted by many of India's SAARC neighbours—Bhutan, Bangladesh, Sri Lanka and Pakistan.

Today, however, India has no formal system for government performance management and all performance reviews are done in an old-fashioned way. The focus is not on the whole-of-department performance but only on projects within departments that are important to the government. The story of the spectacular rise of performance management from 2009 until 2014 and its subsequent speedy demise offers valuable lessons for future reformers in democracies.

Outside observers often marvel at the Indian government. There is a perception that India is run by a bureaucracy that is often rated by outsiders to be the worst in Asia.[2] Yet, India has a highly competitive

[1]Mehrotra, Santosh, *The Government Monitoring and Evaluation System in India: A Work in Progress*, ECD Working Paper Series No. 28, IEG World Bank, p.15, https://bit.ly/3WMTVHA.

[2]'India's Bureaucracy Is "Worst in Asia"', BBC, 12 January 2012, https://bbc.in/3CisfmK. Accessed on 3 January 2023.

civil service recruitment system and regularly recruits the crème de la crème of the available pool of talent through a rigorous screening process. Having taught recent recruits to All-India Services, I can affirm that they are indeed as good as they come anywhere in the world. Thus, there is a consensus that Indian bureaucracy represents a classic case of good people caught in a bad system.

Indian policymakers have been painfully aware of this dilemma for a very long time. Several committees and commissions have been set up over time to find a solution to this problem and prime ministers have complained about it. Consequently, most of these recommendations have gathered dust.

I was invited to join the Government of India, in 2009, to implement two major interrelated recommendations of the following landmark reports on administrative reforms in India:

a. November 2008: Tenth Report of the Second Administrative Reforms Commission (ARC) titled, 'Refurbishing of Personnel Administration: Scaling New Heights'
   Recommendation:
   'The performance agreements should be signed between the departmental Minister and the Secretary of the Ministry as also between the departmental Minister and heads of Department, well before the financial year. The annual performance agreement should provide physical and verifiable details of the work to be done by the Secretary/Head of the Department during the financial year. The performance of the Secretary/Head of the Department should be assessed by a third party—say, the Central Public Services Authority with reference to the annual performance agreement. The details of the annual performance agreements and the results of the assessment by the third party should be provided to the legislature as a part of the Performance Budget/Outcome Budget.'[3]

[3]*Refurbishing of Personnel Administration-Scaling New Heights*, Second Administrative Reforms Commission, Tenth Report, November 2008, p. 241, https://bit.ly/3QapZUc. Accessed on 4 January 2023.

b. March 2008: Report of the Sixth Central Pay Commission (CPC) Recommendation:
   'The Commission has recommended introduction of a new performance based pecuniary benefit, over and above the regular salary, for the Government employees. The benefit will be called Performance Related Incentive scheme (PRIS) and will be payable taking into account the performance of the employee during the period under consideration. It is based on differential reward for differential performance.'[4]

Both recommendations dealt with the performance of the central government departments and the Government of India decided to appoint me as the secretary (Performance Management), in the Cabinet Secretariat with the primary responsibility for implementing these two recommendations. In my earlier position as Economic Adviser to Government of India, I was tasked with implementing a performance management system for India's public enterprise sector. That system, called the Memorandum of Understanding (MoU), was similar in concept to Performance Agreements, recommended by the Second ARC. This essay documents my lessons of experience in implementing these two major recommendations during the five and half years I served in the Government of India from January 2009 through August 2014.

The rest of the paper is divided into three broad sections. The first deals with the design and implementation of the recommendation of the Second ARC dealing with Performance Agreements in the central government. The second section deals with the design and implementation of the recommendation of the Sixth CPC regarding the Performance-Related Incentive Scheme (PRIS) for central government employees. The third section summarizes the key lessons of experience from implementing these two major administrative reforms in India.

---

[4]*Report of the Sixth Central Pay Commission*, Government of India, March 2008, p. 146, https://bit.ly/3jInyff. Accessed on 4 January 2023.

Performance Agreements in Central Government

Today, the world can be divided into two broad groups of countries. In one group, they pretty much do what they say and in the other, the gap between what they say and what they do is wide. No prizes for guessing which group of countries develops faster. Experts agree that the competitive and comparative advantage of nations depends on the performance and effectiveness of its government, implementation of sound policies and optimal utilization of limited resources.

Enhanced delivery of public services and effective implementation of public policies, programmes and projects affects the welfare of all citizens. The guiding principle is 'to do the right things' and also 'to do things right'. This means operating and delivering in ways that are responsive and accountable, as well as more efficient and effective. Our focus, therefore, needs to be on ensuring that public systems are streamlined and managed to work better, faster and cheaper in order to deliver what is promised and what is needed.

The Second ARC argued, 'Performance agreement is the most common accountability mechanism in most countries that have reformed their public administration systems. [...] At the core of such agreements are the objectives to be achieved, the resources provided to achieve them, the accountability and control measures, and the autonomy and flexibilities that the civil servants will be given.'[5]

The Government of India accepted the recommendation of the Second ARC in this regard, but the then prime minister decided to call this instrument Results-Framework Document (RFD) rather than Performance Agreement, as suggested by the Second ARC.

Rationale for performance agreements

In the opening session of Parliament in June 2009, the Dr Manmohan Singh government declared that within 100 days the government would 'establish mechanisms for performance monitoring and

[5]'Chapter-11: Performance Management System', *Refurbishing of Personnel Administration-Scaling New Heights,* Second Administrative Reforms Commission, Tenth Report, November 2008, https://bit.ly/3QapZUc. Accessed on 4 January 2023.

performance evaluation in government on a regular basis'.[6] Three months later, the Prime Minister issued an order to implement 'Performance Monitoring and Evaluation System (PMES) for Government Departments'.

The Government of India created a new department within the Cabinet Secretariat called the Performance Management Division (PMD) to implement these recommendations. The Prime Minister invited me to move from the World Bank to head PMD as India's first Secretary for Performance Management. Lateral entry at the highest level of the Indian bureaucracy remains a rare phenomenon. I fit the bill as an outsider but not a rank outsider. In 1992–94, I had served as Economic Adviser in the Government of India. This completed the celestial alignment required for any successful reform in the Indian context—a Prime Minister with strong political will to implement accountability for results, a knowledgeable Cabinet Secretary who is the head of the civil service and first among equals (with similar convictions and clarity of purpose to manage the whole of government) and a Secretary for Performance Management (a technocrat) to work on the details.

Before launching implementation of Results-Framework Documents/PMES, we diagnosed what was wrong with the existing approach to performance management in 2009 and made the following discovery. First, our diagnosis of the prevailing situation revealed that the Indian civil servants actually faced an excessive amount of performance monitoring. Many institutions within the Indian governmental system felt that they had a right to supervise a government department. This long list included Parliament, the Comptroller and Auditor General of India (CAG), the Controller General of Accounts (CGA), the Planning Commission, the finance ministry, investigative agencies and the media. This might not seem to be a problem; after all, listed companies have thousands of shareholders. The difference is that while all the shareholders of a

[6]Trivedi, Prajapati, 'Administrative Reforms Must for Nation's Long-Term Growth', *Business Today,* 4 January 2015, https://bit.ly/3YzBLuT. Accessed on 19 December 2022.

listed company have roughly the same goal for the company, the stakeholders of a government department have multiple objectives that are often conflicting. This had led to fragmented institutional responsibility for performance management.

Second, it was noted that several important government initiatives had divided responsibilities for implementation, with the result that accountability for results was diluted. For example, e-governance initiatives were being led by the Department of Electronics and Information Technology, the Department of Administrative Reforms and Public Grievances, the National Informatics Centre, as well as individual ministries.

Third, existing performance management tools suffered from selective coverage and time lags in reporting. For example, the performance audit reports of the CAG were restricted to a small group of schemes and institutions (only 14 such reports were laid before Parliament in 2008) and were published with a substantial time lag. By the time these reports were produced, both management and the issues facing the institutions had changed.

Fourth, existing performance evaluation systems in government suffered from two fatal flaws. The lack of prioritization of goals, objectives and tasks meant that no meaningful assessment could be made at the end of the year. Similarly, most, if not all, performance evaluation systems in the government were using a single-point target to measure performance. This made it difficult to judge deviations from the agreed target. For example, how are we to judge the performance of the department if the target for rural roads for a particular year is 24,140 km and the achievement is only 23,335 km? In the absence of an ex-ante agreement, one can reasonably reach many different conclusions.

A new system

We realized that the most competent and well-intentioned civil servant could not have survived in the dysfunctional system that existed in the Government of India in 2009. It confirmed my belief that it was the system that needed to be fixed and not the people.

Our task was made easier because the Second ARC had already recommended a system based on 'performance agreements' to deal with these dysfunctionalities. Performance Agreements were a cornerstone of the New Public Management model and were first tried in New Zealand in the 1980s and in the United States in the 1990s (under its Reinventing Government initiative and the Government Performance and Results Act of 1993).

After reviewing the design and implementation issues of past attempts, we designed a new and improved version of the performance agreement model. Prime Minister Manmohan Singh preferred to call them Results-Framework Documents (RFDs). They overcame the flaws that had limited the effectiveness of the performance agreements in other countries by introducing an explicit prioritization of objectives and an ex-ante agreement on how to judge deviations from the targets. These two innovations allowed the Indian government to calculate a composite score for each department at the end of the year. Thus, for the first time in India, we had a bottom line for the government departments. This also allowed and engendered benchmark competition among departments—which research tells us is the source of true efficiency improvements. It also gave us a measure of performance to which the performance incentives could be tied.

To ensure that the RFD targets were not manipulated, three quality assurance mechanisms were put in place. First, all RFDs had to be put on the web. Second, a non-government body of former secretaries, distinguished academicians and private sector experts was charged by the Cabinet Secretary to vet RFDs at the beginning of the year, as well as the results at the end of the year. Finally, the Ministry of Finance was tasked with ensuring that the targets in RFDs were compatible with budgetary targets. After some initial teething troubles, the RFD system stabilized by 2011–12, as shown in Table 1:

Table 1
RFD Results for Four Years[7]

	2009–10	2010–11	2011–12	2012–13
Mean score	89.4	85.2	82.35	76.11
No. of depts above mean	37 (63%)	39 (63%)	38(57%)	39 (57%)
Excellent	23 (39%)	11 (18%)	5(7%)	4 (6%)
Very good	19 (32%)	26 (42%)	25(37%)	19 (28%)
Good	11 (19%)	12 (19%)	19(28%)	18 (26%)
Fair	1 (2%)	8 (13%)	11(17%)	12 (18%)
Poor	5 (8%)	5 (8%)	6(11%)	15 (22%)

By 2014, much had been achieved in putting in place a solid government performance management system, but much more was needed to be done. The Prime Minister's order had mandated that the RFDs and results at the end of the year should be placed in the public domain. While RFDs were placed on every department's website, the results were only conveyed to each Secretary of the relevant department by a letter from the Cabinet Secretary. This was done because some departments were headed by members belonging to parties whose support was critical for the survival of the government in Parliament.

The impact of performance agreements

Any system takes a long time to implement and reach its full potential and its impact thus, cannot be evaluated in the short term. In addition, it is important to keep in mind that the RFD or PMES system has not been fully implemented. Some of the key features are still in a disabled mode. For example, not all departments were covered by the RFD system. Some argued that unless finance and planning are brought under this common accountability framework, they will

[7]Report submitted to government in 2013 by the author.

remain the weak links in the chain of accountability. Similarly, it was argued that the government needs to demonstrate consequences for performance, or lack thereof.

Despite incomplete implementation, it is encouraging to note preliminary evidence that is beginning to trickle in. As you can see from Figure 1, before the introduction of a success indicator for measuring performance, with respect to Grievance Redress in RFD, the difference between grievances received and disposed was significant.

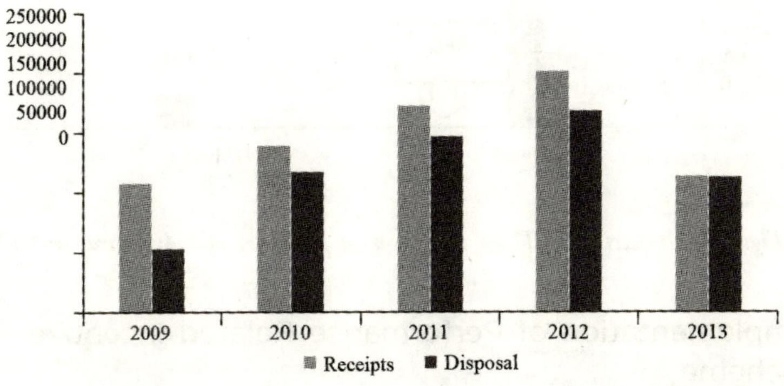

Figure 1: Impact of RFD on Grievance Redress Mechanism

In 2009, only about 50 per cent of grievances registered on the computerized grievance redress system were disposed. In 2013, after three years of RFD implementation, the disposal rate for grievances filed electronically was 100 per cent. The data for this statistic is generated and owned by the Department of Administrative Reforms and Public Grievances (DARPG), so there is no conflict of interest in presenting it as evidence on behalf of PMD. According to the staff of DARPG, before Grievance Redress became a mandatory performance requirement in RFDs, it was widely ignored. If RFD has modified behaviour in this area, it is reasonable to believe that it has had an impact in other areas as well.

Similarly, at the request of the Ministry of Finance, mandatory indicators dealing with the timely disposal of CAG audit reports were introduced in the 2011–12 RFDs. At the time of introduction, the total pendency of paras was 4,216. As can be seen from Figure 2, by 2013–14, the pendency of CAG paras had come down to 533.

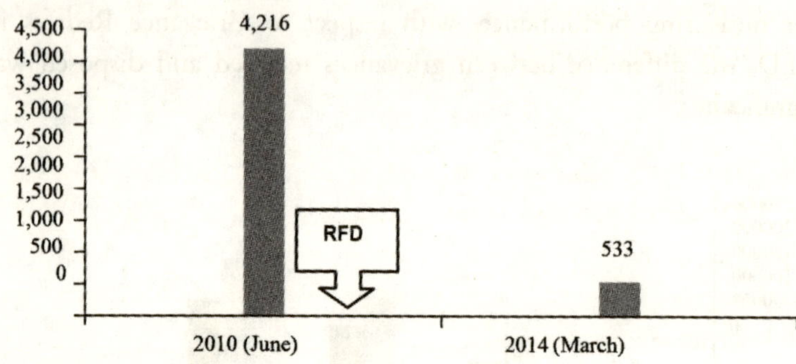

Figure 2: Impact of RFD on reduction in pendency of CAG Paras in GoI

Implementation of Performance Related Incentive Scheme

The Government of India accepted the Sixth CPC recommendation to implement a PRIS in August 2008. Successive governments have accepted the recommendation of CPCs to implement a PRIS over the years, but they have not implemented their decision on PRIS for the past 35 years.

The potential benefits as a result of efficient operations and savings from the Plan Revenue Expenditure, resulting as externalities of this decision, would significantly increase the opportunity cost of non-implementation of PRIS.

What is Performance-Related Incentive?

A Performance-Related Incentive (PRI) is defined as the variable part of pay which is awarded each year (or on any other periodic basis) depending on performance. PRI schemes are applied at the individual employee level and at the team or group level. The definition of PRI excludes:

- Any automatic pay increases by, for example, grade promotion or service-based increments (not linked to performance);
- Various types of allowances which are attached to certain posts or working conditions (for example, overtime allowances, allowances for working in particular geographical areas, etc.).

Why PRIS?

The Sixth Pay Commission was set up by the Government of India on 5 October 2006 and it submitted its report on 24 March 2008. These recommendations were considered by the government and a decision was taken to accept them (with some modifications) as a package on 29 August 2008.

These recommendations can be broadly divided into two categories dealing with: (a) level and structure of benefits; and (b) PRIs. The former have since been implemented, whereas the latter have not.

The Sixth Pay Commission, in Paragraph 2.5.8 of its report[8], recommended the introduction of a new performance-based pecuniary benefit, over and above the regular salary, for central government employees. The Government of India accepted the recommendations and decided that the detailed guidelines would be issued by the nodal ministry. The government, after due consideration and wide consultations, approved the PRIS and a set of guidelines were prepared by the PMD, Cabinet Secretariat, in collaboration with the Department of Expenditure, Ministry of Finance. PRI was to be payable taking into account the performance of the organization and employee during the period under consideration. It is based on the principle of differential reward for differential performance.

The earlier two pay commissions, i.e. fourth and fifth pay commissions, had also commented on the issue of rewarding

[8] *Report of the Sixth Central Pay Commission,* Government of India, March 2008, Paragraph 2.5.8, pp. 146–7, https://bit.ly/3VB2GUJ. Accessed on 3 January 2023.

performance. The Fourth CPC had recommended variable increments for rewarding better performances in 1987. The Fifth CPC had recommended in 1997, a scheme of performance-related increments for all central government employees wherein, an extra increment was to be paid to the exceptionally meritorious performers with the underperformers being denied even the regular or normal increment.

Given the central role that incentives play in improving performance of employees in public and private sectors, it was a matter of urgency to implement a PRIS. I was directed by the then Cabinet Secretary to give the implementation of PRIS a high priority. The chief hurdle, it became clear soon, was the definition of performance in government. There was no system in government to measure performance of the department. The individual Annual Performance Assessment Reports (APAR) was not linked to departmental performance. Hence, a strange dichotomy was common. While all officers in the department were rated excellent, the overall performance of the government department was rated poor. Thus, it became clear that the PRIS could not be implemented in full measure, or even in half measure, without developing a bottom line for government departments. Thus, my work in performance management (and measurement) became inextricably linked to my work in PRIS. That is why I chose to discuss both for this paper.

There are three constituents of an effective Performance Improvement System: Performance Information System, Performance Evaluation System and Performance Incentive System. All three constituents are to be appropriately addressed to achieve sustainable performance improvement of an organization. The PRIS Guidelines developed by us in the Cabinet Secretariat, however, dealt only with the performance incentive system. The accountability for performance and incentivizing the same must go together at all levels of the government, from the top to the bottom.

Who would be eligible for PRIS?

i. Funding for PRIS was to come exclusively from cost savings from non-plan revenue expenditure.

ii. To qualify for financial incentives, the department will have to get a performance rating of more than 70 per cent on its RFD. Thus, to receive the maximum bonus, the department must not only reduce costs compared to previous year but also achieve excellence in the delivery of services and other performance commitments.

iii. The department should implement a biometric access control system in its offices to ensure punctuality and availability of officials.

iv. A department gets eligible for payment of incentives for its employees only after it has prepared RFD for two full years. Hence, the earliest period for which incentive could be paid to government employees would be for the year 2012–13.

v. The incentive scheme would be required to cover all employees of a department. While the incentives paid to secretaries, special secretaries and additional secretaries would depend entirely on departmental performance reflected in the RFD, the incentives paid to the joint secretaries or heads of divisions would depend on the weighted average of their division's performance and departmental performance. Incentives for officials below the joint secretary level would depend mainly on their individual performance.

vi. The incentive scheme for categories of employees below the level of joint secretaries is to be framed by divisions or departments concerned so as to have flexibility to build the specific requirements of a department. The scheme will have to be approved at the beginning of the year for which the payments will be made. When the incentive scheme is implemented for the first time for a department, the concurrence of the Department of Expenditure would be required. Thereafter, the scheme may be implemented by the departments themselves (involving their Financial Advisor and Chief Controller of Accounts) in consultation with PMD of Cabinet Secretariat.

vii. As the amount payable under PRIS is based on annual performance of the department and cost reduction, the employees who are not posted in the department for a full year and are either transferred out or transferred in, are to be paid on proportionate basis for the period of their stay in the department; subject to the condition that their period of stay in that department should be for a minimum of three months.

viii. The present guidelines are for those departments that have not yet implemented performance-related incentives as recommended by the Sixth Pay Commission.

ix. The departments already having their own PRIS will have the choice to adopt this scheme in place of the existing scheme(s). If the departments desire to continue with their existing scheme(s), the same will need to be cleared by the PMD of the Cabinet Secretariat as well as the Department of Expenditure.

Status of implementation

After half-a-dozen meetings of Committee of Secretaries (COS), when everything seemed agreed between departments, one member of the COS put his foot down and insisted that this matter be taken up by the Seventh CPC.

The report of the Seventh CPC has, once again, endorsed PRIS and its linkage to RFD. Yet, no decision has been taken. Primarily because the RFD policy has been discontinued.

Lessons of Experience

Before summarizing the lessons of experience regarding the implementation of two major recommendations—one from the Second ARC and the other from the Sixth CPC, it may be useful to recapitulate the broad conclusions reached above.

1. Implementation of Performance Agreement: This recommendation was implemented fully throughout the central government. As mentioned earlier, in 2014, the PMES of the Government of India covered 80 departments in the Government of India and 800 responsibility centres (subordinate offices, attached offices

and autonomous bodies) under these departments. Seventeen states of the Indian Union, cutting across political lines, were also at various stages of implementing PMES and it was also hailed and adopted by many of India's SAARC neighbours—Bhutan, Bangladesh, Sri Lanka and Pakistan. Today, the Indian methodology and the software have become the standard in the Commonwealth Secretariat and have been widely hailed and many Commonwealth countries have adopted instruments similar to RFD in India. However, for some unexplained reason, this policy was abandoned in the central government.

2. Implementation of PRIS: After accepting the recommendation of the Sixth CPC in 2008, the Cabinet Secretariat in the Government of India piloted the development of PRIS for two years. As mentioned previously, a consensus was reached among all departments, one department reversed its earlier stand and blocked its implementation. It would be fair to say, that the department that eventually reversed its earlier decision was among the staunchest supporters of PRIS to start with.

These two somewhat discouraging outcomes with respect to RDF and PRIS are in sharp contrast with my experience of implementing the policy of MoU in the Government of India. MoU policy for public enterprises is similar to RFD policy for government departments. Like the RFD policy, I was the prime mover behind the design and implementation of the MoU policy as full time Economic Adviser to the Government of India from 1992 to 1994. Earlier from 1988 to 1992, I was a part-time Economic Adviser to the Government of India while serving as a chaired professor at the Indian Institute of Management, Calcutta (IIMC). Unlike the RFD policy, the MoU policy is still thriving even after more than 30 years. We do not have the space to go through the MoU experience in detail, but it is certainly relevant in drawing lessons of experience.

There are several lessons to be learnt from these experiences. They relate to lessons learnt regarding technical specifications, methodological approach, communications and administrative implementation. Here, I will confine myself to a few broad lessons of my experience only.

a. It is certainly true that political will matters, but it is equally true that bureaucratic skill matters too. As a World Bank economist and a director in the Commonwealth Secretariat, I have had the opportunity to work with innumerable political leaders. I was invariably impressed with their innate capacity to identify a good policy. However, they often were more worried about having the staff that had the knowledge and experience to implement a particular policy outside the regular work of their ministry.

   In my experience, all successful policies have a leader with the necessary vision and political will accompanied by a civil servant with the skills to implement the vision. In a majority of the cases, leaders have competent teams under them. However, when they wish to implement something that is outside the experience and competence of the regular civil servants, leaders must have the confidence, courage and determination to supplement bureaucratic skill with appropriate technocratic skill.

b. Key policies that cut across government departments and deal with organizational effectiveness should be codified in law as soon as possible and desirable. Policies dealing with organizational effectiveness affect the widest possible constituency and potentially the intensity of impact is also significant. Thus, it stands to reason that such policies are likely to be resisted. Both RFD and PRIS fall in this category.

Hence, I now believe that such administrative reform policies that have a wide impact on organization performance should be codified in law as soon as possible.

14

ETHICS IN THE CIVIL SERVICES

A Primordial Necessity

Vinod Rai

'Jharkhand IAS officer Pooja Singhal arrested in Rs 18 crore MGNREGA scam.'[1]; '₹28 crore cash, 5kg gold seized from flat of Bengal minister Partha's aide.'[2]; 'Action initiated against officials responsible for construction of Noida twin towers but none in jail.'[3]

These are the headlines that stare back at you when one opens the newspapers in recent days. Not a day passes without a news item alleging misdemeanour by a public servant. Each of these points to lack of integrity, acts of collusion for financial gains, political alignment for nepotism, etc. It is a distressing fact that lack of ethics has become very widespread among public officials and civil servants.

Is this the new normal? Must we get accustomed to this reality that morality, ethics and probity do not find any place in the public domain? Does the civil service lexicon no longer contain these expressions? This would imply that accountability, transparency and fairness also have to be given the go-by. Is the country facing a deficit of ethical governance and has the civil service either gotten embroiled in the widely prevailing climate or is unable to deal with

---

[1]Deogharia, Jaideep, and Sanjay Sahay, 'Jharkhand IAS Officer Pooja Singhal Arrested in Rs 18 Crore MGNREGA Scam', *The Times of India*, 12 May 2022, https://bit.ly/3hwrmjf. Accessed on 19 December 2022.

[2]'₹28 Crore Cash, 5kg Gold Seized from Flat of Bengal Minister Partha's Aide: ED', *Hindustan Times*, 28 July 2022, https://bit.ly/3W8AKbT. Accessed on 19 December 2022.

[3]Kunal, Kumar, and Santosh Kumar Sharma, 'Action Initiated Against Officials Responsible for Construction of Noida Twin Towers but None in Jail', *India Today*, 28 August 2022, https://bit.ly/3G3C1LK. Accessed on 19 December 2022.

it? Government also seems to be seized with this widely prevailing phenomenon.

Government has launched a comprehensive programme of capacity building for the civil services, Mission Karmayogi, 'to address the changing needs and aspiration of the citizen'.[4] The central theme of the mission is to prepare a competent workforce to discharge its role in a dynamic environment. The programme lays emphasis on creating a culture of accountability and transparency. While capacity building to infuse greater professionalism in any organization is an ongoing process and has rightly been emphasized by the government, it is the culture of probity, integrity and accountability that has to be embedded into the DNA of any public service. It need not be emphasized that integrity is the obligation, of those holding power, to take responsibility for their behaviour and actions. In any parliamentary democracy, a culture of probity encompasses the principles of equality before law; and respect for the rights and duties of leaders towards their citizens. With greater awareness among citizens, there is a greater demand for transparency. Civil servants need to espouse the fact that they sit and operate in glasshouses. Each action of theirs is open to scrutiny and question. They will have to be accountable for each of their actions and any political, regional or partisan decision will be at their own peril. Imbibing high standards of probity is a societal requirement and any deficiency in maintaining these standards will lead to a breakdown of trust between an administration and its citizens.

Ethical Governance

Ethical governance and integrity in public actions has attained iconic status. Even among corporates, ESG (environmental, social and corporate governance factors), have become an essential subset

[4]https://dopttrg.nic.in/igotmk/; The National Programme for Civil Services Capacity Building (NPCSCB) envisioned by the government, addresses the changing needs and aspirations of the citizen. Anchored by an apex body and headed by the Prime Minister, it is designed to enhance the civil services under a national programme.

of non-financial parameters which point to the ethical, sustainability and corporate governance issues such as ensuring accountability and ethical governance.

The need for ethical governance has never been so strongly felt as in the present-day world. Only efficient and effective governance can meet these challenges. It is increasingly becoming evident that efficiency and effectiveness in governance are not sustainable without probity and accountability. We need to be conscious of this factor and hence, the need to ensure ethical conduct in all our operations.

A country is not respected for its forests and mountains, roads and rivers, monuments and structures but the quality of administration in terms of ethics in society and government; integrity in public agencies; and moral standards set by public leaders. A value-driven society is the hallmark of a progressive nation. Today, as democracy takes root all over the globe, people demand and expect ethical governance from its public institutions. This is the edifice, the basic foundation upon which any responsive and open organization can be built. From time immemorial, probity in public life has been a major concern of society, since probity in public organizations is an important element in building the character of a nation and its citizens. A modern nation sustains itself on the commitments of its citizen to the core principles and values of public service. It is a quality that can neither be imbibed in a B-school nor a training academy. It has to be ingrained in the growing-up process of every individual. It thus, has to start from the home, be continued in school and become the fundamental core of a person's being.

The professional integrity of public officials would dictate that they adopt values and integrity in their dealings with citizens' issues. Sound moral and ethical beliefs and basic honesty are highly valued characteristics in any civil servant. Acting with integrity and honesty is an actual advantage for any administration. It builds trust and people are drawn towards such honest and dependable behaviour. Thus, we need to recognize that integrity in governance is not the end in itself. It is merely a means to create an enabling environment in which every individual gets to benefit from the fruits of economic development. For this, the bureaucracy, at all levels, has to perform its role with impartiality, transparency and probity. It is a system in which the rule of law is allowed to take its course and the ultimate pursuit is that of the collective good and not any partisan interests. No organization's success can be sustainable unless it is built on an edifice of integrity and credibility. Ethical management and leadership are the cornerstone of any successful public organization and has to set the tone and create a culture of honesty and integrity.

The civil service needs to imbibe a fresh code of ethics. It needs to adopt zero tolerance for lack in integrity among its officials. Today, more than ever in the history of India, every patriot at heart wants to build an India that is truly a world leader. But, today more than ever before, each one of us faces the dilemma of how we can introduce ethics and morality in public life and give to the next generation a heritage that they can be proud of. There is a churning in civil society; citizens' groups have become very discerning. What was earlier the silent and hence, suffering majority has begun to speak up. This group of citizens want to take on the responsibility of cleansing public life. Public opinion is an important weapon in a democracy in shaping the destiny of a nation. Adherence to ethics and integrity needs to be ingrained in our subconscious and not compromised under any circumstance, so that we do not succumb to short-term temptations. Government functionaries have to be made aware that they live and function in glasshouses, that all their actions have to be based on morality and hence, be transparent.

Constitutional Protection

The civil service officials enjoy constitutional protection in terms of their job security. This has come up for adverse notice and debate. Citizens have begun to question this protection and feel that the corrupt and incompetent should be weeded out. Article 311 of the Indian constitution that provides protection for officials and a five-year tenure for elected representatives, is not for immunity, but merely to provide protection from uncertainty or insecurity. The political executive, bureaucracy and lower judiciary cannot assume that they are immune to accountability.

Questions being raised against such protection is justified, as there is no justification for the incompetent, corrupt or ineffectual to be provided job security despite their failings. Such elements tend to distort the legitimacy of the service and they are the ones who often enough become the face of the system, thereby painting all the others in the same colour. Such a reputation has made it fashionable to believe that a permanent bureaucracy is an anachronistic, obsolescent, undesirable and non-viable form of administration. To be able to build the trust of the citizens and credibly convey that the actions of the administration are indeed for their welfare and benefit, it is paramount to have a service that projects probity and accountability. Such an image builds trust towards the administration and thereby ensures a cooperative and participative citizenry.

Political Vulnerability

The supremacy of the elected political executive in a parliamentary democracy cannot be denied. The administrative bureaucracy is meant to advise and facilitate policy parameters enunciated by the political executive, which is commonly understood to be the Council of Ministers. However, while the political executive is superior to civil and uniformed bureaucracy, they owe their allegiance to the ultimate stakeholder, on whose behalf they act. Hence, public and judicial oversight of government policy is essential. Also, as has been demonstrated by subsequent governments through the 73rd and 74th Constitutional Amendments, Right to Information Act and implementation of flagship programmes through gram panchayats, participative governance has come to stay. However, it will be a terrible tragedy if the elected elements in the local self-governments imbibe the culture of permanent administration, such that they fall prey to using public funds for personal gains while they occupy elected offices.

Signs of such malfeasance are already being observed in rural areas.

Government has attempted to plug such leaks with fairly effective procedures such as direct benefit transfer, but the innovative capacity of the human mind is remarkable when self-interest is involved. Successive governments have been guilty of diluting the effectiveness of certain watchdog institutions in the misplaced belief that their acts, possibly bordering on irregularity, would go 'unnoticed' by these institutions which are being rendered 'toothless'. They are sanguine in their belief that theirs would be a perennial administration and no other political set-up would ever displace them. It is only when they sit in the Opposition that they begin to realize that an emaciated institution becomes incapable of checking the wrong doings of others too. Thus, the need to ensure institutional efficacy of oversighting bodies is a very healthy practice. If the benefits of economic growth are to be made inclusive and sustainable, the involvement and oversighting by the public to ensure transparency of decision-making and accountability for actions will have to be ensured.

Functioning in Glasshouses

Modern-day civil servants have to be cognizant of the fact that their actions and decisions are constantly under scrutiny. The scrutiny need not be from formal governmental bodies such as the Central Vigilance Commission or Comptroller and Auditor General of India (CAG). It is more the public and the media who are the 'oversighting' agencies. It is thus, essential for all officers to act and portray the administration to be objective and ethical. A politically, religiously or regionally aligned administration loses its credibility and hence, its efficacy. It further leads to erosion in the trust that the citizen would have in the administration.

The casualty in all this is the quality of governance. A transparent and ethical set-up will invariably be a check on any insidious attempts to polarize the administration towards vested interests. Each organization should serve as a check and watchdog for the wrongdoing of the other. The fairness of decision-making of the administration should never be in doubt. It is to serve this function that civil service officers are exhorted to maintain probity in all their actions and not act in a partisan manner. Due to the constant public contact of the civil service, especially during their field tenures, they act as the face of the administration. The tenet, 'honesty is the best policy', applies most aptly to all their actions and decisions. Moral and professional integrity is an outcome of their honesty and truthfulness. Honesty would help in inculcating a spirit of discipline and decorum. Honesty encourages officials to speak the truth, be straightforward in their approach and transparent in their words and actions.

Quite often shortcuts taken for short term gains, which border on being amoral, become the norm in one's behaviour. We may believe that the act will only be a one-time action, merely to contend with any particular situation that has arisen, but once that course is resorted to, its appeal in the future becomes compelling. We often take these shortcuts for short-term gains, but these short-term gains may have long-term consequences that we tend to ignore. To be above board in all our actions is a powerful tool as one can take the superior upper ground and dictate to others from a position of moral and professional strength.

The integrity factor becomes paramount when the management of public funds is involved. The government spends a huge amount of money in creating infrastructure, providing services and running various schemes for the welfare of its people. A large chunk of the government's money comes from tax, which is compulsorily collected from its citizens. The government is, therefore, obligated to work in the interest of its citizens and deliver ethical governance. It is answerable to the public for its policies, decisions and performance. It is here that the transparency factor comes into play. Public officials, nominated or elected, carry the trust of the people to ensure that the money collected from them is expended for activities that upgrade the quality of life and ease of living. A public servant can no longer believe that his act of misdemeanour will go unnoticed or that he would have covered his tracks so well that he will not be found out. This is a fallacy. It is living in a 'fool's paradise'. We have to be cognizant of the fact that all our actions are being watched—all our decisions are subject to public scrutiny and we will be held accountable for each of these. This thought has to be ingrained, chewed and digested. There is no escape from such public scrutiny.

Do Ends Justify the Means?

We live in a world where the tenet, 'the end justifies the means', has become an acceptable school of thought for far too many. Officials tweak rules under political pressure, convincing themselves that after all, the political executive is supreme. Quite often, officials also convince themselves that helping themselves to a share in the spoils is a part of what is due to them as well. It is a false belief in that, if the higher-ups are acquiring ill-gotten gains, there is no harm in the lower rungs also availing of their own 'share'.

Heads of departments overpromise as they are worried about losing their prized assignment.

Public sector chief executive officers overstate their company's performance because they do not want to incur the minister's ire.

Employees turn a blind eye to wrongdoing as objecting to it may cost them a cozy place of posting they are in.

The list could go on and in each case, the person committing the act of dishonesty would have convinced himself that he had a perfectly valid reason for having committed the amoral act.

It may seem like people can gain power quickly and easily if they are willing to cut corners and act without the constraints of morality. Dishonesty may provide instant gratification in the moment, but it will never last. We can think of several examples around us, of people without integrity who are successful and who win without ever getting caught; these examples create a false perception of the path to success that one should follow. After all, each person in such examples could have gained the result they wanted in the moment, but unfortunately, that momentary result comes at an incredibly high price with far-reaching consequences. That person has lost their ability to be trusted as a person of integrity, which is the most valuable quality anyone can have in their life. Profit in rupees or power is temporary, but profit in a network of people who trust you as a person of integrity is forever.

A dominating factor in a lack of desire to maintain one's integrity is the apathetic public attitude towards bureaucratic misconduct. A case in point are the CAG reports. Reports indicating revenue losses of ₹16,000 crore towards import of pulses or ₹32,000 crore in setting up Ultra Mega Power Projects did not cause any major public reaction. There was the usual media hype, a couple of mentions in Parliament and the customary noise from the Opposition and then the issue was forgotten. It was only when the nation was told of presumptive loss amounting to ₹1.75 trillion that the public conscience was awakened. That has become our capacity to digest misdemeanour.

The most oft repeated statements by public officials, over a large number of misdemeanours which have been reported are that the law would be allowed to take its course. It is unfortunate that this is exactly what does not happen and there are any number of impediments in the law taking its course, within a limited time span. History speaks of enlightened kings and vibrant democracies being successful and popular only because the rule of law was allowed to prevail. This is a very fundamental requirement if we have to make the government of the people, by the people and for the people. These have become the moral flaws in public apathy.

A Strict Code of Conduct and Morality

A new code of morality and ethics will not only have to be put in place but oversighted by citizens' groups. This is not new. We have the Jansunwai programme in Rajasthan architectured by Smt. Aruna Roy. Ethical behaviour will have to be ingrained in public functionaries. The spirit will have to be that of being a 'government servant' and not 'official', as in representative of the Raj. It is undeniable that good governance can come only when it is premised on probity and transparency. We have to reintroduce a culture of morality and ethics. We have remarkable instances wherein lack of probity—both in the government and the corporate sector, though detected—could not be brought to the logical conclusion due to failure of administration and protracted litigation. There have been any number of cases of corrupt officials and confirmed acts of misdemeanour, which have not been brought to the logical conclusion due to procedural delays. There are an equal number of instances of offenders, having been caught red-handed, not being punished due to protracted litigation delays and thus experiencing no deterrence.

Such delays in delivering justice serve to encourage the wrongdoers.

The Road Ahead

It need hardly be emphasized that success will come and go, but integrity is forever. Integrity means doing the right thing at all times and in all circumstances, whether or not anyone is watching. It takes courage to do the right thing, no matter the consequences. Building a reputation of integrity takes years, but it takes only a moment to lose, so civil servants should never allow themselves to ever do anything that would damage their integrity. This would imply neither indulging in any wrongdoing or allowing others to commit a wrong through you. When the story of India is written, it should be written that ethical governance was the solution and not the problem—wherein the public sector was the facilitator and not the predator. These edicts in our public organizations have to be an essential ingredient, as too much is at stake, for far too many people.

It is with this basic intent in mind that the government set up Mission Karmayogi. Professional sensitization towards the maladies that afflict the service can play a major role in expanding a civil servants' analytical and perceptual skills regarding ethical conflict, through exposure to the various training modules. These should be based on real-life incidents that have come to light and which have shamed the individuals concerned and also brought out the administration in a poor light. Officials should be made to come face to face with the reality of conflicting values and pressures encountered in the course of their careers. Instances of conflict would have come early enough in their career as the public or the public leader, assesses the professional integrity of the official in the nascent stage of his career. He is assessed as: the 'yielding' species of the civil servant; the willing to 'compromise'; or the 'stubborn bound to principles' species. A civil servant must realize that personality attributes or professional reputations get typecast very early on in one's career and unless these are carefully forged and protected, they tend to typify the official throughout their career. We need to create a mental attitude that understands the complexities of present-day government administration and demonstrates an ability to operationalize moral concepts in the face of adverse pressures.

The individual is the fulcrum, in upholding ethics within the civil service.

LIST OF CONTRIBUTORS

Vinod Rai is presently a distinguished visiting research fellow at the Institute of South Asian Studies in the National University of Singapore and a trustee on the board of trustees of the International Financial Reporting Standards Foundation. He has held several important assignments in government and was secretary (Financial Services) before being appointed the eleventh comptroller and auditor general of India in January 2008.

Deepak Gupta has experience of almost 40 years of public service, including a year with the World Health Organization. He retired as secretary, Ministry of New and Renewable Energy, where he initiated the National Solar Mission. He was also the chairman of the Union Public Service Commission. He now speaks and writes on energy, health and governance issues. He has authored several books, including one on the history of the Indian Administrative Service.

Pradeep Kumar has served as the central vigilance commissioner, in which appointment he was responsible for supervision over the Central Bureau of Investigation. He had earlier served as chairman of the National Highways Authority of India and secretary to Government of India in the Departments of Disinvestment and Defence Production and as Defence Secretary.

N. Gopalaswami is the president of the Vivekananda Educational Society and the chairman of the Madras Institute of Development Studies and Voluntary Health Services. Gopalaswami was awarded the Padma Bhushan in 2015 for distinguished public service. He retired as Union home secretary on being appointed as election commissioner in 2004, and was chief election commissioner from 2006–09.

Manish Sabharwal is the vice chairman and co-founder of TeamLease Services, India's largest staffing and human capital firm. Sabharwal serves on the boards of New India Foundation, the National Council of Applied Economic Research and Ashoka University. He is a columnist for *The Indian Express* and has served on the boards of the Reserve Bank of India and the Comptroller and Auditor General of India.

Pushpendra Rai has over four decades of experience as a national and international civil servant and diplomat. He worked for the World Intellectual Property Organization (WIPO) at Geneva and Singapore. In the Indian Administrative Service, he was also national director, United Nations Development Programme projects; secretary-general, Quality Council of India; member, National IP Expert Group; and the country's lead negotiator for WTO/WIPO. Dr Rai managed the historic Development Agenda process, leading negotiations with 193 Member States.

Subhomoy Bhattacharjee is consulting editor at the *Business Standard* newspaper. He works on public policy, primarily finance, energy and urban issues. He is also senior adjunct fellow with the Delhi-based think tank Research and Information System for Developing Countries and adjunct faculty at O.P. Jindal Global University, Sonepat, where he teaches economics and public policy.

Satyananda Mishra was a member of the Indian Administrative Service and worked both in the state of Madhya Pradesh and central government in a variety of job assignments. After superannuation as secretary to the Government of India, he was appointed to the Central Information Commission of India, first as information commissioner and later as chief information commissioner.

S. Ramadorai was instrumental, since taking over as the chief executive officer in 1996, in transforming Tata Consultancy Services into a $6-billion global software company. In recognition of his commitment and dedication to the information technology industry, he was awarded the Padma Bhushan in January 2006. He joined public service in February 2011 and is currently the chairperson of the Karmayogi Bharat mission. He was also the chairperson of the National Skill Development Corporation and National Skill Development Agency from 2011–16.

Naina Lal Kidwai is the chairman of Rothschild India, a senior advisor at Advent Private Equity, a non-executive director on the boards of global and Indian companies; and former president of Federation of Indian Chambers of Commerce & Industry. She retired as executive director on the board of HSBC Asia Pacific and chairman, HSBC India. She has received the Padma Shri for her contribution to trade and industry.

Sanjeev Chopra served at the Lal Bahadur Shastri National Academy of Administration, Mussoorie, as its director till 31 March 2021 and previously as the additional chief secretary to the Government of West Bengal in the Department of Industry, Commerce and Enterprises. He also served as the director general of the Administrative Training Institute, Kolkata.

Kiran Mazumdar-Shaw is a leading biotech entrepreneur who has been at the forefront of taking up civic issues with the government for several years. As the honorary president and co-founder of B.PAC along with Mohandas Pai and K. Jairaj, she has led the crusade for good and transparent governance, better civic infrastructure and has actively supported B.PAC's activities.

Prajapati Trivedi is currently the Commonwealth Secretary-General's Special Envoy for SDG Implementation, Commonwealth Secretariat, London, UK; and a distinguished professor at the School of Public Policy and Governance, Management Development Institute, India. He has served in several key positions in the Government of India, including, Secretary to the Government of India in the Cabinet Secretariat; chairman, National Authority Chemical Weapons Convention from 2009–14 and economic adviser to the Government of India from 1992–94.

public service in February 20[illegible] and [illegible] the [illegible] of [illegible] Karnataka [illegible] mission. He was also the [illegible] of the National Skill Development Corporation and National Skill Development Agency from 20[illegible].

Naina Lal Kidwai [illegible] chairman [illegible] India [illegible] advisor [illegible] equity [illegible] for the [illegible] and Indian [illegible] and former president of Federation of Indian Chambers of Commerce and Industry. She [illegible] director [illegible] HSBC Asia [illegible] and chairman [illegible] HSBC India. She has received the Padma Shri [illegible] for her contribution to [illegible].

Sanjeev Chopra [illegible] Lal Bahadur Shastri National Academy of Administration [illegible] March 2021 and [illegible] currently [illegible] and [illegible] Festival [illegible]. He is also [illegible] of India [illegible]

Kiran Mazumdar-Shaw [illegible] who has been [illegible] with the government [illegible] and [illegible] Bengaluru [illegible] infrastructure [illegible] and [illegible] government [illegible]

Prajapati [illegible] Institute of Technology [illegible] Commonwealth [illegible] Science [illegible] for [illegible] Technology [illegible] and Governance [illegible] in the Government of India, including [illegible] Government of India in the [illegible] Chemical Weapons Convention from 2009 [illegible] and [illegible] adviser to the Government of India from 1992 [illegible].

INDEX